Tick Tock

Tick Tock

BY

James Patterson

AND

Michael Ledwidge

DOUBLEDAY LARGE PRINT HOME LIBRARY EDITION

LITTLE, BROWN AND COMPANY

NEW YORK   BOSTON   LONDON

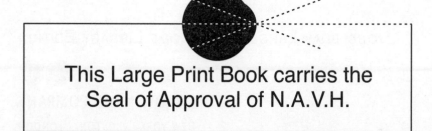

This Large Print Book carries the
Seal of Approval of N.A.V.H.

In loving memory of Thomas Ledwidge
—M.L.

Prologue

SEXY BEAST

One

Like the luxury co-ops and five-star French eateries located in Manhattan's Silk Stocking District, Benchley East Side Parking was outrageously exclusive. Tucked side by side and bumper to bumper within its four temperature-controlled underground levels beneath East 77th Street were several vintage Porsches, a handful of Ferraris, even a pair of his-and-hers Lamborghinis.

The out-of-the-box midnight blue SL550 Mercedes convertible that squealed out of its car elevator at three minutes past noon that Saturday seemed tailor-fit to the high-rent neighborhood.

So did the lean forty-something waiting by the garage's office when the sleek Merc stopped on a dime out front.

With his salt-and-pepper Beckham buzz cut, pressed khakis, silk navy golf shirt, and deep golden tan that suggested even deeper pockets, it was hard to tell if the car or its driver was being described by the purring Merc's vanity plate:

SXY BST

"With this heat, I figured you'd want the top down, as usual, Mr. Berger," the smiling half-Hispanic, half-Asian garage attendant said as he bounced out and held open the wood-inlaid door. "Have a good one, now."

"Thanks, Tommy," Berger said, deftly slipping the man a five as he slid behind the luxury sports car's iconic three-pronged steering wheel. "I'll give it a shot."

The fine leather seat slammed luxuriously into Berger's back as he launched the convertible with a high-torque snarl down East 77th Street and out onto Fifth Avenue. The crisp, almost sweet smell of Central Park's pin oaks and dogwoods fused harmoniously with the scent of the hand-stitched leather. At 59th Street, the park's treetops gave way to the ornate fairy-tale facade of the Plaza Hotel. Moments later, along both sides of the upscale boulevard, glittering signs began to flick past like a *Vanity Fair* magazine come to life: Tiffany's, Chanel, Zegna, Pucci, Fendi, Louis Vuitton. Outside the stores, swarms of summer Saturday tourists took pictures and stood gaping as if they were having trouble believing they were standing in the very center of the capital of the world.

But the world's most expensive avenue might as well have been a dirt road through a shit kicker's cornfield as far as Berger was concerned. Behind the mirrored lenses of his Persol aviators, he kept his gray eyes locked level and forward, his mind blank.

It was his one true talent. In his life, every victory had come down to single-ness of purpose, his ability to focus, to leave out everything but the matter at hand.

Even so, he felt his pulse skitter when he finally arrived at his destination, the New York Public Library's main branch on the west side of Fifth Avenue between 41st and 42nd Streets. In fact, as he slowed, he felt his adrenaline surge, and his heart begin to beat almost painfully in time with the car's indicator.

Even Olivier had stage fright, he reminded himself as he carefully turned onto East 43rd Street. Jack Dempsey. Elvis Presley. All men felt fear. The distinction of great and worthy men like him was the ability to manage it, to act despite the fact that it was breathing down their necks.

By the time he tucked the Merc into a parking spot in front of a Carvel ice-cream truck half a block farther east, he felt somewhat better. To ground himself completely, he patiently watched the hardtop hum into place over his head, precise, symmetrical, a glorious harmony of moving parts. By the time it locked itself down, his fear was still there but he knew he could man it.

Move it, Mr. Berger, he thought. *Now or never.*

He lifted the heavy laptop bag from the passenger-seat foot well and opened the door.

Now it was.

Two

Passing under the Grand Beaux Arts arched portico and through the revolving door of the library, Berger immediately noticed that the steely-eyed ex-cop who usually worked the front hall on Saturdays wasn't there. Instead, there was a young summer-hire slouch in an ill-fitting blazer. Even better. The bored-looking bridge-and-tunneler waved Berger through before he could even lift a finger to his bag's zipper.

The hushed Rose Reading Room on the third floor was about the size of a professional soccer field. It was rimmed with ten-foot-high caramel-colored wooden shelves and lit by brass rococo chandeliers that hung down from its fifty-one-foot-high, mural-painted coffered ceiling. Berger stepped past table after long table of very serious-looking thirty- and forty-somethings, earbuds snug in their ears as they stared intently at laptop screens. Graduate students and ardent self-improvers. No Hamptons this summer weekend for this studious bunch.

He found a seat at the last table along the north wall, with his back to the door of the Rare Book Division of the Brooke Russell Astor Reading Room. He pretended to play Sudoku on his nifty new iPhone until the only other person at the study table, a pregnant Asian woman in a Juicy tracksuit, got up twenty minutes later.

As she waddled away, Mr. Berger took one last deep breath and slowly released it.

Then he slipped on a pair of rubber surgical gloves under the table and slid the bomb out of the laptop bag.

It looked exactly like an Apple Mac-Book seventeen-inch laptop except that there was a hollowed-out space where the keyboard, mouse pad, and computer guts had once been. In their place now sat two kilograms of T4, the Italian version of the plastic explosive RDX. On top of the pale vanilla-colored plastic explosive sat another two-inch-thick layer of barbed stainless-steel roofing nails, like a double helping of silver sprinkles on the devil's ice-cream cone.

There was a gel-like adhesive already attached to the device's bottom. He pressed the bomb firmly down in front of him, gluing it securely to the library desk.

The detonator cap had already been inserted into the explosive and now merely awaited the final connection to an electrical charge, which would occur when someone discovered the laptop and made the mistake of opening the cover. Tied just inside the cover with a snug lanyard knot made of fishing line was a mercury switch, an ingenious little thermometer-like glass tube that was used in vending-machine alarms. When the lid was closed, you could play Frisbee with the IED. Once the lid rose two inches, however, the liquid mercury would spill to the switch's bottom, cover its electrical leads, and initiate instant detonation.

Mr. Berger imagined the bomb's massive shockwave ripping through the crowded Rose Reading Room, blowing apart everything and everyone within forty feet and sending a killing wall of shrapnel in every direction at four times the speed of sound.

He peeled off his gloves and stood with the now-empty laptop bag, careful not to touch anything. He crossed the room and stepped quickly out the exit without looking back.

It was begun, he thought with a feeling of magnificent relief as he found the marble stairs. From here on in, it would be all about timing. A race against the clock, so to speak.

On your mark.

Get set.

"Blow," Mr. Berger whispered happily to himself, and began to take the stairs down two at a time.

Book One

DOWN BY THE SEA

Chapter 1

"Under the boardwalk, down by the sea," I crooned in a high voice, really getting into it with my eyes closed. "On a blanket with my ten big fat babies is where I'll be."

It seemed to me like an appropriate song for walking along a sandy dirt road beside the blue-gray Atlantic. Unfortunately, I was the only one who thought so. A split second later, a fusillade of groans and boos and Bronx cheers sailed back from all ten of my kids.

Still I bowed, displaying my trademark grace under pressure. Never let them see you sweat, even on summer vacation, which is really hard when you think about it.

My name is Mike Bennett, and as far as I know, I'm still the only cop in the NYPD living in his own private TLC show. Some of my more jovial coworkers like to call me Detective Mike Plus Ten. It's actually Detective Mike Plus Eleven if you include my grandfather Seamus. Which I do, since he's more incorrigible than all my kids put together.

It was the beginning of week two of my humongous family's much-needed vacation out in Breezy Point, Queens, and I was definitely in full goof-off mode. The eighteen-hundred-square-foot saltbox out here on the "Irish Riviera," as all the cops and firemen who summer here call it, had been in my mom's family, the Murphys, for a generation. It was more crowded than a rabbit's warren, but it was also nonstop swimming and hot dogs and board games, and beer and bonfires at night.

No e-mail. No electronics. No modern implements of any kind except for the temperamental A/C and a saltwater-rusted bicycle. I watched as Chrissy, the baby of the bunch, chased a tern, or maybe it was a piping plover, on the shoulder of the road.

The Bennett summer White House was open for business.

Time was flying, but I was making the most of it. As usual. For a single father of double-digit kids, making the most of things pretty much went without saying.

"If you guys don't like the Drifters, how about a little Otis Redding?" I called up to everyone. "All together now. 'Sitting on the Dock of the Bay' on three."

"Is that any example to them, Mike? We need to pick it up or we'll be late," Mary Catherine chided me in her brogue.

I forgot to mention Mary Catherine. I'm probably the only cop in the NYPD with an Irish nanny as well. Actually with what I pay her, she is more like a selfless angel of mercy. I bet they'll name a Catholic school after her before long, Blessed Mary Catherine, patron saint of wiseacre cops and domestic chaos.

And as always, the young, attractive lass was right. We were on our way to St. Edmund's on Oceanside Avenue for

five-o'clock mass. Vacation was no excuse for missing mass, especially for
us, since my grandfather Seamus, in
addition to being a comedian, was a
late-to-the-cloth priest.

What else? Did I mention all my kids
were adopted? Two of them are black,
two Hispanic, one Asian, and the rest
Caucasian. Typical our family is not.

"Would ya look at that," Seamus said,
standing on the sandy steps of St. Edmund's and tapping his watch when we
finally arrived. "It must be the twelve
apostles. Of course not. They'd be on
time for mass. Get in here, heathens,
before I forget that I'm not a man of violence."

"Sorry, Father," Chrissy said, a senti-
ment that was repeated eleven more
times in rough ascending order by
Shawna, Trent, Fiona, Bridget, Eddie,
Ricky, Jane, Brian, Juliana, my eldest,
Mary Catherine, and last, but not least,
yours truly.

Seamus put a hand on my elbow as
I was fruitlessly searching for a pew that
would seat a family of twelve.

"Just to let you know, I'm offering mass for Maeve today," he said.

Maeve was my late wife, the woman who put together my ragtag wonderful family before falling to ovarian cancer a few years later. I still woke up some mornings, reaching out for a moment before my brutal shitty aha moment that I was alone.

I smiled and nodded as I patted Seamus's wrinkled cheek.

"I wouldn't have it any other way, Monsignor," I said as the organ started.

Chapter 2

The service was quick but quite nice. Especially the part where we prayed for Maeve. I'm not in line to become pope anytime soon, but I like mass. It's calming, restorative. A moment to review where you've gone wrong over the past week and maybe think about getting things back on track.

Call it Irish psychotherapy.

Therapy for this Irish psycho, anyway.

All in all, I came back out into the sun feeling pretty calm and upbeat. Which lasted about as long as it took the holy water I blessed myself with to dry.

"Get him! Hit him harder! Yeah, boyyyyzzz!" some kid was yelling.

There was some commotion alongside the church. Through the departing crowd and cars, I saw about half a dozen kids squaring off in the parking lot.

"Look out, Eddie!" someone yelled.

Eddie? I thought. *Wait a second. That was one of my kids!*

I rushed into the brawl, with my oldest son, Brian, at my heels. There was a pile of kids swinging and kicking on the sun-bleached asphalt. I started grabbing shirt collars, yanking kids away, putting my NYPD riot police training to good use.

I found my son Eddie at the bottom of the scrum, red-faced and near tears.

"You want some more, bitch? Come and get it!" one of the kids who'd been kicking my son yelled as he lurched forward. Eddie, our resident bookworm, was ten. The tall, pudgy kid with the Mets cap askew looked at least fourteen.

"Back it up!" I yelled at the earringed punk with a lot of cop in my voice. More in my eyes.

Eddie, tears gone, just angry now, thumbed some blood from a nostril.

"What happened?" I said.

"That jerk called Trent something bad, Dad."

"What?"

"An Irish jig."

I turned and glared at the big kid with the even bigger mouth. Trent was even younger than Eddie, an innocent seven-year-old kid who happened to be black. I really felt like knocking the fat kid's hat back straight with a slap. Instead, I quickly thought of another idea.

"In that case," I said, staring at the delinquent, "kick his ass."

"My pleasure," Eddie said, trying to lunge from my grip.

"No, not you, Eddie. Brian's not doing anything."

Brian, six foot one and on the Fordham Prep JV football team, smiled as he stepped forward.

At the very last second, I placed a palm on his chest. Violence never solved anything. At least when there were witnesses around. Twenty or thirty loyal St.

Edmund's parishioners had stopped to watch the proceedings.

"What's your name?" I said as I walked over and personally got in the kid's face.

"Flaherty," the kid said with a stupid little smile.

"That's Gaelic for dumb-ass," Juliana said by my shoulder.

"What's your problem, Flaherty?" I said.

"Who has a problem?" Flaherty said. "Maybe it's you guys. Maybe the Point isn't your cup of tea. Maybe you should bring your rainbow-coalition family out to the Hamptons. You know, Puff Daddy? That crowd?"

I took a deep breath and released it even more slowly. This kid was getting on my nerves. Even though he was just a teen, my somewhat cleansed soul was wrestling valiantly not to commit the sin of wrath.

"I'm going to tell you this one time, Flaherty. Stay away from my kids or I'm going to give you a free ride in my police car."

"Wow, you're a cop. I'm scared," Flaherty said. "This is the Point. I know more cops than you do, old man."

I stepped in closer to him, close enough to head butt, anyway.

"Do any of them work at Spofford?" I said in his ear.

Spofford was New York's infamous juvy hall. By his swallow, I thought I'd finally gotten through.

"Whatever," Flaherty said, walking away.

Why me? I thought, turning away from the stunned crowd of churchgoers. You never saw this kind of crap on TLC. And what the hell did he mean by *old* man?

"Eddie?" I said as I started leading my gang back along the hot, sandy road toward the promised land of our salt-box.

"Yes, Dad?"

"Stay away from that kid."

"Brian?" I said a few seconds later.

"Yeah, Pop?"

"Keep an eye on that kid."

Chapter 3

An hour later, I was out on the back deck of my ancestral home, working the ancestral grill full-tilt boogie. Dogs on the warming rack. Cheese slices waiting to be applied to the rows of sizzling, freshly ground burgers. Blue smoke in my face, ice-cold bottle of Spaten lager in my hand. We were so close to the water, I could actually hear the rhythmic roll-and-crash of saltwater dropping onto hard-packed sand.

If I leaned back on the creaky rail of the deck and turned to my left, I was actually able to see the Atlantic two blocks to the east. If I turned to the right, to the other side of Jamaica Bay, I could see the sun starting its long descent toward the skyline of Manhattan, where I worked. I hadn't had to look in that direction for over a week now and was praying that it stayed that way until the first of August.

No doubt about it. My world was a fine place and worth fighting for. Maybe not in church parking lots, but still.

I heard something on XM Radio behind me. It was the eighties song "Everybody Wants to Rule the World" by Tears for Fears. I laughed as I remembered dancing to it with Maeve at our wedding. I cranked it. You better believe I was preoccupied with 1985. No Internet. Spiky, gelled hair. Weird Al Yankovic. John Hughes movies. If they build a real hot-tub time machine, I'm going back.

"Bet's to you, Padre," I heard Trent say behind me.

Inside at the kitchen table, a tense game of Irish Riviera Hold 'em was under way. A lot of candy had been trading hands all evening.

"All right, hit me," Seamus said.

"Grandpa, this isn't blackjack," Fiona complained with a giggle.

"Go fish?" Seamus tried.

I thought about what my new young friend Flaherty had said about my multicultural family. It was funny how wrong people got it. My family wasn't a Hollywood social experiment. Our gang had come from my cop cases and from my departed wife Maeve's work as a trauma nurse at Jacobi Medical Center in the Bronx. Our children were the survivors of the most horrible circumstances New York City had to offer. Drug addiction, poverty, suicide. Maeve and I were both from big families, but we weren't able to have kids. So we took them in one by one by one. It was as simple and crazy as that.

I turned as Trent opened the sliders to the deck.

I was prepping my father-son sitdown about racist dumb-asses when I saw that he was holding something. It was my work cell, and it was vibrating. I threw a panicked glance back toward the Manhattan skyline. I knew it. Things had been too good for too long, not to mention way too quiet.

"Answer it," I finally said to him, pissed.

"Bennett," Trent said in a deep voice. "Gimme a crime scene."

"Wise guy," I said, snatching the phone out of his hand.

"That wasn't me," I said, turning down the radio. "And you can keep the crime scene."

"Wish I could," my new boss, Inspector Miriam Schwartz, said.

I closed my eyes. Idiot! I knew we should have gone to the Grand Canyon.

"I'm on vacation," I protested.

"We both are, but this is big, Mike. Homeland Security big. Just got off the phone with Manhattan Borough Command. Someone left one hell of a bomb at the main branch of the New York Public Library."

I almost dropped the phone as a pulse of cold crackled down my spine and the backs of my legs. My stomach churned as memories of working down at the World Trade Center pit after 9/11 began to flash before my eyes. Fear, sorrow, useless anger, the end-of-the-world stench of scorched metal in my clothes, in the palms of my hands. Screw that, I thought. *Not again. Please.*

"A bomb?" I said slowly. "Is it armed?"

"No, thank God. It's disarmed. But it's 'sophisticated as shit,' to quote Paul Cell from Bomb Squad. There was a note with it."

"I hate fucking notes. Was it a sorry one?" I said.

"No such luck, Mike," Miriam said. "It said, 'This wasn't supposed to go boom, but the next one will.' Something like that. The commissioner wants Major Case on this. I need my major player. That's you, Mickey."

"Mickey just left," I groaned. "This is Donald. Can I take a message?"

"They're waiting on you, Mike," my boss urged.

"Yeah, who isn't?" I said, dropping the spatula as my burgers burned.

Chapter 4

A day or two after 9/11, a dramatic photograph of a firetruck crossing the Brooklyn Bridge on its way to the burning Twin Towers was splashed across the front page of the *Daily News*. It's an incredible shot, even before you learn that every fireman on the truck, Ladder 118, ended up dying in the subsequent collapse.

As I rolled my beat-up Suburban along the same route under the famous bridge's arches back into the city toward my date with a bomb on 42nd Street, for some strange reason, I couldn't stop thinking of that picture.

I skipped the backed-up FDR Drive and took the side streets, St. James to the Bowery to Park Avenue South. Half a block west of Grand Central Terminal, wooden NYPD sawhorses had been set up, cordoning off 42nd Street in both directions. Behind the yellow tape, a crowd of summering Asian and European tourists stood front-row-center, cameras aloft, taking in some action.

After I badged my way through the outer perimeter, I parked behind a Seventeenth Precinct radio car half a block south of 42nd Street. As I was getting out, I spotted a shiny new blue Crown Vic and a couple of tall and neat-looking guys in JTTF polo shirts sitting on its hood, talking on their cell phones.

I doubted they were here to play polo. Calling in the Joint Terrorism Task Force Feds at the slightest hint of the *T* word was standard operating procedure in our jittery post-9/11 metropolis. The Feds didn't seem too impressed with me or my gold shield as I walked past them. I knew I should have put a jacket on over my Hawaiian shirt.

When I arrived at the corner diagonal to the library, I could see more barricades far down 42nd Street at Sixth

Avenue and three blocks in both directions up and down Fifth Avenue. The silence and lack of traffic on what was usually one of the busiest intersections on earth was zombie-movie eerie.

"¿Sarge, qué pasa?" I said, showing my bling to the Hispanic female uniform at the inner perimeter's aluminum gate.

"Seems like some skell forgot his overdue books so he returned a booby-trapped bomb to the library instead," she said as I signed into her crime scene logbook. "We got the place evacked, including Bryant Park. The Bomb Nuts are inside. Midtown North Squad took a bus of witnesses and staff back to the precinct, but I heard it ain't looking too good."

Among the library's columns and fountains, I passed nervous-looking Midtown North Task Force and Seventeenth Precinct uniforms. Some of the cops were holding what appeared to be radar guns but were really radiation detectors. An unmarked van geared with god knew what kind of testing equipment was parked at the curb.

At the front entrance of the library, a redheaded guy in a white marshmallow-man Tyvek suit was walking out with a yellow Lab on a leash. The Labrador wasn't a seeing-eye dog, I knew, but an EDC, an explosive-detecting canine. I loved dogs, just not at crime scenes. A dog at a crime scene means bombs or dead bodies, and I wasn't particularly jazzed about seeing either one.

Ain't looking too good seemed like the midsummer evening's theme, I thought as I climbed the stairs between the two giant stone lions.

Chapter 5

A big bald guy with a twirly black mustache and tactical blue fatigues met me beneath the landmark building's massive portico. With his mustache, Paul Cell bore a striking resemblance to the guy on the Bomb Squad's logo patch, depicting a devil-may-care Red Baron–looking guy riding a bomb in front of the skyline of Manhattan.

"We got the parked cars and street furniture sniffed, so I'm pretty sure there aren't any secondary devices," Cell said. "Think about it. Draw in the first responders with a decoy. That's what I'd do. Look at all these windows. Some jihadist could be behind any one of them right now with his finger on the button, watching us, aching for that glorious thump and flash of holy light."

"Christ, Paul, please," I said, clutching my chest. "I skipped my Lipitor this morning."

Cell and his guys were the world's elite in bomb handling, as tight and quick and efficient as an NHL team. More so probably since the penalty box on this squad was made of pine. All cops are crazy, but these guys took the cake.

"Fine, fine. You ready to see the main attraction?" Cell said, ushering me through the library door with a gracious wave of his hand.

"No, but let's do it, anyway," I said, taking a breath.

We passed another half dozen even more nervous-looking cops as we crossed the library's monster marble entry hall to a flight of stone stairs. More bomb techs were helping their buddy out of the green astronaut-like Kevlar bomb suit in the ostentatious wood-paneled rotunda on the third floor. Another guy was putting away the four-wheeler wireless robot and the X-ray equipment.

"Uh, won't we need that stuff?" I said.

Cell shook his head.

"We already deactivated the device. Actually, we didn't have to. It wasn't meant to go off. Here, I'll show you."

I reluctantly followed him into the cavernous reading room. The space resembled a ballroom and was even more impressive than the entry hall, with its massive arched windows, chandeliers, and nineteenth-century indoor football field of books. The last library table in the northern end zone of the elaborate room was covered by a thick orange Kevlar bomb-suppression blanket. I felt my pulse triple and my hands clench involuntarily as Cell lifted it off.

In the center of the table was what looked like a white laptop. Then I saw the nails and wires and claylike plastique explosive where the keyboard should have been, and shivered.

On the screen, the chilling and redundant words *I AM A BOMB* flashed on and off before the scrolling message:

THIS WASN'T SUPPOSED TO GO BOOM,
BUT THE NEXT ONE WILL. I SWEAR IT
ON POOR LAWRENCE'S EYES.

"This guy has style," Cell said, looking almost admiringly at the bomb. "It's
basically like a Claymore mine. Two K's
of plastique behind all these nails, one
huge mother of a shotgun shell. All wired
to a nifty motion-sensitive mercury
switch, only the second one I've ever
seen. He even glued it to the desk so
someone would have to open it and spill
the mercury."

"How...interactive of him," I said,
shaking my head.

By far, my least favorite part of the
message was the ominous reference to
the next one. I was afraid of that. It
looked like somebody wanted to play a
little game with the NYPD. Considering
I was on vacation, unless it was beach
ball, I really wasn't that interested in
games.

"He used a real light touch with a soldering gun to wire it up to the battery.
He must know computers as well, because even though the hard drive is

missing, he was able to program his little greeting card through the computer's firmware internal operating system."

"Why didn't it go off?" I said.

"He cut one of the wires and capped both ends in order for it *not* to go off, thank God. Security guy said the room was packed, like it is every Saturday. This would have killed a dozen people easily, Mike. Maybe two dozen. The blast wave itself from this much plastique could collapse a house."

We stared silently at the scrolling message.

"It almost sounds like a poem, doesn't it?" Cell said.

"Yeah," I said, taking out my Black-Berry and speed-dialing my boss. "I've even seen the style before. It's called psychotic pentameter."

"Tell me what we got, Mike," Miriam said a moment later.

"Miriam," I said, staring at the flashing *I AM A BOMB*. "What we got here is a problem."

Chapter 6

The Alexander Hotel just off Madison on 44th was understaffed, overpriced, and excessively seedy. All the grim, peeling walls, off-white towels, and pot smoke and piss stench $175 a night could buy.

Sitting cross-legged on the desk that he'd moved in front of his top-floor room's window, Berger slowly panned his camera across the columns and entablatures of the landmark marble library seventeen stories below.

The $11,000 Nikkor super-zoom lens attached to his 35-millimeter digital camera could make faces distinguishable at up to a mile. At a block and a half, with the incredibly vivid magnification, Berger could see the sweat droplets on the first responders' nervous faces.

Beside him on the desk was a laptop, a digital stopwatch, and a legal tablet filled with the neat shorthand notes he'd been taking for the past several hours. Evacuation procedures. Response times. He'd left the window open so that he could hear the sirens, immerse himself in the confusion on the street.

He was meticulously photographing the equipment inside the open back door of the Bomb Squad van when someone knocked on the door. Freaking, Berger swung immediately off the desk. He lifted something off the bed as he passed. It was a futuristic-looking Austrian Steyr AUG submachine gun, all thirty 5.56 NATO rounds already cocked, locked, and ready to rock.

"Yes?" Berger said as he lifted the assault rifle to his shoulder.

"Room service. The coffee you ordered, sir," said a voice behind the door.

No way anyone could be onto him this quickly! Had someone in another window seen him? What the hell was this? He leveled the machine gun's long suppressed barrel center mass on the door.

"I didn't order anything," Berger said.

"No?" the voice said. There was a pause. A long one. In his mind, Berger saw a SWAT cop in a ski mask applying a breaching charge on the door. Berger eyed down the barrel, muscles bunching on his wiry forearms, finger hovering over the trigger, heart stopped, waiting.

"Oh, shit—er, I mean, sugar," the hotel worker said finally. "My mistake. It's an eleven, not a seventeen. So sorry, sir. I can't read my own handwriting. Sorry to have bothered you."

More than you'll ever know, Berger thought, rubbing the tension out of the bridge of his nose. He waited until he heard the double roll of the elevator door down the outside hall before he lowered the gunstock off his shoulder.

A man was standing talking to the Bomb Squad chief down on the library's pavilion when Berger arrived back to the zoom lens. After clicking a close-up shot with the camera, he smiled as he examined the looming face on the screen.

It was him. Finally. Detective Michael Bennett. New York's quote unquote finest had arrived at last.

The feeling of satisfaction that hummed through Berger was almost the same as the psychic glee he got when he'd perfectly anticipated a countermove in a game of chess.

Berger grinned as he squinted through the viewfinder, watching Bennett. He knew all about him, his high-profile NYPD career, his *Oprah*-ready family. Berger shot a glance over at the rifle on the bed. From this distance, he could easily put a tight grouping into the cop with the suppressed rifle. Blow him to pieces, splatter them all over the marble columns and steps.

Wouldn't that stir the pot? Berger thought, taking his eyes off the gun. All in due time. Stick to the plan. Stay with the mission.

"Stay tuned, my friends," Berger said,

allowing himself a brief smile as he clicked another shot of the clueless cops. "There's much more where this came from. In Lawrence's honor."

Chapter 7

I didn't have a care in the world as I fought the Saturday-night gridlock on the BQE back to Breezy Point. No, wait a second. That's what I was wishing were true. My real mood was closer to depressed and deeply disturbed after my face time with the sophisticated booby-trapped bomb and cryptic e-note.

Cell and his crew had ended up cutting off the entire library tabletop to transport the bomb out to their range in the Bronx. A quick call to Midtown North revealed that no one in the library or its staff had noticed anyone or anything particularly out of the ordinary.

With the absence of security cameras at the location, we were left with basically nada, except for one extremely sophisticated improvised explosive device and a seemingly violent nut's promise to deliver more. To add insult to injury, a briefing about the incident had been called for the morning down at One Police Plaza, my presence required.

I hate seemingly violent nuts, I thought as I got on the Belt Parkway. Especially ones who really seem to know what they're doing.

Even though it was ten and way past everyone's bedtime, all the windows of the beach house were lit as I parked the SUV and came up our sandy path. I could hear my kids inside laughing as Seamus held court. It sounded like a game of Pictionary, the old codger's favorite. He was a born ham.

I went around back and grabbed a couple of beers to wind down with on the porch. When I came back, I spotted a good-looking blonde sitting on the steps.

Hey, wait a second, I thought after my double-take. That's not just a good-looking blonde, that's my au pair, Mary Catherine.

"Psst," I called to her, waving the Spatens temptingly from the shadows. "Come on. Run before someone sees."

We crossed the two blocks to the beach and walked out on the dunes, drinking, taking our time. We made a left and headed north toward a firemen's bar nearby called the Sugar Bowl that we'd been to a couple of nights after the kids had gone to sleep.

If you haven't guessed by now, my relationship with Mary Catherine was more than merely professional. Not *that* much more, but who knew where it was heading? Not me, that was for sure. Mary Catherine was a nice-looking female. I, of course, was a handsome gentleman. We were both hetero. Add vacation and cramped quarters, and trouble was bound to happen. At least, that's what I was kind of hoping.

"How's the thesis coming?" I said as we walked along the beach.

In addition to being the Bennett nanny, Mary Catherine had an art history degree from Trinity College in Dublin and was now in the midst of getting her master's from Columbia. Which made her as smart and sophisticated as she was pretty and kind. She was truly a special person. Why she insisted on hanging around all of us remained a mystery that even I hadn't been able to crack.

"Slowly," she said.

"What's the summer course again?"

"Architectural history," she said.

I drew a massive blank. Dead air.

"How about those Yanks?" I tried.

As we approached the loud, crowded bar, Mary Catherine stopped.

"Let's keep going, Mike. It's so nice out," she said, hooking a right and walking across some more dunes and sea grass down toward the Atlantic.

I liked the sound of that. No dead air this time.

"If you insist," I said.

We were strolling beside the rumbling waves at the shoreline when she dropped her beer. We went to grab it at the same time and bonked heads as the surf splattered around our ankles.

"Are you okay?" I said, holding her by her shoulders. We were so close our chins were almost touching. For one delicious second, we looked into each other's eyes.

That's when she kissed me. Softly, sweetly. I put my arms around her waist and pulled her toward me. She was lighter than I thought she would be, softer, so delicate. After a minute as we continued to slowly kiss, I felt her warm hands tremble against the back of my neck.

"Are you okay, Mary?" I whispered. "Are you cold?"

"Wait. Yes. I mean, no. I mean, I'm sorry, Mike," she said, suddenly breaking away.

In the faint light from the bar's neon signs, I watched her cross the beach at a fast walk that turned into a jog. Rooted to the wet sand, feeling about fifteen emotions at once, I noticed my hands were also trembling a little now. She passed the bar at a sprint, heading back toward the house.

"Sorry?" I said to myself as I rubbed my hot and sore head by the water. "That's the best thing to happen to me all day. Maybe even all year."

Chapter 8

After that casanova moment, instead of heading straight home, I decided to stop in at the Sugar Bowl to apply something cold to my wounded—What? Heart? Ego? I couldn't decide. I sipped a crisp Heineken as I watched the Mets lose to the Cubs at Citi Field. It seemed like there was an epidemic of striking out all over Queens tonight.

As I drowned my sorrows, I thought about what had just happened between me and Mary C. Or to be more precise, I lamented what hadn't happened.

Because I had to admit, it had been a nice kiss. Tender and sweet and surprisingly sensual. I definitely would have liked to stay down there along the water line with her, perhaps reconstructing an outer-borough version of that famous beach make-out scene in *From Here to Eternity*. Instead, she'd run like it was a scene from *Jaws*.

"Hey, you're cute," said a young dark-haired woman next to the pool table as I was coming out of the men's room five minutes later.

I stopped in my tracks and took in the attractive thirty-something's barely-there tank and tight shorts, her slightly drunk-looking cute face, the Tinker Bell tattoo on her left ankle. I couldn't remember the last time a tipsy young woman with a Disney tattoo had hit on me. Probably because it had never happened before. My summer hookup radar was going like gangbusters. Maybe the night wasn't such a bust after all.

But before I could come up with a snappy, charming response, the text jingle sounded from my cell.

I glanced at it. It was from Mary Catherine. Of course it was. Now she wants to connect? I thought, thumbing the message open.

Sorry I freaked on you, Mike. Putting the kids to bed. Left the back door open.

"The kids?" Tinker Bell said, reading my BlackBerry smartphone over my shoulder. "Where's your wedding ring? In your back pocket? Get a life, creep."

I opened my mouth to explain myself but then closed it as I realized Tinker Bell actually was right. What was I doing? I wasn't some barhopping kid anymore. I definitely wasn't Peter Pan. I was more like the old lady who lived in a shoe. Someone had to be the grown-up, and unfortunately that someone was me.

I dropped a five on the bar on my way out.

I came in through the cottage's back door ten minutes later. I tiptoed through what we called "the dorm," the big, rambling family room where all the boys slept on pull-out couches and air mattresses. They were all asleep, sunburned, exhausted, and dreaming happy midsummer-night dreams after another day of all the beachside heaven the tri-state area would allow.

My baby, Chrissy, giggled in her sleep as I kissed her good night in the girls' tiny, crowded bedroom next door. I looked at the massive pile of seashells on the table. At least someone was still having a good time.

As I was heading to my own bunk, I saw Mary Catherine through the crack of an open door. With her eyes closed, she looked ethereal, otherworldly, serene as a cemetery angel.

I tore my eyes away and forced myself to continue down the hallway before I succumbed to the urge to go in and kiss her good night, too.

Chapter 9

It seemed like I'd just fallen asleep when my eyes shot open in the dark, my heart racing. Confused, I lifted my cell phone off the bedside table to see if its ringing was what woke me up. That's when I heard glass breaking.

"Dad!" one of the kids called from down the hall.

It was coming from the dorm. I jumped out of bed and began turning on lights as I ran.

Beside Ricky's bed by the bay window, there was broken glass and a chunk of concrete. I ran to the window, then ducked as a beer bottle ricocheted off the glassless frame and whizzed past my ear.

I could see a small car parked in front of the house with its lights off. Two or three people were in it.

"You suck, Bennett!" called a voice. "Get out of the Point while you still can!"

On the wings of hate, I flew out of the room toward the front door. I was past pissed, more like enraged. Those bastards could have hurt or killed one of my kids. In bare feet, wearing just my boxer shorts, I ran out the front door, picking up an aluminum baseball bat from the porch as I ran.

The car's engine raced as I hit the street. Its tires barked as the car peeled out. I could hear teenage kids inside laughing and yelling. Instead of trying to get the plate, like the trained law enforcement professional I was, I went another route. I hauled back and threw the bat as hard as I could at the car's taillights. It clinked across the empty asphalt as they rounded the corner.

I ran to the corner, but there was no sign of them. They'd gotten away. I was absolutely wide awake as I stood there in the dark. My adrenaline was definitely pumping. I didn't care how old Flaherty was. No one messes with my kids. I really felt like killing someone.

Brian came up behind me as I was retrieving the bat.

"Was that the Flaherty kid, Dad?" he said. "Had to be, right?"

"I didn't see any faces, but it's a pretty safe assumption," I said.

"I asked around about him, Dad. They say he's bad news. Actually, his whole family is crazy. He has five brothers, each one badder than the next. They even have a pit bull. Someone said they're Westies, Dad."

I thought about that. The Westies were what was left of the Irish mafia, latent thugs and gangsters who still ran some rackets on the West Side of Manhattan. One of their signature moves was dismembering bodies. And we'd apparently just gotten into a feud with them?

Brian looked at me, worried.

I put an arm around his shoulders.

"Look at me, Brian," I said, indicating my lack of attire. "Do I look sane to you?

In the meantime, try to stay away from them. I'll take care of it."

I wasn't sure how, but I kept that to myself.

Everyone, and I mean everyone, was awake and on the porch as we came back.

Some joker from the cottage across the street gave a cat-calling whistle out the window at my shirtless bod as I stepped up the stairs.

"Daddy, get in here!" Chrissy commanded. "You can't walk around in just your underpants."

"You're right, Chrissy," I said, actually managing a smile. "Daddy forgot."

Chapter 10

I left for work early the next morning. Which, if you're vacationing in the ass end of Queens and want to avoid the traffic back into the city, means being in the car by a bleary-eyed five thirty.

I hadn't gotten much sleep thanks to the late-night cinder-block delivery from the Breezy Point welcoming committee. My guys were pretty shaken up, and though I didn't want to admit it, so was I. The kid Flaherty really did seem kind of crazy, and I, more than most, knew what crazy people were capable of.

After the incident, I had called the local One Hundredth Precinct, or the 1-0-0 in cop parlance, who'd sent over a radio car about half an hour later. We'd filled out a report, but from the shift commander's ho-hum expression, I didn't get the impression that finding the culprits was too high on his night's priority list. So much for professional courtesy. The best we could do was have a guy come fix the window later today and hope that was the end of it.

I checked my BlackBerry in the driveway before leaving and learned that the morning's case meeting locale had been changed from NYPD's One Police Plaza headquarters to the fancy new NYPD Counterterrorism Bureau on the Brooklyn/Queens border. Though I was glad I didn't have to drive as far, I didn't like how quickly the case was escalating. My dwindling hopes of salvaging the remainder of my vacation seemed to be diminishing at an increasingly rapid clip.

As I was coming in, Miriam suggested we meet for breakfast at a diner near the Counterterrorism HQ beforehand to get on the same page. I arrived first and scored us a window booth overlooking an expansive junkyard vista.

A muted Channel Two news story

about the bomb threat was playing on the TV behind the counter. An overhead shot of the cop-covered public library was followed by another one of a pretty female reporter standing by a police barricade.

A truck driver in the adjacent booth glared at me as I loudly groaned into my white porcelain cup. I knew this was coming. Media heat meant heat on the mayor, which I knew through bitter experience would roll quickly in one direction—downhill, straight at me.

About ten minutes later, I watched from the window as my boss, Miriam, got out of her Honda. Stylish and athletic and irritatingly serene, Miriam looked more like a hot upscale soccer mom than a razor-sharp city cop.

Despite the fact that she had ordered me back from my vacay, I still liked my feisty new boss. Running the Major Case Squad, the Delta Force of the NYPD, was a near-impossible job. Not only was Miriam's head constantly on the chopping block with high-profile cases, but she had the added challenge of having to garner the respect and loyalty of the department's most elite detectives, who were often prima donnas.

Somehow Miriam, a former air force pilot, managed to pull it off with wily intelligence, humor, and tact. She also backed her people unconditionally and took absolutely no one's shit. Including mine, unfortunately.

"What's the story, morning glory?" my boss said as she sat down.

"Let's see. Hmm. Today's headline, I guess, is 'Vacationing Cop Gets Screwed,'" I said.

"Hey, I feel you, dawg. I was up in Cape Cod, sipping a fuzzy navel when they called me."

"Who's was it? Anyone I know?" I said

"A gentlewoman never tells," she said with a sly wink. "Anyway, hope your shoes are shined. Sander Flaum from Intel is going to be at this powwow, as well as the Counter-terrorism chief, Ciardi, and a gaggle of nervous Feds. You're today's featured speaker, so don't let them trip you up."

"Wait a second. Back up," I said. "I'm

primary detective on the case? So now I'm on vacation when? Nights?"

"Ah, Mike," Miriam said as the waitress poured her a coffee. "You Irish have such a way with words. Yeats, Joyce, and now you."

"For a nice Jewish girl from Brooklyn, you're not too bad at throwing the blarney around when you have to," I said. "Seriously, two chiefs? Why all the heavies on a Sunday?"

"The lab came back on the explosive. It's T-four from Europe—from Italy apparently. You know how squirrelly the commissioner gets about anything remotely terrorist-related."

The new commissioner, Ken Rodin, was a pugnacious, old-school former beat cop who still wore a .38 in an ankle holster above his Italian wingtips. With crime down in the city, his primary directive—some said his obsession—was to prevent another terrorist act during his watch. Which wasn't as paranoid as it might sound, considering NYC was still terrorist organizations' Top of the Pops, so to speak.

"Though it's still far from conclusive

that this is a terrorist thing, we have to go through the DEFCON One motions for the time being. There's been smoke coming out of my BlackBerry all night."

"Is McGirth going to be there?"

Tom McGinnis, or McGirth, as he was more casually known due to his not-so-girlish figure, was the department's chief of detectives, Miriam's boss and perhaps the most egregious power-hungry ballbuster in the NYPD.

Miriam rolled her eyes in affirmation.

"What's up with bullshit internal politics?" I said. "What happened to the commissioner's pep talk last month about how the mayor wanted a new role for Major Case? 'Kick ass, no politics, just results?' Ring a bell?"

"Yeah, well, the mayor and the commish aren't going to be at the meeting, unfortunately," Miriam said. "It's our sorry lot to deal with the department's evil henchmen. Why am I saying *we?* It's your job, Mike, since you're the briefing DT."

"Well, lucky old me," I said, sipping my coffee as the sun crested over the crushed cars outside the window.

Chapter 11

The NYPD's Counterterrorism Bureau was extremely impressive. Outside, it looked like a faceless office building in the middle of a crappy industrial neighborhood. Inside, it looked like the set of *24*.

There were electronic maps, intense-looking cops at glass desks, and more flat-screen TVs than in the new Yankee Stadium. Walking through the center behind my boss, I felt disappointed that we hadn't been able to enter through a trick manhole and down a slide, like James Bond or Perry the Platypus.

I began to realize why there was so much heat on the library threat. The last thing the commissioner wanted was to have his big, new, expensive initiative to protect the city fail in some capacity.

The meeting was held in a glass fish-bowl conference room next to something called the Global Intelligence Room. I immediately spotted the assistant commissioner and the Counterterrorism chief. Though they wore similar golfing attire, their physical contrast was pretty comical. Flaum was tall and thin, while Ciardi was short and stocky. Rocky and Bullwinkle, I thought. Laurel and Hardy.

Unfortunately, I also spotted Miriam's boss, McGirth, who, with his puffy, pasty face, looked like a not-so-cute reincarnation of Tammany Hall's Boss Tweed. Beside him were Cell from the Bomb Squad and the two superfit Feds who had been at the library the day before. Intelligence briefings about the most recent terrorist bombings across the globe were stacked at the center of the long table. I took one as I found a seat.

"Why don't you start with what you've got, Mike?" Miriam said the second my ass hit the cushion.

"Uh, sure," I said, giving her a dirty look as I stood back up. "Basically, sometime yesterday afternoon, a bomb was left in the main reading room at the main branch of the New York City Public Library. It looked like a Macintosh laptop wired to plastic explosives. It was a sophisticated device, capable of killing dozens of people. A cryptic electronic note left on the laptop stated that the device wasn't intended to go off, but the next one would, sworn 'on poor Lawrence's eyes,' whatever that means. There were no witnesses, as far as we can tell at this point."

"Jesus Christ. On whose eyes? Lawrence of Arabia's?" said Chief McGinnis, making a spectacle of himself as usual.

"Who found the device?" asked Flaum, the tall, professorial-looking Intel head.

"An NYU student pointed out the unattended laptop to a security guard," Cell said, jumping in. "The guard opened it, saw the message, ordered an evac, and called us."

"Don't they have a security check there?" Ciardi said.

"Yeah, some summer kid checks bags," I said, looking at my notes. "But that's just so people don't steal books. Patrons can take laptops in. He said that white Apple laptops are all he sees every day."

"What about security cameras?" said the stocky Counterterrorism chief.

"Deactivated due to a huge ongoing reno," I said.

"Any threats from your end that might be relevant to this, Ted?" Assistant Commissioner Sander Flaum asked the senior FBI rep.

The taller of the two Feds shook his head.

"Chatter hasn't increased," he said. "Though Hezbollah likes to use plastique."

Hezbollah? I thought. That was crazy. Or was it?

"You always seem to be in the middle of this kind of crap, Bennett," the chops-busting chief of detectives, McGinnis, said. "What's your professional opinion?"

"Actually, my gut says it's a lone nut," I said. "If it were Hezbollah, why not just set it off? An attention-seeking nut with some particularly dangerous mechanical skills seems to be a better fit."

There was a lot of grumbling. The idea that the bomb might not be terrorism wasn't a particularly popular one. After all, if it was just a lone, sick freak, then why were we all here?

"What about the explosive?" the Intel chief said. "It's from overseas. Maybe the whole nutcase note thing is just window dressing in order to get us off balance. Are nuts usually this organized?"

"You'd be surprised," Miriam said.

"If there aren't any objections, I say we keep it in Major Case until further notice," said the Counterterrorism head as he glanced impatiently around the table.

I was thinking about voicing an objection of my own about how I was supposed to be on vacation, until Miriam gave me a look.

"And try to keep your face from appearing on TV, huh, Bennett? This is a confidential case," McGirth said as I was leaving. "I know how hard you find that at times."

I was opening my mouth to return a pithy comment when Miriam appeared at my back and ushered me out.

Chapter 12

With that bureaucratic hurdle painfully tripped over, we headed back to Manhattan. Sunday or no Sunday, we needed to go to our squad room on the eleventh floor of One Police Plaza in order to put together a Major Case Squad task force on the Lawrence Bomber Case, as we were now calling it.

I followed Miriam's Honda through Queens and over the 59th Street Bridge. Beyond the windshield, Manhattan's countless windows seemed to stare at me through the bridge's rusty girders. The thought that somebody behind one of them might be right now meticulously plotting to blow up his fellow human beings was not a comforting one. Especially as I hurried across the rattle-trap bridge.

I received a text on my smartphone as we arrived downtown and snuck in through the back door of HQ.

It was from Emily Parker, an FBI agent I'd worked with on my last case. We'd stayed close since the investigation, so I knew Emily worked a desk at the Bureau's VICAP, Violent Criminal Apprehension Program, which dealt with cheerful things like homicides, sexual assaults, and unidentified human remains.

Just heard about ur performance at NYCT Blue. Don't u love working weekends? U the primary on the Library Bomb thing?

Talk about a security leak, I thought. How the hell had she found out about our secret meeting this fast on a Sunday? One of her fellow FBI agents at the meeting must have told her, I surmised. She wouldn't actually go out with one of those organic-food-eating geeks, would she?

The fact was, Emily was an attractive lady to whom I'd become quite attached. Not quite firmly enough for my liking, but I did get to sample her lipstick in the back of a taxi after the case's conclusion. I remembered its taste fondly. Very fondly, in fact.

Thinking about it, I suddenly remembered the kiss I'd shared with Mary Catherine on the moonlit beach the night before. That was pretty good, too, come to think of it. Being single was fun, though confusing at times.

Affirmative, I thumbed. Mike Bennett, Chief of the Library Cops.

LOL, she hit me back as I was getting into the elevator. I heard ur leaning toward a single actor. U need something to bounce, don't forget ur cousins down here at Quantico.

Kissing cousins, I thought.

"You coming or what, text boy?" my boss, Miriam, said as the elevator door opened on eleven. "You're worse than my twelve-year-old."

"Coming, Mother," I said, tucking away my phone before it got confiscated.

Chapter 13

Berger's hair was still wet from his shower as he drove his blue Mercedes eastbound out of Manhattan on the Cross Bronx Expressway. Spotting a seagull on the top rail of an exhaust-blackened overpass, he consulted the satellite navigation system screen on the convertible's polished wood dash. Not yet noon and he was almost there. He was running just the way he liked to, ahead of schedule.

He sipped at a container of black coffee and then slid it back into the cup holder before putting on his turn indicator and easing onto the exit ramp for I-95 North. Minutes later, he pulled off at exit eleven in the northbound lane toward the Pelham section of the Bronx. He drove around for ten minutes before he stopped on a deserted strip of Baychester Avenue.

He sat and stared out at the vista of urban blight. Massive weeds known as ghetto palm trees commanded the cracks in the stained cement sidewalk beside him. In the distance beyond them were buildings, block upon block of massive, ugly brick apartment buildings.

The cluster of decrepit high-rises was called Co-op City. From what he'd read, it was the largest single residential development in the United States. Built on a swampy landfill in the 1960s, it was supposed to be the progressive answer to New York City's middle-class housing problem. Instead, like most unfortunate progressive solutions, it had quickly become the problem.

Berger wondered what the urban wasteland had looked like in December of 1975. Worse, he decided with a shake of his head.

Enough nonsense, he thought as he drained his cup. He closed his eyes and cleared his mind of everything but the job at hand. He took several slow, deep breaths like an actor waiting back-stage.

He was still sitting there doing his breathing exercises when the kitted-out pearl gray Denali SUV that he was wait-ing for passed and pulled over a couple of hundred feet ahead.

"What have we here?" Berger said to himself as a young Hispanic woman got out of the truck. Berger lifted a pair of binoculars off the seat beside him and quickly focused. She was about fifteen or sixteen. She was wearing oversize Nicole Richie glasses, a lot of makeup, a scandalously slight yellow bikini top, and denim shorts that were definitely not mother-approved.

Berger flipped open the manila folder that the binocs had been sitting on. He glanced at the photograph of the girl whose name was Aida Morales. It was her, Berger decided. Target confirmed.

The Denali pulled away from the curb, and the girl started walking down the sidewalk toward where Berger sat in the parked car. Berger held back a smile.

He couldn't have set up his blind better in a dream.

He quickly checked himself in the rearview mirror. He was already wearing the clothes, baggy brown polyester slacks and an even baggier white shirt, butterfly collar buttoned to the neck. He'd padded the shirt with a wadded-up laundry bag to make himself look heavier.

When she arrived at the turn for her building's back entrance, he took out the curly black wig from the paper bag beside him and put it on. He checked himself in the mirror, adjusting the shaggy wig until he was satisfied.

She was halfway down the back alley of her building with her all-but-naked back to him when he started running and yelling.

"Excuse me, miss. Excuse me. Excuse me!" he cried.

She stopped. She did a double take when she saw the wig. But by then he was too close, and it was too late.

Berger pulled the knife from the sheath at his back. It was a shining machete-like military survival knife with a nine-inch blade. Rambo would have been proud.

"Yell and I'll carve your fucking eyes out of your skull," he said as he bunched her bathing suit top at her back like puppet strings. He hauled her the quick twenty steps to the loading dock by the building's rear even faster than he had visualized. He dragged her into the space between the dock's truck-size garbage compacter and the wall. A little plastic chair sat in the space next to the dock. It was probably where the building's janitor fucked off, he thought.

"Here, have a seat. Get comfy," Berger said, sitting her down on it hard.

Instead of taping her mouth as he had planned, he decided to go ahead and start stabbing her. The garbage stench and the buzzing of the flies were too much for him.

The first quick thrust was to her right shoulder. She screamed behind his cupped hand and looked up at the windows and back terraces of her twenty-story building for help. But there were just humming, dripping air conditioners and blank, empty panes of glass. They were all alone.

She screamed two more times as Berger removed the knife with a slight tug and then thrust it forward into her left shoulder. She started to weep silently as her blood dripped to the nasty, stained cement.

"There, see?" he said, patting her on the cheek with his free bloody hand. "It's not so bad, right? Almost done, baby. In a minute, we'll both be out of this stinking hole. You're doing so fine."

Chapter 14

Still at my desk late Sunday afternoon, I'd spent the last two hours scouring the NYPD and FBI databases for any open cases involving the name Lawrence. Though there were quite a few, not one of them seemed to have anything to do with explosives or serial bombings. My eyes felt like blown fuses after I'd sifted through case after irrelevant case.

I glanced up from my computer at the cartoon on the wall of my cubicle, where two cops were arresting a guy next to a dead Pillsbury Doughboy. "His fingerprints match the one on the victim's belly," one of the cops was saying.

If only I could catch a slam dunk like that, I thought, groaning as I rubbed my tired, nonsmiling Irish eyes with the heels of my hands.

Scattered around the bullpen behind me, half a dozen other Major Case detectives were running down the lead on the European explosive and questioning potential witnesses and library staff. So far, just like me, they had compiled exactly squat. Without witnesses or likely suspects to connect to the disturbing incident, I was betting it was going to stay that way. At least until our unknown subject struck again. Which was about as depressing as it was gut-churning.

It was getting dark when I finally clocked out and drove back to the Point. Fortunately, most of the traffic was in the opposite lane, heading back into the city from Long Island, so I made decent time for a change.

My gang had quite a surprise for me as it turned out. It started innocently enough. Trent was sitting by himself in the otherwise empty family room when I opened the front door.

"Hey, buddy. Where is everyone?"

"Finally," Trent said, putting down the deck of Uno cards he was playing with. He lifted up my swim trunks sitting on the couch beside him and tossed them at me.

He stood and folded his arms.

"You need to put these on and follow me," he said cryptically.

"Where?" I said.

"No questions," Trent said.

My family was nuttier than I was, I thought, after I got changed and let Trent lead me down the two blocks toward the dark beach. Down toward the water's edge, I saw a crowd beside a bonfire. The Black Eyed Peas song "I Gotta Feeling" was blasting.

"Surprise!" everyone yelled as I stepped toward them.

I staggered over, unable to believe it. All my guys were there. They'd brought out the grill, and I could smell ribs smoking. A tub of ice and drinks and a tray of s'mores sat on a blanket. A Bennett beach party was in full swing.

"What the heck is this? It isn't my birthday."

"Since you couldn't be here for a day at the beach," Mary Catherine said, stepping out of the shadows and handing me a gigantic Day-Glo blue plastic margarita glass, "we thought you might like a night at it. It was all the kids' idea."

"Wow," I said.

"We love you, Dad," Jane said, dropping a plastic lei around my neck and giving me a kiss. "Is that so surprising?"

"Oh, yes, Daddy-Waddy. We wuv you so much," said Ricky, tossing a soaking-wet Nerf football at my head. I even managed to catch it without spilling a drop of booze.

After a few more stress-killing margaritas and laughter from watching Seamus dance to "Wipe Out," I was ready for the water. I gathered everyone up and drew a line in the sand with the heel of my bare foot.

"Okay. On your mark, get set..."

They were already bolting, the little cheating stinkers. I hit the ocean a second behind them. I collided with the water face-first, a nail bomb of salt and cold exploding through my skull. Damn, I needed this. My familia was awesome. I was so lucky. We all were.

I let the water knock me silly, then got up and threw someone small who smelled like a s'more up onto my shoulders and waited for the next dark wave. Everyone was screaming and laughing.

I stared up at the night sky, freezing and having an absolute panic. There was a roar, and another wave came straight at us. We howled as if to scare it away, but it was having none of it. It kept on coming.

"Hold on tight!" I screamed as tiny sticky fingers dug into my hair.

Chapter 15

It was dark when Berger pulled the Mercedes under the cold, garish lights of a BP gas station at Tenth Avenue and 36th Street back in Manhattan.

He'd bagged his bloody clothes and changed back into jeans and a T-shirt immediately after the stabbing. Directly from the scene, he'd driven over the Throggs Neck Bridge, where he'd tossed everything, including the knife and the wig. For the past several hours, he'd been driving around the five boroughs, winding down, blowing off steam, and, as always, thinking and planning. He actually did some of his best thinking behind the wheel.

He'd pulled over now not just to fill

his tank, but because his braced left knee was starting its all-too-familiar whine. *Hey, greetings from down here, big guy,* his knee seemed to say. *Remember me? Iraq, RPG, the piece of shattered rebar that burned through me, cooking all my muscles, ligaments, nerves, and blood vessels into tomato soup? Yeah, well, I'm sorry to bring it up, but I'm starting to hurt like a bitch down here, bud, and was just wondering what you were planning to do about it?*

Gritting his teeth at the pain, Berger popped the gas cap and dragged himself up and out of the car, rubbing his leg. He dry-swallowed a Percocet, or "Vitamin P," as he liked to call it, as he filled the tank.

Twenty minutes later, he was piloting the convertible uptown near Columbia University in the Morningside Heights neighborhood. He went west and found meandering Riverside Drive, perhaps the coolest street in Manhattan. He passed Grant's Tomb, all lit up, its bright white Greek columns and rotunda pale against the indigo summer night sky.

He smiled as he cruised Riverside Drive's elegant curves. He had a lot to smile about. Beautiful architecture on his right, dark water on his left, Percocet in his bloodstream. He started blowing some red lights just for the heck of it, cutting people off, putting Stuttgart's latest V8 incarnation through its paces.

He really couldn't get enough of his new $100,000 toy. Its brute propulsion off the line. How low it squatted in the serpentine curves. Like Oscar Wilde said, "I have the simplest tastes. I am always satisfied with the best," he thought.

Tired of screwing around, Berger picked it up. Slaloming taxis, he hit the esplanade at 125th doing a suicidal eighty. When he spotted the full moon over the Hudson, he actually howled at it.

Then he thought of something.

Why not?

He suddenly sat up on the seat and drove with his feet the way Jack Nicholson did in a movie he saw once.

Wind in his face, holy madness roaring through his skull, Berger sat high up above the windshield, his bare feet on the wheel, arms folded like a genie riding a magic carpet. A woman in a car he flew past started honking her horn. He honked back. With his foot.

Nicholson wished he had balls as big as mine, Berger thought.

He really did feel good. Alive for the first time in years. Which was ironic, since he'd probably be as dead as old Ulysses S. back there in a week's time.

All in Lawrence's honor, of course.

Berger howled again as he dropped back down into his seat and pounded the sports car's German-engineered accelerator into its German-engineered floor.

Chapter 16

A silver Bentley Arnage with a Union Jack bumper sticker pulled away from the hunter green awning as Berger came hobbling up 77th Street with the cane he kept in the Merc's trunk.

Did the Bentley belong to landed gentry? he thought. The Windsors visiting from Buckingham Palace? Of course not. It was Jonathan Brickman from 7A, the biggest WASP-aspiring Jew since Ralph "Lifshitz" Lauren.

Berger was only joking. He actually liked Brickman. He'd sat on the board when they reviewed the businessman's co-op application. He had the trifecta of impeccable creds, Jonathan did. Princeton, Harvard, Goldman Sachs.

His financials were mind-boggling even for the Silk Stocking District.

Jonathan was a pleasant fellow, too. Amiable, self-deprecating, handsome, and crisp in his bespoke Savile Row pinstripe. The only thing the gentleman financier had left to do was get a *Times* wedding announcement for his debutante daughter so he could die and go to heaven, or maybe Greenwich.

Berger even liked Brickman's Anglophile Ralph Lauren yearnings. What wasn't to like about Ralph Lauren's *Great Gatsby*–like idealized aristocratic world, filled with beautiful homes and clothes and furnishings and people? Brickman was attempting to become brighter, happier, better. In a word, more. What could be more triumphant and life-affirming than that?

When Berger entered the bird's-eye maple-paneled lobby, he saw the Sunday doorman packed down with Brickman's Coach leather bags. His name was Tony. Or at least that was what he said it was. His real name was probably Artan or Besnik or Zug, he figured, given the Croatian twang in his voice.

Welcome to New York, Berger thought with a grin, where Albanians want to be Italians, Jews want to be WASPs, and the mayor wants to be emperor for life.

"Mr. Berger, yes, please," Tony said. "If you give me a moment, I'll press the elevator door button for you."

He was actually serious. Literally lifting a finger was considered quite gauche by some of the building's more obnoxious residents.

"I got this one, Tony," Berger said, actually pressing the button himself to open it. "Call it an early Christmas tip."

On the top floor, the mahogany-paneled elevator opened onto a high coffered-ceiling hallway. The single door at the end of it led to Berger's penthouse.

Brickman had actually made a discreet and quite handsome offer for it several years before. But some things, like seven thousand multilevel square feet overlooking Central Park, even a billionaire's money couldn't buy.

As he always did once inside the front door, Berger paused with reverence before the two items in the foyer. To the left on a built-in marble shelf sat a dark-lacquer jug of Vienna porcelain, a near flawless example of Loius XV–style chinoiserie. On the right was Salvador Dali's devastating *Basket of Bread,* the masterpiece that he painted just before being expelled from Madrid's Academia de San Fernando for truthfully telling the faculty that they lacked the authority to judge him.

Standing before them, Berger felt the beauty and sanctuary of his home descend upon him like a balm. Some would say the old, dark apartment could probably use a remod, but he wouldn't touch a thing. The veneer of the paneled dusty hallways made him feel like he was living inside an Old Master's painting.

This place had been built at a time when there was still a natural aristocracy, respect for rank and privilege and passion and talent. An urge to ascend. There were ghosts here. Ghosts of great men and women. Great ambitions. He felt them welcome him home.

He decided to draw himself a bath. And what a bath it was, he thought, entering his favorite room. Inside the four-hundred-square-foot vault of Tyrolean marble sat a small swimming pool of a sunken tub. On its right stood a baronial fireplace big enough to roast an ox on a spit. On its left, a wall of French doors opened onto the highest of the sprawling apartment's many balconies.

Berger particularly loved being in here in the wintertime. When there was snow on the balcony, he'd open the doors and have the fire roaring as he lay covered in bubbles, looking out at the lights.

He opened the doors before he disrobed and lowered himself slowly into the hot bath.

He floated on his back, resting while staring out at the city lights, yellow and white, across the dark sea of trees.

Tomorrow he would be "kickin' it up to levels unknown," to borrow the words of some obnoxious Food Network chef. This weekend was nothing compared with what people would wake up to tomorrow morning.

Tomorrow was going to be one hell of a day.

Chapter 17

Way past all our bedtimes and loving it, the kids and I were soaked to the skin and shivering around the bonfire. I heard Seamus clear his throat to tell one of his famous ghost stories.

I remembered them from when I was a kid. Run-of-the-mill ghost stories were for pansies. Seamus's tales were H. P. Lovecraft–inspired yarns about fish creatures so horrifying, just the sight of them made people go insane. I mean, anyone can scare a little child. Few can introduce them to cosmic horror.

"Make it a PG tale, huh, Padre?" I said, taking him aside. "I don't want the kids to have nightmares. Or me, either."

"Fine, fine. I'll water it down, ya party pooper," Seamus grumbled.

"Mike?" Mary Catherine whispered to me. "Would you help me get some more soda?"

She didn't even make a pretense of heading toward the house. We walked north along the dark beach parallel to the waterline. Mary Catherine was wearing a new white-cotton sheer summer dress I'd never seen before. Over the past two weeks, she'd become quite brown, which made her blue eyes pop even paler and prettier than usual. She turned those eyes on me and held them there as we walked, an adorably nervous look on her fine-boned face.

"Mike," she said as I followed her on our mystical soda quest.

"Yes, Mary?"

"I have a confession to make," she said, stopping by an empty lifeguard chair. "This party wasn't the kids' idea. It was mine."

"I'll forgive you on one condition," I said, suddenly holding her shoulders.

There were no head butts this time or hesitating. We kissed.

"This is crazy. What the hell are we doing?" Mary Catherine said when we came up for air.

"Looking for soda?" I said.

Mary Catherine smiled and gave me a playful kick in the shin. Then we climbed up into the lifeguard chair and started kissing again.

We went at it for quite some time, holding each other, warm against the cold. I didn't want to stop, even with the skeeters biting the crap out of my back, but after a while we climbed back down.

We headed back to the party, but everyone was gone and the fire was out.

"Oh, no. We're so busted," Mary Catherine said.

"Who knows? Maybe we'll be lucky and Seamus's fish monsters got them," I tried.

I knew we were in trouble when I saw Shawna and Chrissy on the front porch.

"They're coming. They're coming. They're not dead," they chanted, running back into the house.

"Oh, yes, we are," Mary Catherine said under her breath.

"Now, where could the two of you have been for the last eon?" Seamus said with a stupid all-too-knowing grin on his face.

"Yeah, Dad," Jane said. "Where'd you go to get the soda? The Bronx?"

"There was, uh, none left, so I tried, I mean, we, uh, went to the store."

"But it was closed, and we walked back," Mary Catherine finished quickly.

"But there's a case of Coke right here," Eddie said from the kitchen.

"That can't be. I must have missed it," I said.

"In the fridge?" Eddie said.

"Enough questions," I said. "I'm the cop here and the dad, in fact. One more question and it's everyone straight to bed."

I saw Seamus open his mouth.

"With spankings," I added, pointing at him as everybody burst into giggles.

"Fine, no questions," Seamus said. "How about a song? Ready, kids? Hit it."

"Mike and Mary sitting in a tree.

K-I-S-S-I-N-G," they regaled us. Seamus was by far the loudest.

"First comes love, then comes marriage," they said, making a circle and dancing around us like evil elves. "Then comes Mary with a baby carriage."

"You're all dead, you know that," I said, red-faced and unable to contain my laughter. "As doornails."

Chapter 18

It was already hot at seven fifteen in the morning when Berger downshifted the massive Budget rental box truck with a roar and pulled over onto Lexington Avenue near 42nd Street. Even this early on Monday morning, people in office clothes were spilling out of Grand Central Terminal like rats from a burning ship.

He threw the massive truck into park and climbed out, leaving it running. He was wearing a Yankees cap backward, cutoff jeans, construction boots, and yellowish-green cheap CVS shades. A wifebeater and a gold chain with a massive head of Christ topped off his outerborough truck-driver look.

He made a showy display of dropping the back gate and rattling up the steel shutter before wheeling out the hand truck. On it were three thick plastic-strapped bundles of *New York Times* newspapers. He rolled them to the truck's hydraulic ramp and started it humming down.

Weaving around morning commuters on the sidewalk, he quickly navigated the hand truck into the massive train station. Inside, hundreds of people were crisscrossing through the cathedral-like space, running like kids playing musical chairs to get into place before the Stock Exchange's golden opening bell.

A pudgy antiterror cop strapping an M16 yawned as Berger rolled right on past him. He dropped his bundles by a crowded stationery store called Latest Edition that adjoined the main waiting room. The short, mahogany-colored Asian guy behind the counter came out of the store with a puzzled look on his face as Berger spun the hand truck around with a squeal.

"More *Times*?" the little brown guy

said. "This is a mistake. I already got my delivery."

"Wha'?" Berger said, throwing up his arms. "You gotta be f——ing kiddin' me. I should be finished my deliveries already. Central just called and said to drop these off. Let me call these jag-offs back. Left my cell phone in the truck. I'll be back in a second."

The Asian guy shook his head at the chest-high stack as Berger quickly rolled the hand truck away.

As Berger passed the antiterror cop on his way out, he went into his pocket and slid ballistic ear protectors into his ears. Then he turned into the long Lexington Avenue Corridor exit, took the cell phone from his pocket, and dialed the number for the trigger in the massive paper-wrapped bomb he'd just planted.

He winced as fifty pounds of plastic explosive detonated with an eardrum-splitting *ba-bam!* Ten feet from the exit door, a chunk of cream-colored marble the size of a pizza slid past him like a shuffleboard disk. A man's briefcase followed. A cloud of dust and hot smoke followed him out the door into the street.

Outside on Lexington, cars had stopped. On the sidewalk, people were turned toward the station's entrance, arrested in place like figures in a model-train display. The hand truck clattered over as Berger rolled it off the curb. Passing the rear of the truck he'd parked, he crossed the street and turned the corner of 43rd Street, walking quickly with his head down, the iPhone still in his hand.

When he was halfway up the block, he took a breath and dialed the other mobile phone trigger.

The one attached to the incendiary device in the cab of the truck.

Someone screamed. When he glanced over his shoulder, a pillar of thick black smoke was billowing up between the office towers.

Instead of creating just a distracting blazing truck, he'd seriously thought about filling the rear of the truck with diesel-soaked ammonium nitrate, like the Oklahoma City bomber did, but in the end he'd decided against it.

He chucked the hat and the glasses and the Christ head, feeling unsure for a moment, shaking his head.

All in due time, he thought.

He glanced back at the ink black pin-wheeling mushroom cloud sailing into the July morning sky as he hit Third Avenue and started walking uptown. The first sirens started in the distance.

He hadn't crossed the line this time, Berger knew.

He'd just erased it.

Chapter 19

I got up early the next morning. In the predawn gray, I threw on some flip-flops and biked over to a deli a couple of blocks north of our beach bungalow. After I bought a dozen and a half Kaiser rolls and two pounds of bacon, I sat with a cup of coffee on a beat-up picnic table in the deli's still-dark parking lot, gazing out at the beach.

As the sun came up over the ocean, it reminded me of the summer I was seventeen. A buddy and I pulled a Jack Kerouac and hitchhiked down to the Jersey Shore to visit a girl that he knew. My friend cut out with the girl, and I ended up sleeping on the beach. Waking alone to the sound of gulls, I was depressed at first, but then I turned to the water and sat there, wide-eyed and frozen, overwhelmed for the first time by what a flat-out miracle this world could be.

I smiled as I remembered being with Mary Catherine last night. No wonder I was thinking about my teen years, I thought, finishing the dregs of my Green Mountain French vanilla. After last night, I certainly felt like I was seventeen all over again. I was definitely acting like a kid. Not a bad thing, by any stretch in my book. I highly recommend it.

Seamus was on the porch waiting for me when I got back. I could tell by the bloodless look on his face that something was very wrong. He had my phone in his hand for some reason. I screeched to a stop and dropped the bike as I bolted up the stairs.

"No! What is it? One of the kids?"

Seamus shook his head.

"The kids are fine, Michael," he said with a surreal calm.

Michael?

Shit, this was bad. The last time I remembered him using my Christian name was the morning I buried my wife.

I noticed that the radio was on in the house behind him. A lot of silence between the announcer's halting words. Seamus handed me my vibrating phone. There were fourteen messages from my boss.

"Bennett," I said into it as I watched Seamus close his eyes and bless himself.

"Oh, Mike," my boss, Miriam, said. "You're not going to believe this. A bomb just went off in Grand Central Terminal. Four people are dead. Dozens more wounded. A cop is dead, too, Mike."

I looked up at the pink-and-blue-marbled sky, then at Seamus, then finally down at the sandy porch floorboards. My morning's peaceful Deepak Chopra contemplation session was officially over. The big bad world had come back to get my attention like another chunk of cinder block right through my bay window.

"On my way," I said, shaking my head. "Give me an hour."

Chapter 20

Inbound Manhattan traffic was lighter than usual due to the heart-stopping news. I'd taken my unmarked Impala home the day before, and as I got on the LIE, I buried the pin of its speedometer, flashers and siren cranked.

Keeping off the crowded police-band radio, I had my iPod turned up as far as it would go, and blasted the Stones' "Gimme Shelter." Gritty, insane seventies rock seemed extremely appropriate theme music for the world coming apart at its seams.

The Anti-Terror Unit in full force had already set up a checkpoint at the 59th Street Bridge. Instead of stopping, I killed some cones as I put the Imp on the shoulder and took out my ID and tinned the rookie at the barricade at around forty. There were two more checkpoints, one at 50th and Third, and the final one at 45th and Lex. Sirens screaming in my ears, I parked behind an ambulance and got out.

Behind steel pedestrian barricades to the south, dozens of firefighters and cops were running around in all directions. I walked to take my place among them, shaking my head.

When I arrived at the corner and saw the flame-gutted box truck, I just stood gaping.

I spotted Bomb Squad chief Cell through a debris-covered lobby. It looked like a cave-in had happened. One of the fire chiefs at the blast site's command center made me put on some Tyvek and a full-face air mask before letting me through.

"Guess our friend wasn't lying about the next one," Cell said. "Looks like the same plastique that we found at the library."

He smiled, but I could see the frozen rage in his eyes. He was angry. We all were. Even through the filters of the mask, I could smell death. Death and concrete dust and scorched metal.

There was no predicting what would happen next.

Chapter 21

The rest of the day was as hellacious as any in my career. Later that morning, I helped an EMT dig out the body of an old, tiny homeless man who'd been buried under the collapsed Grand Central Lexington Avenue Corridor. When I went to grab his leg to put him in the body bag, I almost collapsed when his leg separated freely from his body. In fact, all of his limbs had been dismembered by the bomb's shock wave. We had to bag him in parts like a quartered chicken.

If that wasn't stressful enough, I spent the afternoon in the on-site morgue with the medical examiner, compiling a list of the dead. The morgue was set up in the Campbell Apartment, an upscale cocktail bar and lounge, and there was something very wrong about seeing covered bodies laid out in rows under a sparkling chandelier.

The worst part was when the slain police officer was brought in. In a private ceremony, the waiting family members were handed his personal effects. Hearing the sobbing moans, I had to get out of there. I walked out and headed down one of Grand Central's deserted tracks. I peered into the darkness at its end for a few minutes, tears stinging in my eyes. Then I wiped my eyes, walked back, and got back to work.

I met Miriam that afternoon at the Emergency Operations trailer set up by the main entrance of Grand Central on 42nd Street. I spotted a horde of media cordoned off on the south side of the street by the overpass behind barricades. National this time. Global newsies would be showing up pretty soon to get their goddamn sound bites from this hellhole.

"We got Verizon pulling recs of the

nearest cell sites to see if it was a mobile trigger," Miriam said to me. "The rest of our guys are getting the security tapes from the nearest stores up and down the block. Preliminary witnesses said a large box truck pulled up around seven. A homeless guy sleeping in the ATM alcove in the bank across the street said he looked out and saw a guy pushing a hand truck with something on it before the first explosion."

Miriam paused, staring at me funny, before she pulled me closer.

"Not only that, Mike. You need to know this. A letter came to the squad this morning. It was addressed to you. I had them X-ray it before they opened it. It was a typed message. It had today's date along with two words: *For Lawrence*."

I closed my eyes, the hair standing up on the back of my neck.

Addressed to me?

"For Lawrence?" I said. "What the hell? I mean, give me a break. This is insane. There's no rationale, no demand for ransom. Why was it addressed to *me*?"

Miriam shrugged as Intelligence chief Flaum came out of the trailer.

"ATF is flying in their guys as we speak to help identify the explosive," he said. "You still think we have a single actor, Mike? Could that be possible? One person caused all this?"

Before I could answer, the mayor came out of the trailer, flanked by the police and fire commissioners.

"Good morning, everyone," the mayor said into a microphone. "I'm sorry to have to address you all on this sad, sad day in our city's history," he said.

Not as sorry as I am, I thought, blinking at the packs of popping flash bulbs.

Around four o'clock, I was at Bellevue Hospital, having just interviewed an old Chinese woman who'd lost one of her eyes in the blast, when my cell rang.

"Mike, I hate to tell you this," Mary Catherine said. "With everything going on, I know it's not the right time, but—"

"What, Mary?" I barked.

"Everyone's okay, but we're at the hospital. St. John's Episcopal."

I put down the phone for a minute. I took a breath. Another hospital? Another problem? This was getting ridiculous.

"Tell me what happened."

"It's Eddie and Ricky. They got into a fight with that Flaherty kid. Ricky got the worst of it, five stitches in his chin, but he's fine. Really. They both are. Please don't worry. How is it down there? You must be going through hell."

"It's not that bad," I lied. "I'm actually leaving now. I'm on my way."

Chapter 22

Angry, dirty, and emotionally hollow, I parked in my driveway and sat for a moment. I smelled my hands. I'd scrubbed them at the hospital, but they still smelled like burnt metal and death. I poured another squirt of Purell into them and rubbed until they hurt. Then I stumbled out and up the porch steps and through the front door.

The dining-room table was packed full with my family having dinner. It was silent as a graveyard as I came through the kitchen door. I stepped down to the end of the table and checked out Ricky's chin and Eddie's shiner.

While I was carrying out the dead, some sick kid had savagely beaten up my ten- and eleven-year-old sons. This was my sanctuary, and even this was under siege. Nowhere was safe anymore.

"What happened, guys?"

"We were just playing basketball at the court by the beach," Ricky said.

"Then that Flaherty kid came with his older friends," Eddie jumped in. "They took the ball, and when we tried to get it back, they started punching."

"Okay, guys. I know you're upset, but we're going to have to try to get through this the best we can," I said with a strained smile. "The good news is that everyone is going to be okay, right?"

"You call this okay?" Juliana said, pointing at Ricky's chin. She made Eddie open his mouth to show me his chipped tooth.

"Dad, you're a cop. Can't you just arrest this punk?" Jane wanted to know.

"It's not that simple," I said, my voice calm, and a convincing fake smile plastered on my face. "There's witnesses and police reports and other adult stuff you guys shouldn't worry about. I'll take care of this. Now, until then, I want everyone to lay low. Stick around the house. Maybe stay away from the beach for a few days."

"A few days? But this is our vacation," Brian said.

"Yeah, our *beach* vacation," Trent chimed in.

"Now, now, children. Your, uh, father knows best," Seamus said, sensing how I was about to snap. "We need to be Christian about this. We need to turn the other cheek."

"Yeah," Brian said, "so the next time we get socked, the first stitches don't get reopened."

Brian was right. We were getting our asses kicked, and I was too drained to come up with some good bullshit to bluff them that everything was fine.

That's when Bridget started crying from the other end of the table, followed almost simultaneously by her twin, Fiona.

"I want to go home," Fiona said.

"I don't like it here anymore," Bridget added. "I don't want Ricky and Eddie to be hurt, Daddy. Let's go to Aunt Suzie's for the rest of our vacation." Aunt

Suzie lived in Montgomery, New York, where she and Uncle Jerry owned a mind-blowingly fabulous restaurant called Back Yard Bistro. We had vacationed at nearby Orange Lake the previous summer.

"Girls, look at me. No one's going to get hurt again, and we can still have fun. I really will take care of this. I promise."

They smiled. Small smiles, but smiles nonetheless.

I couldn't let them down, I thought. No excuses. New York City under attack or not.

I'd have to think of something. But what?

Chapter 23

It was dark when Berger crossed the Whitestone Bridge. He buzzed up the hardtop as he pulled the Mercedes convertible off 678 onto Northern Boulevard in Flushing, Queens.

Traffic, crummy airports, an even crummier baseball team. Was there anything that *didn't* suck about Queens?

He slowly cruised around the grid of streets, trying not to get lost. It wasn't easy with all the small, tidy houses and low apartment buildings set in neat, boring rows everywhere he looked. Thank God for the car's navigation system.

After five minutes, he finally stopped and pulled over behind a parked handi-

cap bus near a wooded service road
alongside the Cross Island Parkway. He
turned the Merc's engine off but left the
radio on. He listened to a talk show for
a bit, then found a soothing Brahms
concerto.

When it was over, he sat silently in
the darkness. Just sitting there waiting
was torture when there was still so much
to do. He'd seriously debated contract-
ing this part out, but in the end he had
decided against it. Every small thing
was part of the effort, he reminded himself. Even Michelangelo, when painting
the Sistine Chapel, built the scaffolds
himself and mixed his own paint.

It was almost half an hour later when
a new Volvo Crossover passed him and
turned off the road onto the secluded
lover's lane that ran up the wooded hill
alongside an electrical tower cutout.

He waited ten minutes to let them get
going. Then he slipped on his trusty
surgical gloves, got out his new black,
curly wig, and grabbed the sack.

Fireflies flickered among the weeds
and wildflowers as he stepped up the
muggy deserted stretch of service road.

It could have been upstate Vermont but for the massive electrical pylon that looked like an ugly, sloppy black stitch across the face of midnight blue sky at the top of the hill.

Even though the parked Volvo's lights were off, Berger caught a lot of motion behind the station wagon's steamed windows as he approached. If the Volvo's a rockin', don't come a knockin', Berger thought, taking the heavy gun out of the paper sack.

He arrived at the passenger-side window and tapped the snub-nosed chunky .44 Bulldog against the glass.

Clink, clink.

"Knock, knock," he said.

They were both in the lowered passenger bucket seat. The young lady saw him first over the guy's shoulder. She was pretty, a creamy-skinned redhead.

Berger took a few steps back in the darkness as she started to scream.

As the man struggled to pull up his pants, Berger walked around the rear of the car to the driver's side and got ready. The Weaver shooting stance he adopted was textbook, two hands extended, elbows firm but not locked, weight evenly distributed on the balls of his feet. When the guy finally sat up, the Bulldog was leveled exactly at his ear.

The two huge booms and enormous recoil of the powerful gun were quite surprising after the light, smooth trigger pull. The driver-side window blew in. So did most of the horny middle-aged guy's head. The girl in the passenger seat was splattered with blood and brain matter, and her sobbing scream rose in pitch.

With the elbow of his shirtsleeve, Berger wiped cordite and sweat out of his eyes. He lowered the heavy revolver and calmly walked around the front of the car back to the passenger side. In situations like this, you had to stay focused, slow everything down. The woman was trying to climb over her dead lover when he arrived at the other side of the car. Berger took up position again and waited until she turned.

Two more dynamite-detonating booms sounded out as he grouped two .44 Bulldog rounds into her pale forehead.

Then there was silence, Berger thought, listening. *And it was good.*

Recoil tingling his fingers, Berger dropped the gun back into the paper sack and retrieved the envelope from his pocket.

He flicked the envelope through the shattered window. There was something typed across the front of it.

MICHAEL BENNETT NYPD

Humming the concerto he'd just been listening to, Berger tugged at a rubber glove with his teeth as he hurried back down the hill toward his car.

Chapter 24

"Going out for ice cream," I said, getting up from the game of Trivial Pursuit that we started playing after dinner. Mary Catherine gave me a quizzical look as I was leaving. Her concern only seemed to increase when I gave her a thumbs-up on the way out the screen door.

But instead of getting ice cream, I hopped into the Impala and called into my squad to get the address for the Flaherty family in Breezy Point. Was that a little crazy? It was. But then again, so was I by that point.

Their house was on the Rockaway Inlet side of the Point about ten blocks away. I drove straight there.

They really did have a pit bull chained in their front yard. It went mad as I stepped out of my car and made my way up the rickety steps.

It wasn't madder than me, though. I actually smiled at it. After today and everything that I had seen, I was in a man-bites-dog sort of mood.

I pounded on the door.

"Oh, this better be good," said the bald guy who answered it.

The guy was big. He was also shirtless and in damn good shape, I could see: huge bowling-ball shoulders, six-pack abs, prison-yard pumped. There was another man, just as big and mean-looking and covered in tattoos, standing behind him.

I should have been cautious then. I knew a violent criminal mobster asshole when I saw one. But I guess I was through giving a shit for the day.

"You Flaherty?" I said.

"Yeah. Who the fuck are you?"

"My name's Bennett. You have a kid?"

"I got five of 'em. At least. Which one we talkin' about here?"

"Fat, freckles, about fourteen. Did I say *fat?*"

"You talking about my Seany? What's up?"

"Yeah, well, your Seany split my eleven-year-old's chin open today is what's up," I said, staring into Flaherty's soulless doll's eyes. "He had to go to the hospital."

"That can't be right," the man said, stone-faced. He smiled coldly. "We went fishing today. All day. It was sweet. Got some blues. Hey, Billy, remember when Sean caught that blowfish today?"

"Oh, yeah," the thug behind him said with a guffaw. "Blowfish. That was the puffy balloon thing, right? That shit was funny."

"See. Guess you made a mistake," Flaherty senior said. "Wait a second. Bennett. I know you. You got all those rainbow-coalition crumb crunchers, right? You're a cop, too. Look, Billy. It's the Octo-cop in the flesh."

"I do have a gun," I said with a grin. "You want me to show it to you?"

I really did feel like showing it to him.

In fact, I actually felt like giving him a taste of my Glock.

"I know what they look like, but thanks, anyway," Flaherty said, cold as ice. "If you don't mind, though, I'd like to get back to the ballgame. Mets might even win one for a change. Have a nice night, Officer."

That's when he slammed the door in my face. I felt like kicking it in. The pit was in a frenzy. So was I. But even in my stress-induced hysteria, I knew that wasn't a good idea. I chose to retreat.

An empty Miller High Life can landed beside me as I was coming down the steps.

Young Flaherty himself waved to me from the rattletrap's second-story window.

"Gee, Officer, I apologize. Must have slipped out of my hand."

Even over the dog's apoplexy, I heard raucous laughter from inside.

Death all day and ridicule for dessert. What a day. I crushed the can and hit the stairs before I could take my gun out.

Chapter 25

Returning to the house with a full head of steam, I decided I needed some alone time. Wanting to make it both relaxing and constructive, I opted for doing what any angry, overworked cop in my situation would do. Inside the garage, I tossed down some old newspaper on a workbench and began field-stripping my Glock 21.

For half an hour, I went to town, cleaning the barrel and slide until everything was ship shape and shining like a brand-new penny. I'm not proud to admit that as I went through the motions meticulously, some un-Christian thoughts went through my mind concerning certain Breezy Point residents. As I reloaded the semiauto's magazine and slapped it home with a well-oiled snick, I made a mental note to set up a confession the next time I saw Seamus.

I discovered a bottle of Johnnie Walker Black Label on a shelf behind a bolt-filled coffee can as I was cleaning up. One of my cousins must have left it there after his own Clark W. Griswold family vacation fiasco, no doubt. I drummed my fingers on the workbench as I eyed the half-full bottle.

Why not just get drunk and let the world go straight to hell? I certainly had a good excuse. Several, in fact.

As I stood there weakly and wearily pondering the Scotch bottle, beyond the front door of the garage I heard steps on the porch and the doorbell ring.

"Hey, is Juliana around?" a voice called out.

The voice belonged to Joe Some-body-or-other, some tall, friendly nonpsychotic high-school kid from up the block who kept coming around because he had a crush on Juliana.

"Hey, Joe," I overheard Juliana say a second later.

"Do you and Brian and the guys want to play roundup again?" the sly Breezy Point Romeo wanted to know.

"Can't tonight, Joe, but I'll text you tomorrow, okay?" Juliana said curtly before letting the door close in his face with a bang.

That was odd, I thought, heading outside and up the porch steps after Joe left. I knew my daughter had a bit of a crush on the lad as well. What was up?

I figured it out when I saw Juliana through the new front window. She was sitting on the couch, laughing, painting Bridget's toenails as Fiona and Shawna and Chrissy waited their turns. I spotted Jane sitting in the recliner with cucumber slices over her eyes.

I stood there shaking my head, amazed. Juliana knew how upset this whole Flaherty thing had made her little sisters, so she had scratched her plans in order to comfort them with some sister spa time. While I was itching to crack the seal on a bottle of booze, Juliana was stepping in, stepping up.

"Let's have a hand for father of the year, Mike Bennett," I mumbled as I plopped myself down on the front porch swing. I was still there when Mary Catherine came out. She frowned at my sad, self-pitying ass as she sat down beside me.

"And how are the Flahertys?" she asked.

I looked at her, about to deny my visit to the neighbors. Then I cracked a tiny smile.

"Bad news, Mary," I said, looking off down the sandy lane. "Which is about par for the course lately, isn't it? For this vacation. This city. This planet."

She wisely went back inside and left me alone with my black mood. When my work phone rang a half hour later with my boss's cell number on the display, I seriously thought about throwing it as hard as I could off the porch. Maybe taking a couple of potshots at it before it landed, my own personal Breezy Point clay shoot.

Then I remembered what my son

Trent had said two days before. Who was I kidding? Vacations were for real people. I was a cop.

"This is Bennett," I said into the phone with a grim smile. "Gimme a crime scene."

"Coming right up," Miriam said.

Chapter 26

As I drove through Queens twenty minutes later, I thought about a documentary I once saw on cable about the annual NYPD Finest versus the FDNY Bravest football game.

At halftime with the score tied, the firemen's locker room was about what you'd expect: upbeat, healthy-looking players and coaches encouraging one another. The NYPD locker room, on the other hand, was about as cheerful as the visitor's room at Rikers. In place of a traditional pep talk, red-faced, raging cops opted for screaming horrendous obscenities at one another and punching the lockers like violent mental patients.

No doubt about it, we're a funny bunch. Not funny ha-ha, either, I thought as I arrived at the latest atrocity, a murder scene along an industrial service road in Flushing.

I was a little fuzzy as to why I, of all people, needed to come to this godforsaken place in the middle of the night when I was already up to my eyeballs in the bombing case. But I was pretty sure I was about to find out.

Beside an electrical pylon at the top of the access road, half a dozen detectives and uniforms were taking pictures and kicking through the weeds, accompained by police-band radio chatter. In the far distance behind them, cars continued zipping by on the lit-up Whitestone and Throggs Neck Bridges. With the red-and-blue police strobes skipping through the trees, there was something bucolic, almost peaceful, about the whole scene.

Too bad peace wasn't my business. Definitely not tonight.

A short, immaculately dressed Filipino detective from the 109th Precinct pulled off a surgical glove and introduced himself to me as Andy Hunt while I was signing the homicide scene log. The death scene Hunt guided me to was a new Volvo Crossover with a nice tan-leather interior.

Formerly nice, I corrected myself as I stepped up to the driver's-side open door and saw the ruined bodies.

A middle-aged man and a younger woman leaned shoulder-to-shoulder in the center of the car, both shot twice in the head with a large-caliber gun. Green beads of shattered auto glass covered both bodies. I waved away a fly, staring at the horrible constellation of dried blood spray stuck to the dash.

"The male victim is one Eugene Keating. He was a professor at Hofstra, taught International Energy Policy, whatever the hell that is," Detective Hunt said, tossing his Tiffany Blue silk tie over his shoulder to protect it as he leaned in over the victims.

"The redhead is Karen Lang, one of his graduate students. Maybe they were testing the carbon output on this electrical cutout, but I have my doubts, considering her panties on the floor there.

two kids and his pregnant professor wife is due for a C-section in two days. Guess she'll have to call a cab to the hospital now, huh?"

"I don't understand, though," I said, resisting the urge to pull down the poor female victim's bunched-up T-shirt. "Why does anyone think this twofer has something to do with today's bombing?"

Hunt gave me an extra-grim look. Then he moved the light onto something white that was sitting in the dead man's lap. It was an envelope with something typed across the front of it.

I squatted down to get a better look. You're not supposed to let the job get inside you, but I have to admit that when I read my name on the envelope, I absolutely panicked. I froze from head to toe as if someone had just pressed an invisible gun to my head.

After a few minutes, I shrugged off my heebie-jeebies and decided to go ahead and open it. With thoughts of Ted Kaczynski, the Unabomber, dancing in my head, I retrieved the envelope with the pliers of Hunt's multi-tool. I borrowed a folding knife from one of the uniforms and slit the envelope open on the hood of the nearest cruiser.

If I thought opening the letter was a hair-raising experience, it couldn't hold a candle to what it said on the plain sheet of white paper inside.

Dear Detective Michael Bennett:
I am deeply hurt by your calling me a woman hater. **I am not.** *But I am a monster.*
I am the Son of Sam.

Book Two

DOUBLE DOWN

Chapter 27

Wearing a pink Banana Republic button-down shirt, pillow-soft J. Crew khakis, and Bass penny loafers, Berger whistled as he carried a brimming tray of Starbucks coffees south down Fifth Avenue with the rest of the early-morning commuters. Shaved and gelled to a high-gloss metrosexual sheen, he even had a corporate ID badge with the improbable name CORY GONSALVES emblazoned across it like a Hello sticker. In this elitist venue of publishing houses and television company offices that was the Rockefeller Center business district, his just-so-casual creative-type office-worker look was better camouflage than a sniper's ghillie suit.

Pounding hammers and clicking socket wrenches and muffled shouts rang off the granite walls as he turned right down Rockefeller Center's east concourse. Berger almost tripped over a gray-haired, potbellied roadie on his knees who was taping down some cables.

Berger knew that the stage was being erected for the *Today* show's outdoor summer concert series, to be broadcast at 8:15 this morning. The musical artist, a young man by the ponderous name of The Show, was going to perform his hit song, "Anywhere Real Slow."

Already people had arrived for the event. Faces painted, holding signs, they were anticipating a fun morning of dancing and singing along with the ex–drug-dealing rapper as he performed his soulful ode to the joys of public sexual activity.

Berger had a catchphrase for today's young that he was waiting for the ad firms to pick up on. First, you had Generation X, then Generation Y, now welcome, ye one and sundry, I introduce De-generation 1.

Because "Anywhere Real Slow" wasn't a mockery of just music but of civilization, too. It didn't glorify raunch and stupidity and low urges. It worshipped them. Anyone who didn't see the cheerful acceptance of this gutter dirt by the general public, and especially by the young, as a sign of the coming new Dark Ages lacked a working mind or was madder than Alice's hatter.

Once upon a time Rome fell. Now it was our turn. The Show was here to provide the background music.

Berger passed a group of giggling high-school girls. Enjoy the bottom-feeding, he thought as he carefully left one of his coffees on the ledge of a planter that he passed. Without looking back, he stepped out onto Sixth Avenue and hailed a taxi.

Chapter 28

It was almost eight a.m. by the time Berger got back to his apartment.

Inside the high, dim alcove, he actually genuflected before Salvador Dali's first painting, praying to the great Spaniard for help and strength.

He remembered a quote from the Master. "At the age of six, I wanted to be a cook. At seven, I wanted to be Napoleon. And my ambition has been growing steadily ever since."

Berger stood, smiling. Each moment, each breath, came that much sweeter the closer he approached his death. In the beginning, he had been afraid when he thought about how things would turn out. Now he saw that it all made perfect sense. He was glad.

In the apartment's imposing library, Berger slowly removed all of his clothing. He lifted the remote control and stood before the massive screen of the $50,000 103-inch Panasonic plasma TV. He glanced at the butter-soft leather recliner where he'd sat to watch all his favorite movies, but he didn't sit down. For this, he preferred to stand.

He clicked on the set. There was a commercial for a feminine product and then Matt Lauer filled the wall of the room.

"Without further ado," Lauer said, "let's cut to the Plaza and The Show."

A young black man in a full-out orange prison jumpsuit covered in gold chains winked from the screen.

"Ya'll ready to make some noise?" The Show wanted to know. Behind him, a retinue of other prison-suited young male and female backup singers and dancers of every race were standing, still as Buckingham Palace guards, waiting for the first drop of bass to start kicking it freestyle.

Many of the young people in the crowd had cell phones in their hands and were recording the momentous occasion. Berger lifted his own phone, but it wasn't to take a picture.

It was to paint his own.

He pressed the speed dial.

"And one, two," The Show said.

"Show's over," Berger said.

There was a flash of light. A startling blast of sound followed by a long, cracking echo. The Show stood there, microphone to his gaping mouth, as the camera panned over his shoulder onto a plume of smoke. In 1080 HD with Dolby Surround, Berger was psyched.

He changed to Channel Two.

CBS's *Early Show* was on. The host, some slutty-looking bimbo, was grilling fish out on the studio's 59th and Fifth Avenue plaza with none other than celebrity chef Wolfgang Puck.

"Ja, you see? Ja," Wolfgang said.

"Ja, Volfie, I see, I see," Berger said

as he thumbed another speed-dial button for the second device he'd planted next to the corner garbage can at the chef's back.

Another explosion, even louder than the first, happened immediately. Someone started screaming.

"That's what you get," Berger chided, clicking over to ABC.

Diane Sawyer was interviewing a sportswriter who was shilling his latest vapid tear-jerking bestseller. They were outside on one of ABC's Times Square Studios' roof plazas.

"Tell me, where do you get your ideas?" Diane wanted to know.

"On second thought, don't," Berger said as he dialed the third bomb that he'd left in the center of Times Square, down on the street beneath her.

The sound was softer, which made sense due to the elevation, Berger thought, looking down at the Oriental carpet. Had there been a little glass-shattering in that one? He nodded with a grin. Indeed, there had been. Exceptional!

Satisfied, he shut off the massive set. Watching the ensuing chaos would prove—What? People were afraid of explosives? He knew that already. Better than most. Now it was time to rest up before lunch.

He was actually pretty proud of the bombs. They were simple, Venti-size sticks of dynamite attached to a Wi-Fi antenna wired to a watch battery with a thin piece of detcord for the boost. Not huge, but just big enough to make everybody scared shitless. Big enough to make everyone start to carefully ponder their next step.

With high explosives, it was all about the real estate. Location, location, location.

He went into his bathroom and opened the tap. He dropped in the bubble soap and bath crystals and lit some candles. On the sound system, he put on a new CD that he'd gotten at Bed Bath & Beyond. He popped a couple of Vitamin P-is-for-Percocets and slid into the warm water as a woman's voice rang like an angel's off the glowing white Tyrolean marble walls.

"Who can say where the road flows?" Berger sang along.

He closed his eyes.

"Where the day goes?
Only time."

Chapter 29

I buried my head deeper under my pillow as a little hand shook my big foot. By the brightness of the light trying to crash through my sealed eyelids, I knew I was late for work, and I couldn't have cared less.

I didn't even want to start thinking about, let alone dealing with, the mind-blowing letter I'd received last night from the Son of Sam.

Then there was a giggle and more fingers wrapped around my other foot. Two someones were now having some silly fun at Daddy's expense. Two about-to-be-spanked someones.

"Daddy," Shawna said, wiggling my ear.

"No es Daddy here-o," I said in my best Speedy Gonzales voice as I peeled her hand off. *"Daddy es mucho nighty-night."*

"But Daddy, you have to come," Shawna said. "Grandpappy is cooking breakfast. *Grandpappy.*"

"What?" I said, rolling to my feet in my Manhattan College boxers.

Seamus cooked breakfast on one occasion only. Christmas morning. The funny thing was, it was so good, it was worth the yearly wait.

I couldn't believe it as I came into the kitchen and the smell hit me. It was true. Seamus, in a chef's hat, was working all the burners, and the table was already a feast of pecan bacon, links from heaven called Pork King Sausages, eggs, home fries, and pancakes. Seamus had gone to town. All the way downtown, in fact, I thought as I saw a stack of homemade doughnuts covered in powdered sugar.

"What gives, Seamus?" I said as he laid down some sizzling blood pudding. "You leaving us? Is that it? You're heading back to the ol' sod, Danny boy. Is this farewell?"

"You wish," he said, pointing the spatula at me. "If you haven't noticed, this family is in need of some cheering up ever since we went to war with Clan Flaherty."

"Dad?" said Juliana as I took my place at the head of the table. "Could you at least, like, I don't know, put on a bathrobe?"

Everyone was smiling around the crowded dining-room table. Even poor Ricky with his stitches.

"Why do I have to be so formal, Juliana?" I said, smiling back at everyone. "Is Joe coming by?"

"Ooooh!" everyone said.

"Ooooh yourselves," Seamus said, coming in with a platter of buckwheat pancakes. "How about we say grace instead. Mr. Bennett, you lead us, if you can even remember it."

"Bless us, O Lord, and these thy gifts," I said as we all joined hands, "which we are about to receive from thy bounty through Christ our Lord."

"AMEN!" everyone agreed heartily.

Joking aside, I actually did say a prayer for the professor's poor wife who was about to give birth. I even asked for help to catch the insane son of a bitch who blew her husband's head off at point-blank range.

I was in a breakfast-grease coma and biting into my first doughnut when someone made the mistake of putting on the TV.

"Dad! Dad! You have to see this!" Ricky yelled.

"I'm a cop," I said, calling into the family room. "Don't mess with a cop when he's anywhere near a doughnut."

I winked at Mary Catherine across the table. She seemed to be in a good mood, having slept in while Seamus cooked. Maybe today would turn out better than yesterday, after all. I was due for a small miracle. Past due.

"But it's another bombing, Dad. At Rockefeller Center. No one dead, it says at the bottom of the screen. But a dozen people are in the hospital. The mad bomber strikes again!"

Rockefeller Center? This loser didn't

quit, did he? Or was it two people? One Son of Sam copycat and another fool?

I didn't even look for my phone. I didn't need my boss to tell me where I needed to be.

Running for the shower, I passed Seamus coming in with the coffee.

"I'll need to take that to go."

Chapter 30

Pedal to my city-issued Impala's metal, flashers and siren cranked to full amplification, I plowed a swath through the BQE's left lane that morning.

A scraggly red Ford pickup that had missed out on the Cash for Clunkers deal tried to cut in a hundred feet in front of me. His mirrors must have been broken, as well as his ears. I roared up until I was practically in his rusting truck bed before I sent him packing with a fierce barrage of machine-gunning *yawps* and *whoops*.

No wonder I was on the warpath. What was happening was beyond incredible. Police presence had been beefed up at all major public places around the city, and still our bomber had managed to set off even more explosives. At the same time as all three network morning shows were being broadcast, no less!

I thought about the crime scene from the night before.

I lifted my BlackBerry as I pounded past a nasty stretch of Queens tract housing and half-finished construction sites. Talking on the phone was beyond stupid and reckless, considering I had my cop car up near the three-digit range, but what was I going to do? *Stupid* and *reckless* happened to be my middle and confirmation names this crazy morning. It was time to brainstorm with Emily Parker down at the FBI's Violent Criminal Apprehension Program in Virginia.

"Parker," Emily said.

I quickly told her about the previous night's murder scene and the Son of Sam letter addressed to me.

"So not only is someone setting off bombs every three seconds, but the Son of Sam has apparently returned," I said in conclusion. "And to top things off, the only connection between the crimes so far seems to be a desire to correspond with lucky old me."

"You think the three terrorist acts are connected to the Son of Sam copycat killer?" Emily said. "That is truly bizarre."

That's when I remembered what Ricky had said as I was leaving. I almost ran off the elevated expressway.

The mad bomber strikes again!

"Wait! The Mad Bomber. Of course!" I cried. "It isn't a terrorist act, Emily. The bombings are copycats, too. There actually was a Mad Bomber who terrorized New York in the forties or fifties, I think."

"Hold up, Mike. I'm at a computer," Emily said.

I could hear her typing.

"My God, Mike, you're right. It's right here on Wikipedia. The guy's name was George Metesky. He was known as the Mad Bomber, and it says here that in the forties and fifties, he planted bombs at New York landmarks. Wait! It says he planted bombs at the Public Library and Grand Central Terminal."

I shook my head.

"Is that what this is?" I said. "Someone or more than one person is copycatting two famous crime sprees at once?"

"But how?" Emily said, sounding astounded. "Think about the logistics. How could it be coordinated? Four bombings and a double murder in a little over twenty-four hours?"

"Well, from the sophistication of the bombs, we're not dealing with dummies," I said as I fumbled my grip on my phone. I was just able to catch it against my chest.

When I looked back up, I immediately stopped thinking about the case. In fact, my entire brain stopped functioning. Then my lungs.

Because around a curve in the expressway, being approached at roughly the speed of light, were three packed lanes of dead-stopped traffic.

Chapter 31

For a few precious fractions of a second, I did nothing but gape at the frozen red wall of brake lights.

Then I did four things pretty much simultaneously. I screamed, released the phone, let off the gas, and slammed on the brakes.

Nothing happened. In fact, the brakes felt suddenly looser than normal. Were they broken? I thought, pissed. Or possibly *cut?* I knew the car had ABS. It was perhaps the only thing on my shock-scrambled mind as I hurtled toward the rapidly approaching rear of a Peter Pan tour bus.

I wondered in my panic if I was doing it right. Was I supposed to pump or hold the brakes? I couldn't remember. My fear-locked leg decided for me, keeping the pedal down as far as it would go.

The brake pedal gave a couple of hard jerks under my foot and then felt even looser. The line had snapped under the strain, I decided. The massive steel wall of bus in my windshield got larger and closer by the millisecond.

It was over, I decided. I was going to hit it head-on, and it was going to be very bad.

That's when a slow-motion, life-flashing-before-your-eyes sensation kicked in. I glanced to my right as I lasered past a white Volkswagen Jetta. The pretty young brunette behind the wheel was putting on mascara. Turning back toward the rear of the bus that I was about to become part of, I wondered if she was the last human face I would ever see.

My last thought as I braced my arms against the steering wheel was of my kids. How hard and royally shitty it was going to be for them to lose not just their biological parents, not just their adoptive mother, but now their careless adoptive father as well.

I closed my eyes.

And the car just stopped.

No skidding. No warning. There was a brief scream of rubber, and it was like God slipped his hand between my car and the bus, and I went from sixty to zero in zero point zero seconds.

Too bad I was still moving. My sternum felt like it was hit with an ax handle as I chest-bumped my locked shoulder belt. My dropped BlackBerry catapulted off the passenger seat like an F-14 off a carrier. It ricocheted off the glove box and whizzed past my ear like a bullet.

Guess I should have bought that merchandise insurance after all, I thought, as I sat blinking and shuddering behind the wheel.

Was I still alive?

I decided to check. I took a sweet drink of oxygen and, like magic, turned it into carbon dioxide. Then I did it again. My heart was still beating, too. Actually, it felt like it was trying to tear itself out of my chest, but that was neither here nor there. Being alive was fun, I decided.

Chapter 32

I waited a few more seconds to see if St. Peter was going to show. When he didn't, I backed away from the rear of the idling bus. Ignoring the dumbstruck looks from my fellow motorists in the other lanes, I reached into the back of the car and retrieved my phone. The battery cover was shot, but the phone was actually still working. Miracles were abounding this morning.

Since traffic was at a standstill, I decided to call Emily back.

"Mike, what happened?" Emily said when I got her on the line.

"Oh, nothing," I said, wiping cold sweat out of my eyes with my free palm. I was going to leave it at that, but then the fear and adrenaline caught up with me, and my hands started to shake so badly, I had to lay the phone down and put it on speaker.

"Actually, I almost just killed myself, Emily," I said. "I was flying back into Manhattan and turned a corner and came within an inch or two of embedding myself in the rear end of a tour bus. Who needs coffee?"

"My God! Are you okay?"

"My hands won't stop shaking," I said. "I thought I'd bought it there for a second, Emily."

"Pull over and take some deep breaths, Mike. I'm right here with you."

I followed her advice. It wasn't just what she said but the way she said it. Emily really was a supportive person. I remembered her on our previous case together. How caring she was with one of the young kidnapping victims. She knew when to push and when to hold back. She was a terrific agent and a deeply caring person. She was good-looking, too. We kind of fell for each other during the case. Well, I know I fell for her.

"Mike? You still there?"

"Barely," I said.

She laughed.

"Well, I, for one, am glad your head's still attached to your shoulders, Mike. I like the way it thinks. The way it looks isn't half bad, either."

What did she say? I thought, squinting at the phone.

"Ah, you're just saying that to keep me from going into shock," I said.

"That's what friends are for," Emily said. "Actually, they want to send someone from our team up to New York to help you guys out, Mike. I was wondering if you thought it was a good idea if I volunteered?"

I thought about that. It went without saying that her expertise on the case would be invaluable. And it really would be awesome to see her. We had definitely made a connection, something special.

Then I suddenly remembered Mary Catherine, and how things were going on that front.

I must have still been loopy with

shock, because the next thing I said surprised me.

"Come up. We need all the help we can get. We need the best people on this. Besides, it would be great to see you."

"Really?" she said.

"Really," I said, not knowing what the hell I was doing or saying. "Call me as soon as you get up here."

Chapter 33

I somehow managed to complete the rest of my commute safely and arrived at the closest bombing scene, at 59th Street and Fifth Avenue, around nine thirty a.m.

The area across from the Plaza Hotel and Central Park was usually packed with rich ladies who lunch and tourists looking for overpriced horse-and-buggy rides. Now an occupying force of assault rifle–strapping Emergency Service Unit storm troopers had cordoned off the corner, and instead of Chipoos peeking from Fendi clutches, bomb-sniffing Labradors were sweeping both sides of the street.

I noticed an aggravating CBS News

camera aimed directly between my eyes as I came under the crime scene tape in front of the GM Building. I guess I couldn't complain that the media had already gotten here, since, including ABC and NBC, they seemed to be the targets.

As if Tiffany's and the network studios weren't high-profile enough, the world-famous FAO Schwarz toy store sat on the other side of the outdoor space, as well as the funky transparent glass cube of the wild Fifth Avenue sunken Apple store.

I found the Bomb Squad's second in command, Brian Dunning, chewing gum as he knelt on the intersection's southeast corner in front of a blast-blackened streetlight. At the Grand Central scene, Cell had told me that the blond pock-faced tech was fresh from Iraq, where he'd been part of a very busy army EOD team. Since it seemed New York was currently at war as well, I was glad he was on our side.

The toppled garbage can beside him had a hole in its steel mesh the size of a grapefruit. What looked like tiny pieces

of confetti were scattered on the sidewalk and street beside it. It reminded
me of firecracker paper on the day after
the Fourth of July. I scooped some of it
up to get a better look.

"It's cardboard," Dunning said, standing. "From a coffee cup, is my guess.
Which would blend in perfectly in a garbage can. You want an IED to appear
totally innocuous."

"Was it plastic explosive, like the last
one?" I said.

Dunning smelled the piece of cardboard.

"Dynamite, I'd say off the top of my
head. About a stick or so, I'd guess.
Mobile phone trigger with a fuse-head
electric blasting cap packed in a coffee
cup all as neat as you please. This cop-
killing freak's got skills. I'll give him
that."

Great, I thought. Our guy was using
new materials. Or maybe not, I thought,
letting out a breath. It could have been
someone else catching the heat of the
moment and getting in on the act.

More questions without any answers,
I thought. What else was new?

I caught up to my boss, who was talking with a group of shaken-up *Early Show* staffers.

"No one seems to have seen a thing, Mike," Miriam said as we walked toward the corner. "They have security out here on the Plaza, of course, but they don't detour pedestrian traffic. Sanitation said they collected this morning at five. Our guy must have dropped the coffee cup sometime after that, probably as he was waiting for the light. This guy's a ghost."

I quickly went over the double copycat theory that Emily and I were working on.

"He's not just copying Sam the Man," I said. "In the forties, a disgruntled Con Ed employee named George Metesky planted bombs in movie theaters and public places. For sixteen years, he set off gunpowder-filled pipe bombs in the same places this guy has hit. The library, Rockefeller Center, Grand Central. It fits, boss."

She stepped off the sidewalk into the street. We looked down Fifth Avenue at the Empire State Building for a few beats.

"So you're saying this guy isn't just some regular run-of-the-mill violent psycho?" she said.

I nodded.

"I think we have some kind of super-competent and super-loony NYC crime buff out there giving nods to those he admires," I said.

Chapter 34

For the remainder of the day, I visited the other crime scenes at Rock Center and Times Square, where I learned absolutely nothing new. No one in Times Square had seen a man dropping a coffee cup, not even the Naked Cowboy.

The entire Major Case Squad was going blind reviewing security video footage from surrounding stores and buildings, but so far nothing had made itself evident. It was the same story for the red-balled forensics test on the letter from the Flushing double murder. There was a brief moment of hope when I learned that the VIN for the truck involved in the Grand Central bombing had been traced. But that hope had been dashed with authority when it turned out that it was a *stolen* rental truck.

Who steals a rental truck? A psycho, was the answer to that one. A very neat and tidy anal psycho. The worst kind of all. And to top it all off, I still couldn't shake how I'd almost died on the BQE through my own sheer stupidity.

It was around ten that night when I got off the exit for Breezy Point. There was no music when I pulled up in front of the Bennett beach house. Definitely no margaritas waiting for me. In fact, all the lights in the house were off. I remembered Mary Catherine was at her night class at Columbia. Not good.

Somebody was on the porch. It was my son Brian, pacing back and forth, holding a baseball bat. It didn't look like he was working on his swing.

"Don't tell me something else happened," I groaned. "Wasn't today any better?"

"No one told you, Dad? Eddie and Ricky went out to get ice cream, and a bunch of a-holes threw some eggs at them from a passing car. Not only that, but when Jane rode the bike to the store, she came out and found this."

He rolled the bike over and showed me the front tire sliced to ribbons.

"I'm going to kill this kid, Dad. I swear, I'm going to kill him."

"And I'm going to absolve him when he does," Seamus said, stepping onto the porch with a golf club.

I let out a breath. Home Insane Home.

"The worst thing," Seamus said, "is that all the fookin' Flahertys go to Sunday mass. Like it's going to keep them out of Hell, which it isn't, the little heathens. The host should burn holes in their tongues."

"Enough about going on the warpath, you fighting Irishmen," I said. "Brian, listen. I know you're mad, but we need to be smart about this. You let this punk bait you, you'll be the one who gets arrested."

"Maybe we should do what Bridget said, then, Dad," Brian said, dropping the mangled bike. "Maybe we should just clear out, because this vacay is starting to suck."

I lifted up the bike and carried it off the porch and into the garage. I popped off the tire with a screwdriver and looked through the shelves for a patch kit.

"He's right, you know," Seamus said, coming in as I put rubber cement over the first gash.

"About what?" I said.

"This vacay is starting to suck. Big time," Seamus said.

Chapter 35

Later that night, I sat on the porch swing, having pulled guard duty. I had a plastic cup of cheap red wine in one hand and Brian's Louisville Slugger in the other. Summer of Love, part two, this was not.

"Hark, who goes there?" I said as Mary Catherine came up the stairs, home from her art class. She was wearing tight jeans with a jazzy leopard-print tank and looked amazing.

"We're arming ourselves? It's that bad, huh?" Mary Catherine said as she shrugged off her laptop bag and sat her long legs down beside me.

I poured my nanny a glass of Malbec.

"Worse," I said, handing it to her.

"Are they all asleep?"

"At least pretending to be," I said. "All except the big one."

"Brian?"

"No, Father Pain-in-the-Ass. He went out for a few jars, quote unquote, to soothe his troubled mind. Even the saints are hitting the suds tonight," I said, clinking plastic cups.

"Are you any closer to catching the bomber guy?" she asked, kicking off her flats. "Because the people in my class are completely bonkers. Half of them didn't even show up for tonight's test. They told the professor they're too afraid to ride the trains."

"Smart kids," I said. "You might want to follow their example. If the color code thing were still in place, we'd be looking at orange, dark orange."

"I'm a big girl, Mike. I know my way around the city now. I can take care of me own self."

"I know that, but if something happens to you, who's going to take care of me?" I said.

We swung back and forth for a while,

talking and having more wine. She told me some funny stories about her summer vacations with her big family when she was a kid back in Tipperary. Even after the day I'd had, I was actually starting to relax.

I don't remember who started kissing whom. For a while we held each other, just listening to the sound of the surf two blocks away. The waves were incredibly choppy and loud, making a relentless pounding noise. The first hurricane of the season was heading up the East Coast from Florida, I remembered I'd heard on the radio.

That's when I remembered something else. The hurricane wasn't the only thing coming up to New York.

Why had I told Emily Parker to come again? I thought as Mary Catherine undid the buttons on my shirt. Because she was a competent law enforcement expert? Even I knew that was bull. Emily was cute, and I liked her. But Mary Catherine was cute as well, and I liked her, too.

One thing led to another, and after a bit I found my hand under the back of

Mary's shirt. Mary suddenly pulled back and sat up.

"Talk about dark orange," she said.

She was right. We both knew we were on the threshold of something either wonderful or terrible. Neither one of us knew what to do about it.

"What now?" Mary said.

"You tell me."

"We're so Irish, Michael."

"Well, technically, I'm Irish-American," I said, pulling her in again and kissing her sweet hot mouth.

"Eh-hem," someone yelled.

I don't know who jumped higher, me or Mary. There was a jangle of chains as we almost ripped the porch swing off its moorings.

Seamus came up the steps, a smile from ear to ear.

"And how was your class tonight, Mary Catherine? Your art class that is, if you don't mind me askin'?"

"Oh, fine, Seamus. Look at the time. So much to do tomorrow. Good night," Mary said, off like a shot into the house, absolutely abandoning me.

Seamus looked at my completely open shirt with disdain.

"Michael Sean Aloysius Bennett. What in the name of the good Lord do you think you're doing? And don't be telling me you've been catching some rays," Seamus said.

"I'm...going to bed, Father," I said, hitting the screen door at mach two. "It's been a long day. G'night."

Chapter 36

I woke up extra early for work the next morning.

And not just to beat the traffic this time. A stealthy exit after last night's questionable tonsil-hockey session with MC on the porch seemed just the thing.

In addition to probably breaking several employer sexual harassment laws, I didn't know where to start in sorting through my conflicting feelings. I really had no idea at all what to say to Mary in the light of day. I definitely didn't want to face another inquisition from Seamus.

Red wine always gets me into trouble. No, wait, that's my big mouth.

As I tiptoed out of Dodge, holding my shoes, I noticed a strange bluish light coming from the girls' room. I knew I should keep on going and leave the culprits to their own mischievous devices, but the cop in me couldn't resist a righteous bust.

I retraced my toe tips back into their room. The light was coming from under a suspiciously lumpy blanket on the bed in the corner. There was a lot of suspicious excited whispering going on as well.

"What's this?" I said, whipping away the blanket like a magician.

What I saw wasn't a rabbit, though it was still quite cute.

"AHHHHH!" Chrissy and Shawna screamed in unison, lying on their bellies in front of a laptop computer.

"A computer?" I said, clapping a hand against my head in mock outrage. "You smuggled in a computer on our vacation? Don't tell me that's *Phineas and Ferb* on that screen. No electronic toys, remember? No video games. Sound familiar?"

"It was Ricky," Shawna said, pointing toward the boys' room frantically.

"It's true. It's Ricky's. We're just borrowing it," Chrissy said.

"What's going on?" Mary Catherine whispered suddenly there, yawning in the doorway.

Uh-oh. I knew I should have gotten out while I could. The girls weren't the only ones who were busted.

"We're sorry, Mary," Chrissy said.

"Yes. We're so sorry," Shawna added quickly. "So sorry that Ricky brought a computer when he wasn't supposed to."

"We'll deal with this later," Mary said as she confiscated the computer and tucked the girls back in.

"You're up early," she said, glancing suspiciously at the shoes in my hand as we left the room. "Come to the kitchen. I'll make you coffee before you go."

"I'd love to, but I don't have time. Early briefing," I said.

"It's five-thirty," Mary Catherine said, peering at me.

"Duty calls," I said with a hopefully

convincing smile and a wave as I headed toward the front door.

I stopped as I came out onto the porch. Even in the predawn murk, I could see it. Somebody had spray-painted the wall behind the porch swing.

GO HOME STUPID BASTERDS!

I stood there holding my hungover head in my hands. The sons of bitches had come onto my porch in the middle of the night? I guess my scare tactic over at the Flaherty compound hadn't gone as well as I'd hoped. This was really getting nuts now.

"Seems like Flaherty gets his spelling lessons from Quentin Tarantino," Seamus said in his bathrobe from the doorway.

I shook my head. Like it or not, I really did need to get to work. I couldn't stay to sort through this latest outrage. I glanced at Seamus.

"Seamus, I'm swamped at work. Do you think you could take care of this for me before the kids see it?"

Seamus gave me a hard glare.

"Oh, don't worry, Michael Sean Aloysius. I'll be cleaning up all the latest *shenanigans* going on around here before the kids see them," Seamus said.

I winced at his emphasis on the word. I guess I was getting a fresh, un-asked-for heaping of Catholic guilt to go this morning.

"And I'll tell you another thing, jail time or no jail time, I'll blast the first Flaherty I see back to Hell's Kitchen and straight down to Hell, where they belong," he called as I walked down the steps. "This old codger will make Clint Eastwood from *Gran Torino* seem like Santa Claus."

"You already do," I whispered as I hurried for the safety of my police car.

Chapter 37

Instead of heading into the city to my crowded, frantic squad room, I skirted Manhattan altogether and took the Triborough Bridge north to the New York State Thruway. An hour and a half later, I was upstate in Sullivan County near Monticello, sipping a rest-stop Dunkin' Donuts java as I rolled past misty pine forests, lakes, and dairy farms.

The bucolic area was close to where Woodstock had taken place. It had also been home to the "Borscht Belt" vacation resorts, where Jewish comedians like Milton Berle and Don Rickles and Woody Allen had gotten their start.

Unfortunately, my visit had nothing to do with music and even less to do with laughter. This morning I was heading to Fallsburg, home of the Sullivan Correctional Facility.

My boss and I had decided it was time to have a chat with its most infamous resident, David Berkowitz, the .44 Caliber Killer. The Son of Sam himself.

There were several reasons why. One of the most compelling was that the Monday night double murder in Queens wasn't the only recent Son of Sam copycat crime.

An hour after we put the Son of Sam lead over the inner department wire, a sharp Bronx detective had called the squad. He told us that on Sunday a teenage Hispanic girl in the Bronx had barely survived an odd stabbing in Co-op City. Her attacker had worn a crazy David Berkowitz–style wig and said some real out-there stuff to her as he slowly cut her up. It mimicked almost perfectly Berkowitz's first crime, the random stabbing of a girl in Co-op City in 1975.

There was a long list of people with whom I'd rather spend my morning, but since Berkowitz seemed to have some connection to the recent string of murders, I thought it might be fruitful to have a sit-down. It was probably a long shot, but with seven people dead and no lead in sight, it was high time to get creative.

Sullivan Correctional was hidden discreetly behind a tall stand of pines, a few miles northeast of Fallsburg's small-town main street. As soon as I spotted the sudden vista of steel wire and pale concrete buildings built terrace-like up a rolling hill, the coffee in my stomach began to percolate for a second time. Sullivan was a maximum-security prison that housed many of New York City's most violent offenders. I knew because I had put a few of them there.

Under the stony eye of a tower guard, I was buzzed into the south complex administrative building, where I reluctantly relinquished my service weapon and signed in. I was escorted to the ground-floor office of Doug Gaffney, the prison manager, whom I'd spoken to the day before to set up the meeting.

Bald and stocky in a polo shirt and khakis, Gaffney reminded me of a middle-aged football coach more than a warden. Books about anger management and drug abuse lined the shelf behind his desk, along with a thick binder with the words "Life Skills" on the spine.

"Thanks for setting this up for me, Doug," I said after we shook hands and sat down.

"This case you're working on? We're talking about the bombing thing?" Gaffney asked as his secretary closed the door.

"Yes, but that's confidential, as is my visit," I explained, sitting up in my folding chair. "The press is already dogging us on this. I'd hate to sell more papers for them than I have to. What should I expect from Berkowitz?"

"Don't worry. We don't have to put him in a hockey mask or anything," Gaffney said with a small grin. "In the six years I've been here, he's been nothing but a model prisoner. Runs a prayer group now. He even helps blind inmates back to their cells."

"I heard about his religious conversion. Do you believe it?" I said.

"I limit my belief to things outside these walls, Mike, but who knows?" he said, lifting a radio out of the charger behind him. "If you're ready, I'll walk you over."

Chapter 38

I met Berkowitz in a bright and airy secure visitors' room in a cell block across the concrete yard behind Gaffney's office.

What struck me first was how surprisingly unthreatening he was. Short, paunchy, and middle-aged, with white hair, he reminded me of the singer Paul Simon. He was clean-shaven and his hair was freshly cut. Even his green prison clothes seemed excessively neat, as if he had had them dry-cleaned. He bore little resemblance to the wild-eyed sloppy young man on the front cover of all the newspapers when he had been apprehended in 1977.

He actually smiled and made eye

contact as he sat on the opposite side of the room's worn linoleum table.

"Hi, David. My name's Detective Bennett from the NYPD," I said, smiling back. "Thank you for agreeing to speak with me this morning."

"Nice to meet you," he said, taking a small Bible from his pocket. He placed it directly on the table before him. "How can I help you, sir?"

"Well, I was wondering if you might be able to give me a little insight into a case I'm investigating right now," I said.

Berkowitz's eyes narrowed as he cocked his head.

"It must be some case for you to come all the way up here from the city."

"It is, David. It seems a person is committing crimes similar to the ones you were involved with back in the seventies."

I reluctantly used the term "involved with" instead of "viciously and cowardly committed" because I needed his cooperation.

"A girl in Co-op City was stabbed,

and two people were shot in a lover's
lane in Queens with a forty-four-caliber
weapon," I continued. "We even received a letter from someone claiming
to be you."

Berkowitz stared at me wide-eyed.
He looked genuinely shaken.

"That's terrible," he said.

"Do you know anyone who might
want to do these things?"

"Not a soul," he said immediately.

"C'mon, David. I know in the past
you've made reference to other people
who might have been involved in your
case. Other satanic cult members,
wasn't it? Have you had any contact
with any of those people lately?"

"Well, to tell you the truth, Detective,
I don't know how helpful I can be in that
area," he said, staring at the Bible. "You
see, what I remember of that tragic time
is really all a blur now."

How convenient for you, I thought.

He began to fan the Bible pages with
his thumb as he continued.

"I was deep into the occult back then
and not really in my right mind. In fact,
ever since giving myself over to Jesus

Christ, more and more of those memories seem to fade every day, thankfully. That's the incredible power of Jesus. His forgiveness can cleanse even a man like me."

I looked across the table for a beat. Berkowitz had his eyes closed and hands clasped in silent prayer. He seemed pretty convinced that Jesus Christ was now his personal savior.

I wasn't so sure. I knew that one of the things serial killers tended to crave was manipulation. They exulted in their superiority over people and liked to lie for the sheer pleasure of it.

"You said you weren't in your right mind," I continued in order to keep the conversation flowing. "Do you think I should look for a person with mental instability? Talk to some psychiatrists maybe?"

Berkowitz nodded, opening his eyes.

"Sure, sure," he said. "Though, like myself, there are a lot of lost individuals out there who never receive any formal psychiatric help."

That's when I dropped my payload, the thing I was truly interested in.

"Does the name Lawrence mean any- thing to you?" I said, staring into his eyes. "Think hard, David. Someone from your past or maybe someone you met in jail?"

He cocked his head again and squinted up at the ceiling.

"No," he said slowly after a few sec- onds. "Should it?"

"Have you ever received any corre- spondence from anyone named Law- rence? An admirer perhaps?"

I kept staring into his eyes.

"Not that I remember," he said, look- ing back at me serenely. "It is possible though. I do receive a lot of mail."

I nodded as I let out a sigh. That was about it. Either Berkowitz wasn't aware of anything or he wasn't going to tell me. There was no connection, no lead. I'd arrived at yet another dead end.

"Thanks, David," I said, frustrated as I stood and nodded at the guard out- side. "I appreciate your time."

"Good luck and God bless you, De- tective Bennett. I hope you catch the poor soul who's out there hurting people," Berkowitz said as the guard led him away.

Poor soul? I thought, rolling my eyes as Gaffney came in. Yeah, I couldn't wait to catch the poor, tragic, homicidal wayward lamb myself.

"Does he get a lot of mail?" I asked Gaffney.

"It's amazing," Gaffney nodded. "From all over the world."

"I know you guys read the mail, but you wouldn't happen to have a record of Berkowitz's correspondence, would you?"

"That we do. For Diamond Dave, we read and make a copy of everything coming and going. Even the stuff we won't let him have."

Maybe my trip wasn't such a bust after all.

"Do you think I could see it?"

"Confidentially?" Gaffney asked with a wink.

"But of course," I said.

"We actually scan everything now. I'll e-mail you the whole ball of wax. Hope you have a big hard drive. Anything else?"

"Just one thing," I said, hurrying behind him toward the block's electric gate and the free world. "Where do I get my gun back?"

Chapter 39

To the clack of kitchen plates, the pale, elegant brunette weaved her way around the dim room's empty linen-covered tables and climbed the little corner stage to reach the ebony Steinway Concert Grand. After a moment, a slow and pretty impressionistic piece began to drift out over the room, Debussy or maybe Ravel.

At the opposite end of the wood-paneled room, Berger nodded with approval. Then he carefully tucked his damask napkin into his shirt, closed his eyes, and *inhaled*.

Invisible ribbons of hunger-inflaming scents from the vicinity of the swinging kitchen door behind him invaded his quivering nostrils. He detected nutty sizzling butters, meat smoke, soups redolent of mushrooms and leeks, decanted vintage wine. His palate was so sensitive, he felt he could actually distinguish the separate odors dissolving against the postage stamp–size tissue called the olfactory epithelium, high in his nasal cavity.

"Now, sir?" whispered the bug-eyed tuxedo-clad maître d' at his back.

The arrangement was that only the maître d' could serve or speak to him. Berger never spoke back, but rather indicated his wishes with a series of predetermined head and facial gestures. He had even asked that the shades be drawn to keep the dining space as dark as possible.

Berger waited a moment longer, holding in the glorious aromas, a junkie with a hit of crack smoke. Then he gave a subtle nod.

The maître d's finger snap was like a starter pistol, and in came the white-jacketed waiters with the plates. They were actually more like platters. There were mounds of brioche, caviar, quiche, a roast duck, a crème brûlée, oysters, a gravy boat filled with a saffron-colored sauce, and more. It was hard to tell which meal was being served.

It was actually *all* of them, a montage of breakfast, lunch, and dinner.

Berger immediately tucked in. The first thing within his grasp was a still-warm baguette. He ripped off a hunk in a detonation of flaky crumbs, stabbed it into a tub of white truffle butter, and slammed it into his waiting mouth. More crumbs went flying as he chewed with his mouth open. He loudly slurped at a glass of Cabernet, spilling much of it. Arterial-red rivulets dripped unnoticed off his chin as he reached for the plate of oysters.

He was well aware that he was breaking every rule of table etiquette. No doubt about it, he had a soft spot for food. When it came to meals, he literally became overwhelmed, almost drugged, with all the smells and tastes and, lately, even textures. He was so unabashedly gluttonous, he didn't even use silverware anymore but went at it with his bare hands like a savage in order to heighten his obsessive pleasure. The consumption of food had become something shameless, almost horrifying, and yet in a very real sense, somehow divine.

Like the famous killers Berger so admired, he possessed an intensity of desire for certain things that other people either couldn't understand or were afraid to even consider.

The maître d' cleared his throat.

"More wine, sir?" he whispered beside his ear.

Berger nodded as he ripped into the duck with his bare hands, fingernails tearing deliciously at the crispy, greasy skin.

More, Berger thought, filling his mouth until his cheeks bulged. My favorite word.

Chapter 40

It was two in the afternoon when Berger got out of a taxi in Brooklyn's Grand Army Plaza. Dapper as can be in a chalk-pinstripe Alexander McQueen power suit, he carried a brown paper bag in his right hand, and in his left his lucky cane. The razor-sharp saber inside it had a grinning pewter skull for a handle that he kept hidden under his palm as he strolled.

He arrived at Sixth Avenue and made a right. A block up the leafy, brownstone-lined street, he paused by the steps of a church. He made the sign of the cross as he glanced at himself in the window of a parked Prius. He unbuttoned his jacket to show off his

Hermès tie and handmade single-stitched Turnbull & Asser shirt. Now was not the time for Christian modesty.

He counted the addresses until he came to 485. He stepped up the stoop and rang the doorbell with the cane.

The forty-something redheaded man who opened the door was wearing a Fordham T-shirt and shiny black basketball shorts, both speckled with primer.

"Mr. Howard?" the man said, patting at his carrot-colored hair as he opened the door. "What brings you here?"

"I was in the neighborhood, Kenneth," Berger said, smiling. "I remembered you lived around here and thought I'd give you a buzz."

The man's name was Kenneth Cavuto. He'd been a real-estate financial analyst working for Lehman Brothers until the investment bank went belly-up in the financial meltdown. Berger had interviewed the man two weeks ago after contacting him from the Classifieds section of Craigs-list. On the Monday following, at $200,000 to start plus bonuses, Kenneth was supposed to begin running the capital market team of Berger's fictitious new investment start-up, Red Lion Investments.

"Here, I brought you a gift," Berger said, handing him the paper sack. "My mother always said when you go for a visit, ring the bell with your elbow."

"Hey, wow, thanks. You didn't have to do that," Cavuto said as he accepted the bag. "What is it?"

"Fresh strawberries and pot cheese," Berger said.

"What kind of cheese?" Cavuto said, looking into the bag.

"Pot. Though it's not the kind you're thinking of, you rascal. It's the latest thing at Whole Foods."

"Is that right?" Cavuto said with a shrug. "Please come in. Let me wash up, and I'll put on some coffee."

"Don't bother yourself," Berger said with a wave. "I just wanted to make sure we were buttoned down on your position. No one else has come in with a higher bid, I hope. You'll be there on Monday?"

"Of course, Mr. Howard. Nine a.m.

sharp," the redhead assured him with a pathetic earnestness.

Berger smiled immediately as a three- or four-year-old blond girl appeared in the hall behind Cavuto.

"Hey, who's that?" Berger called to her. "Angela? Am I right?"

"That's right. You remembered," Cavuto said with happy surprise. "Angela, come here, baby."

Berger got down on one knee as she arrived next to her father. He looked at the funny-looking doll she was holding. It was Boots the Monkey from *Dora the Explorer*.

"Knock, knock," Berger said to her.

"Who's there?" Angela said, peering suspiciously at him.

"Nunya."

"Nunya who?" Angela said, smiling a little.

"Nunya business," Berger said, standing.

The little girl laughed. He always had a way with kids.

"Won't you come in?" Kenneth offered again.

"No, no. I'm off," Berger said. "I have to head over to the zoo in the park now, where my ex is waiting to get my little angel Bethany's fourth-birthday party started and—"

Berger snapped his finger.

"Where are my manners? Why don't you come? A couple of vice presidents from the firm will be there as well. It'll give you a chance to get acquainted before Monday."

"Really?" Cavuto said. "Sounds great. Give me five minutes to get ready."

Berger checked his flashy white-gold Rolex and made a face.

"Ah, but I'm already late, and it starts off with a guided tour for the kids. The ex-wife will lay into me if I'm not right there video-recording every millisecond of it."

Berger fished into his pocket and handed Cavuto his Red Lion Investments business card.

"How's this?" Berger said. "You and Angela can skip the animals and meet us for cake."

"But, Daddy! Animals! The monkeys!

I want to see the monkeys," Angela said, tugging at her father's shirt and on the verge of tears.

"There I go again. Me and my big mouth," Berger said sheepishly as the girl actually started crying.

Berger snapped his fingers.

"I feel terrible, Ken. If you want, Angela and I can start ahead so she doesn't miss the tour. Then when you're ready, call us and we'll tell you what animal we're up to."

This was the do-or-die moment, Berger knew. Hang with the boss versus parental paranoia. Berger was banking on the fact that the unemployed analyst wasn't that used to being a stay-at-home dad, was still unsure of himself, still unsure of his instincts. And of course, if he said no, Berger would quickly switch to Plan B. Stun-gun the father, chloroform the girl, and get out of there.

"Yeah?" Cavuto finally said.

Berger held his breath. The fish was on the hook. Time to reel it in slowly.

"You know, on second thought,"

Berger said, checking his watch as he retreated a step down the stairs. The girl, sensing his departure, broke into full-fledged sobs.

"It's not too much of a pain?" Cavuto said.

"Of course not," Berger said, reaching out for the little girl's hand with a smile. "Bethany will be so happy to make yet another brand-new best friend."

"I won't be long," Cavuto called, fingering the fake business card as they started down the sidewalk.

Oh, yes, you will, Daddy, Berger thought as he waved good-bye. Longer than you'll ever know.

He turned around when they got to the corner. Cavuto had already gone inside. Instead of heading straight for the park and the zoo, he made a left, searching for a taxi.

"Hey, Angela. You thirsty? Want a juice box?" Berger said, taking out the Elmo apple juice that he'd laced with liquid Valium.

"Is it 'ganic?" the white-blond-haired

tot wanted to know. "Mom only likes when I drink 'ganic."

"Oh, it's 'ganic, all right, Angela," Berger said as a taxi pulled to the curb. "It's as 'ganic as 'ganic can be."

Chapter 41

That afternoon back in the city, I glued my butt to my squad room office chair and did nothing but go through Berkowitz's fan mail.

It was unbelievable. There were curiosity seekers, people who wanted autographs, softhearted and softheaded religious people wanting to save the serial killer's soul. Some old cat lady from England had sent him a feline family picture along with a check for $300 to buy himself "some gaspers," whatever they were. I'd have to run it by the Geico lizard next chance I got.

I had just gotten through all the stuff from the 2000s and was tossing my desk for some aspirin when my boss called from a Bomb Squad meeting in the Bronx.

"Something nuts just came out of Brooklyn," Miriam said. "A little girl was abducted from her dad in broad daylight. We got Brooklyn Major Case running over, but I need you to see what in the hell is going on. From the little I've heard, it's completely bizarre, which makes it par for the course for our guy. But I mean, it can't be our bastard, right? How could a child abduction have something to do with the Mad Bomber or the Son of Sam?"

The address was in a pricey part of Brooklyn not too far from the art museum and Prospect Park. Blue-and-whites blocked both sides of the brownstone-lined street as I double-parked and headed toward an elaborately refurbished town house. A funereal-faced female lieutenant from the Seventy-eighth Precinct met me in the bright front hallway.

"How we doing here, boss?" I said.

"We've activated an AMBER Alert and sent Angela's picture to all the media outlets, but so far nothing," she said, lowering the static on her radio. "The missing girl is four. *Four.* The father was totally out of it when the first unit showed, just glassy-eyed. They've got him in the back bedroom now with the mother and a doctor and a priest. A Brooklyn DT went in about five minutes ago."

Another ten long minutes passed before Hank Schaller, a veteran Brooklyn North detective who sometimes taught at the Academy, came out from the back of the house.

"Hank, what's up?" I said. The neat middle-aged man's gray eyes looked wrong as he shouldered past me like I wasn't even there. That wasn't good.

I followed him out of the town house and down the steps. He started speed-walking down Sixth so fast I had to jog to catch up with him. He seemed in a place beyond hurt, beyond angry.

Around the corner, he headed into the first place he came to, a swanky-looking restaurant. He walked around the stick-thin blond receptionist straight to the empty bar. He was loudly knocking an empty beer bottle on the black-quartz bar top when I finally arrived behind him.

"I want a vodka! Yo, a fucking vodka here! Now!" he yelled.

"You some kind of asshole?" said a burly bearded guy who came in from the kitchen.

Hank was trying to launch himself over the bar at the guy when I got in front of him. I flashed my badge and dropped a twenty.

"Just get him a drink, huh?"

"This animal," Schaller whispered, crumpling onto a bar stool. He stared at the empty bottle in his hand as if wondering how it got there. "We need to catch this animal."

"What happened, Hank?"

"I can hardly even say it," he said, biting his lip. "This poor son of a bitch, the father, has been out of work for the past year, right? This guy preyed on him, said he was going to hire him. Then he shows up today out of the blue and invites both him and his daughter to his own daughter's birthday party. Cavuto's thinking, new job, new boss, definitely gotta go, right?"

The lead-assed cook finally poured three fingers of Grey Goose, which Schaller immediately knocked back.

"The dad needs a few minutes to get ready," Schaller said, raising a finger, "so the guy says he'll take the girl ahead because he's running late. Cavuto can catch up with them in ten, call to see where they are. He let her go, Mike. He gave him his kid. They walked away hand in hand. Except, when he gets out of his shower and calls the number, nothing happens. He runs to the zoo, there's no party." A tear ran down the bridge of the veteran detective's nose. "Imagine, Mike. No one's there!"

"Take it easy, brother," I said.

"Four years old, Mike. This girl was a butterfly. How is this guy going to live with himself, Mike? Fucking how?"

"You need to calm down, Hank," I tried.

"Calm down?" the cop said, flicking his tear off his cheek with his middle finger. "I know how this story ends, and so do you. I calm down when this monster is worm food. I catch up with him, this guy isn't going to see the inside of a police car, let alone a courthouse."

I watched Hank storm out of the restaurant.

I stayed back in the empty bar for a second, absorbing all I'd just heard. Hank was right. Our culprit really did seem like a monster out of some primordial ooze, the personification of antihuman evil. Hank's knee-jerk reaction about it was spot-on as well. What do you do when you find a nasty bug crawling up your arm? You slap it off and crush it under your foot and keep squashing it until it isn't there anymore. You do your darnedest to erase it out of existence.

"That all, Officer?" the cook said sarcastically.

"No," I said, pulling up a stool and dialing my phone for my boss. "I need a fucking vodka now, too."

Chapter 42

I finished my drink and made some more calls before I returned to the house. Since I knew that poor Angela had been walked away, I put people on to contact the major taxi companies and the buses and subways in case anyone had seen anything.

When I arrived back to the town house, I spotted the CSU team and stayed out on the stoop coordinating with them. For some reason, the kidnapper had dropped off a bag with the father that contained strawberries and some kind of weird-looking cream cheese. I was hoping the bizarre package might get us a print. If this creep was bold enough to let the father get a good look at him, I was thinking, he might be getting sloppy and prone to making a mistake.

I'd just sent the department sketch artist in to Detective Schaller when Emily Parker called me.

"Hey, Mike. I got the green light. Just got the word from my boss I'm on the task force."

"That couldn't be better news, Emily," I said. "Because this case has just taken another left turn."

"What now?" she said.

"A four-year-old child from Brooklyn has just been abducted. I'm not sure yet how an abduction fits in with the other two sets of copycat crimes, but my gut says it's the same flavor of weird that our perp likes."

"Maybe it's another crime of the century. The Lindbergh kidnapping, maybe?" Emily said. "I'll research it and bring anything I find with me tomorrow on the train. Can you pick me up from Penn Station in the morning?"

I thought about Mary Catherine then and how I was going to manage things. It was like a fifth-grade word problem.

One love interest is waiting for you out at the beach as another one gets on a train from Washington traveling at a hundred miles an hour. How long will it take before you find yourself in the dog-house? I wasn't sure. I knew I definitely wasn't smarter than a fifth-grader.

"Mike, you still there?" Emily said.

"Right here, Emily," I said. "Of course, I'll come get you. What time does your train get in?"

Chapter 43

NYC'S evening rush hour was just getting started by the time I bumper-to-bumpered it back under the arches of the Brooklyn Bridge toward my squad room.

I evil-eyed my vacation-robbing workplace, One Police Plaza, as I crawled across the span. The slab concrete cube of a building had been butt-ugly even before it was surrounded with guard booths and bomb-barrier planters post 9/11. Because traffic from the financial district had been rerouted due to all the security measures, some Chinatown businesspeople had raised a fuss and suggested that headquarters be moved to another area. I had my fingers crossed for Hawaii, but so far I hadn't heard anything.

Finally pulling off the bridge ramp onto the Avenue of the Finest, I spotted all the double-parked TV news vans. Since all the newsies and camera guys on the sidewalk beside them looked especially restless, I did myself a favor and decided to keep on going.

I drove a few blocks south and pulled over in front of a graffiti-scrawled deli on the corner of Madison and James. I got a coffee and one of those little Table Talk Pies and a *Post,* with its ever-subtle tabloid headline "WHO WILL BE NEXT?" on the front page.

Which turned out to be ironic because when I came back out onto the sidewalk, sitting on the hood of my car was Gary Aronson, the *New York Post* police beat reporter, who was probably responsible for the paper's headline. Like most crime reporters, Gary was ruthless. He claimed color blindness and dyslexia for his habit of ignoring crime scene tape.

So instead of heading back for my

vehicle, I hooked a hard left and stepped into Jerry's Old School, an inner-city barbershop I sometimes used as a meeting spot with confidential informants.

And almost tripped over Cathy Calvin, the *New York Times* police beat reporter BlackBerry-ing by the door under a poster for the rapper Uncle Murda.

I glared over at the muscular owner, Jerry, giving some Chinese kid a fade.

"Is nothing sacred, my man?" I asked him as I did an immediate one-eighty back outside.

Calvin had exchanged her phone for a tape recorder by the time she caught up to me on the sidewalk.

"We have a bombing spree, a double murder that looks a lot like the Son of Sam, and now a girl is missing. Rumors are that all three are related. What's going on, Detective?"

As if I had the time to perform in the media circus.

"Didn't I blackball you?" I said as I picked up my pace.

"That was just for the last case," Calvin said.

"Finally," Aronson said, taking out his own recorder as he got off the hood of my Impala.

"I got this one, Gary," Calvin said, waving him away.

The *Post* reporter stepped away, making call-me gestures at Calvin. All the newspaper hacks who covered crime hung out together. They were as thick as thieves and just about as considerate when it came to cops. They actually had some space on the second floor of HQ called the Shack, where they came up with new ways to get cases and cops jammed up.

"No, she doesn't, Gary," I said, opening my car door. "You want info? Talk to the thirteenth floor, Cathy, my lass. I'm sure they'll be willing to hand over everything you need to know."

The thirteenth floor was home to the department's Public Information Office. Because of the logjam in the white-hot case, its under-pressure chief wanted certain vital body parts of mine for breakfast, last I'd heard.

"C'mon, Mike. I do news, not propaganda," Calvin said, rolling her eyes.

"That's not what Fox News says," I shot back before I jumped into the safety of my vehicle.

Chapter 44

I was starting the car to make my escape when the passenger door opened, and Calvin hopped in beside me.

"What class of medication did you forget to take this morning?" I said.

"I'm screwed, Mike," she said, letting out a weary breath. "I'm not kidding. You don't understand how desperate things are in the paper biz right now. The city editor is waiting for any tiny excuse to clear some payroll. Can't you give me anything? I'll take a 'no comment' at this point."

"In that case, No comment," I said as I leaned across her and opened her door. "Good sob story, by the way. I almost fell for it. The first three times you used it. You should update it. Toss in a dying roommate or something."

"You really are heartless, aren't you?" Calvin said.

"Heartless, yes. A sucker, no," I said. "If it bleeds, it leads, right, Cathy? This one is most definitely bleeding. The last thing I'm worried about is your job security."

She gave me a thin smile.

"Fine, fine. I like you, too, by the way, Mike. Hard enough as it is to believe. What's that cologne you're wearing? I like it."

I sniffed. It was some Axe body soap one of my kids had left in the sand-covered shower back at Breezy. It actually did smell pretty good. I knew she was just yanking my chain to get an angle on the case. Or was she?

"Cathy, you seem like a nice enough young woman," I said. "You're educated. You dress nice. I thought covering cops was just a stepping-stone to better things. Is it the street cred? You have a thing for dead bodies? You ever ask yourself?"

"Come to dinner with me and find out, Mike," Calvin said, checking her makeup in my rearview. "I'll tell you the long, sad story of my life over a bottle of Irish wine. I'm partial to Jameson myself."

Then she gave me a naughty-girl stare for a few seconds. Cathy was a tall, slim blonde with soft green eyes. I couldn't help staring back.

"We won't even talk shop. I promise," she said, clicking off her tape recorder with a red-nailed thumb. She smiled. "Well, maybe just a teensy, weensy bit."

It was the click that did it. It snapped me back to what was left of my senses. What the hell was I doing or thinking? Attractive or not, Cathy was nuts and the enemy. Even if she wasn't, I had two young ladies on my dance card already. I needed three?

"Some other time, Calvin," I said. "If you haven't noticed, I'm a tad busy these days."

"Whatever you say, Detective," she said, getting out. She stopped for a moment on the sidewalk and turned slowly, giving me a good look at what I'd be missing.

"My phone is always on."

"I'm sure it is," I mumbled as I pretended to ignore her walking away.

Chapter 45

After another three fruitless hours spent fishing through Son of Sam letters at my desk, I was toast. I was about to leave, when I received a call from Miriam telling me that the commissioner was on his way back from a speech in Philly and wanted me to brief him in person. So I stuck around for another two eye-melting hours at my desk, only to have Miriam call back to say that the Big Kahuna had actually changed his mind and I was free to go.

Tonight out in Breezy was the church-sponsored carnival we'd been looking forward to since our vacation began. For the past couple of weeks, I'd had this grammar-school romantic vision of taking Mary Catherine on all the rides, being next to her as she screamed and laughed, maybe winning her one of those stupid oversize teddy bears.

Traffic was light for a change, so I managed to get back to Breezy Point in just over an hour. Instead of going to the house, I drove straight over to St. Edmund's, hoping to catch the last of the summer carnival.

I was momentarily hopeful when I saw that the rides and tents were still there beside the rectory. But then I realized that all the lights were off. Even the fried-dough cart was shut up tight.

Talk about missing the party, I thought, as I idled beside the darkened parking lot. Even the carnies were snug in their beds fast asleep.

I really felt like crap. I couldn't protect the city. I couldn't even protect my kids from a pack of jackasses. Now I was AWOL from the height of our long-awaited summer vacation.

I stared up at the still and towering black shapes of the rides against the dark sky. It was the most depressing moment of my day, and that was truly saying something. I headed back for the house.

But apparently I'd spoken too soon. My day wasn't over. Not by a long shot. As I was coming alongside the house, Seamus sat up from the front porch steps and waved for me to pull over. He was wearing a black T-shirt and jeans, his priest's collar nowhere to be seen. What now?

"Finally," he said, snapping his phone shut as he got in. "Don't bother parking. We have a meeting."

"What are you talking about?" I said.

"I didn't want to tell you with everything going on in the city."

"Tell me what?"

Seamus let out a breath, his blue eyes cold in his deeply lined face.

"We had another Flaherty incident. It was at the carnival. The fat kid, Sean, pushed Eddie by one of the rides. Eddie fell into Trent, and Trent flipped over the railing beside the ride."

"What?" I yelled.

"No, he's fine. Shaken up, like the rest of us, but fine. I went ballistic and called the local precinct. But a funny thing happened. The two officers who arrived didn't seem too concerned. So I asked the monsignor of St. Edmund's about it. You'll never guess the last name of the precinct's second in command."

"No!" I said. "Another Flaherty?"

"No wonder they made you first-grade detective," Seamus said.

I shook my head, truly steamed. Nothing pissed me off more than a fellow cop abusing his power.

"They're a scourge, these people. From way back. I actually knew their father when I worked in the meatpacking district before I went to college. He was a loan shark as vicious as they come. Used to make his rounds come dinnertime, and if a man couldn't pay, he'd mercilessly beat him in front of his own family."

"Father of the year," I said.

"That's why we need to head over there now and squash this thing. This nonsense has to stop. I pulled some strings and arranged a sit-down."

"A sit-down?" I yelled. "Who are you, Father Tony Soprano?"

"You don't grow up in Hell's Kitchen

without knowing a few people, lad. I called in a few favors. What of it? We're due over there now. It's time to settle this thing man to man, West Side-style."

"Over where?" I cried.

"The Flaherty house, Mike. Pay attention. And keep your gun handy."

Chapter 46

How the hell did I get myself into these things?

As I drove toward the Rockaway Inlet for the second time, I couldn't believe I was actually agreeing to participate in some kind of crazy Irish mobster meeting. Had I fallen asleep at work and was I dreaming this? Of course not. You hang with an old-school Irish lunatic grandfather like mine long enough, the surreal becomes your normal.

We heard the fireworks before we turned the corner for the Flahertys' street. There were whistling bottle rockets and deafening strings of firecrackers. A giant flower burst of yellow lit up the sky behind the Flaherty compound's dilapidated split-level as we pulled up in front of it.

"I thought the Fourth of July was over," I said as we got out. "Are you sure the Vatican would approve of this?"

"You just follow my lead and keep quiet," Seamus said. "These gangster people only listen to man talk."

I shook my head as I spotted my old pal, Mr. Pit Bull, trying to chew a hole in the chain-link fence as we came up the steps. This time I couldn't actually hear the dog going batshit with all the noise of the ordnance from the backyard.

When no one came to the door, we decided to go around the side of the house to the back. The sulfurous smell of gunpowder hung in the air, which I thought was fitting, since we were now walking through the valley of the shadow of death, straight into the gates of Hell.

The rear of the place was almost completely overtaken by a large deck and one of those cheap aboveground pools. On the deck, the muscle-headed punk patriarch of the Flaherty clan, "Tommy Boy," as he was known from his rap sheet, sat with his tattooed brother Billy, book-ending a keg. I realized why no one had called the cops, when I saw the third Flaherty for the first time. I didn't know what his name was, but I noticed that he was still wearing his white NYPD captain's shirt as he tossed a lit bottle rocket toward the house next door.

Tommy Boy looked over with bleary eyes as Seamus cleared his throat by the deck steps.

"What the—?" he said. His pale face split into a grim grin. "Hey, guys. Check this out. How's this for a joke: A cop and a priest walk uninvited into a private party."

"We're here to have that sit-down, Flaherty," Seamus said. "We've come to work this thing out, and we won't leave until we do."

"Sit-down?" the illustrated Flaherty brother, Billy, said, balling his hands into fists as he stood. "Only thing that's gonna happen to you, coot, is a serious *beat*-down."

Chapter 47

I followed my courageous, or maybe just insane, grandfather up the stairs onto the deck.

"Murphy sent me," Seamus said to Tommy Boy, completely ignoring the tattooed man.

"Murphy?" Tommy Boy said, not budging from his cheap plastic seat. *"Frank* Murphy? That dirty ol' little Forty-ninth Street bookie I let operate out of the kindness of my Irish heart? News flash, Father Moron. He's less valid on the West Side than you. Now get your scrawny ass out of here before my brother Billy here makes it so that you have to say mass for the rest of your life on a Hoveround."

As the tattooed brother took a step toward us, I decided it was time to take the lead. My first move was to gently push Seamus to the side. My next and last move was to much less gently kick the seated Flaherty in the side of the head as hard as I could as I drew my Glock.

I helped him up by his long, greasy hair, the barrel of my gun wedged into his ear hole like a pencil into a sharpener.

"Bennett! Whoa, whoa, hold up," the cop brother said, slowly showing me his hands. "We don't need this kind of stuff. We're all friends here. You actually worked with my old partner, Joe Kelly, when you were in Manhattan North homicide."

"That's right, I worked homicide," I said. "And I'm not above committing one right about now. Three of them, in fact. How's this for a joke, Flaherty? Three dumb-ass brothers are found floating facedown dead in their own pool."

"Let me get this straight. You're actually willing to shoot me over this stupid kiddie crap?" Tommy Boy asked from the other side of my Glock.

I nodded enthusiastically.

"Your kid almost killed my seven-year-old tonight at the carnival. To protect my kids, you better believe I'll end your worthless ass."

"I see," Tommy Boy said, looking at me sideways across the gun I was scratching against his eardrum. "I hadn't heard about that. I think I'm starting to understand your position now. I even know what to do. Here, watch. Seany!"

The screen door opened a few moments later, and the fat kid who'd been terrorizing my family stepped out onto the deck. His pudgy jaw dropped in a cartoonish gape when he saw me and his dad down on the deck conversing over the barrel of my Austrian semi-auto.

"Uh...yes, Dad?" he said, fear in his voice.

"Come here," Flaherty senior said.

Quick as a snake, Tommy Boy moved out of my grasp before the kid had made two steps. Before I could tell what was going on, he lifted his portly son up and

threw him off the deck. Instead of landing in the pool, like I was expecting, the
heavy teen slammed into the side of it
with a cracking sound before he fell
face-first onto the backyard concrete.
Right away he started bawling.

Christ, I thought, standing there
shocked, with the gun still in my hand.
Now, that's what you call tough love.

"Dad!" young Sean cried from his
knees as blood poured out of his nose.
Behind him, water began to trickle out
of the crack he'd made in the plastic
pool.

"Don't you 'Dad' me, you little punk.
Stay the hell away from this man's kids,
you hear me?"

"But, Dad," Sean wheezed. "You told
me to teach them a lesson."

"Yeah, well," Tommy Boy said, giving
me a sheepish look. "Lesson learned.
You don't hurt little kids, shithead. I have
to actually explain that to you? Here's
the new orders. If one of Mr. Bennett's
kids skins his knee, you better have a
Band-Aid handy. Any of them gets hurt
again, you're going to spend the rest of
your vacation in the hospital."

"Yes, Dad," Seany moaned as he ran up the deck stairs and back inside.

"Honestly, Bennett," Flaherty said with his palms up. "I'm sorry about the whole thing. It really is my fault. My wife went to Ireland for a week to bury her mother. Guess I'm not so great at this dad thing. Everything's just gone to Hell without her here."

"There's a definite learning curve," I said reholstering my weapon. "I'm just glad we could finally work things out."

"Man to man," Seamus added behind me.

"Hey, it took a lot of guts to come over here. I respect that," Tommy Boy Flaherty said as we were leaving. "You ever need anything—anything—you let me know. That goes for you, too, Father."

"Back, Satan," Seamus mumbled as we took our leave.

I let out the breath of all breaths as I got the car started. Pulling my gun had been beyond reckless. What the hell had gotten into me? As we drove away, I suddenly got a proud pat on the cheek from Seamus.

"We'll make a man out of you yet, Mike, me boy," he said with a blue-eyed wink. "That's how you do things West Side–style."

Chapter 48

Naked in the dark, Berger kicked back on the leather recliner in his massive, magnificent library and hit the play button on his remote control.

There was a chirp and hum from the Blu-ray player and then the 103-inch Plasma blazed with a midday shot of the New York Public Library.

The camera shook a little from the first-person shot, but the picture and colors and sounds of the street were amazingly vivid. You could almost smell the hot pretzels and summer sweat.

It was the film of the first crime, the library decoy bombing that had been shot with a hidden fiber-optic camera.

All of his work, of course, had been filmed.

Now it was time to edit it, clean it up, and polish, polish, polish.

As the images fast-forwarded and re-wound, he thought of his school years at Lawrenceville, the premier boarding school near Princeton.

A pudgy and slow child, he had been enrolled by his father at the über-preppy institution in order to make a gentleman out of him. But it didn't work out. Quite the contrary. By the time Berger entered ninth grade, his physique, unique artistic sensibilities, and uncommon interests had actually earned him an alliterative nickname that had caught on famously: Big Bellied Bizarro Berger.

He was seriously considering suicide for his fifteenth birthday, when he unexpectedly made a friend. His new roommate, Javier Souza, a diminutive boy from a wealthy Brazilian family, not only called him by his Christian name, but he turned out to share some of his strange, dark interests.

It was actually Javier who dared him to burn down the school library during the freshman class movie night the week before Christmas break. Wanting to prove his mettle, Berger had purchased a case of lighter fluid as well as some lengths of chain and padlocks to bar the building's exits.

If the suspicious owner of the Ace Hardware store in town hadn't contacted the headmaster, he would have gone through with his plan of wiping out the entire Lawrenceville class of '68. Instead, he was expelled, and if it hadn't been for a hasty and hefty donation by his father to the school, there might have been criminal charges.

Coulda, woulda, shoulda, Berger thought wistfully. He'd had such passion then. If it hadn't been for the hand of fate, he would become famous then. He would have instantly transformed from Big Bellied Bizarro Berger to The Boy Who Killed the Class of '68!

It was, of course, that singular near brush with greatness that drove him on his little project now. After all the failure and misery and confusion that had clouded his life, he'd finally, miraculously, gotten his gumption back.

In the light of the TV screen, he dabbed at a joyful tear as he watched the bomb get glued to the library desk.

What he had done already, the sheer wondrousness of it, no one could ever take away. No matter what happened next, he had triumphed.

Berger had finally done something that was truly his.

Chapter 49

Though it was only nine a.m., I felt punch-drunk by the time I pulled up in front of Madison Square Garden on Seventh Avenue to pick up Agent Parker at Penn Station. Horns honked as I blatantly and highly illegally sat in my cruiser in a no-standing tow zone, washing down a bagel with a Big Gulp–size coffee.

As the loud, cruel world rushed by the window, I slowly went over what had happened with the Flahertys the night before. Talk about fireworks! I'd broken a few laws there, hadn't I? Improper use of my firearm was a firing offense. Assault was a felony. But I guess the strangest thing about it was that it seemed to have worked. I'd finally spoken to Flaherty in the only language he seemed to understand. Why hadn't I just threatened his life from the get-go?

I shook my head. I'd actually out-crazied a Westie. Was that a good thing? I wasn't sure. Probably not.

The grind of the case wasn't exactly doing wonders for my mental well-being, was it? I needed a vacation. Oh, wait. I was already on one.

I flipped through the *Post*. On page three, a state senator from Manhattan warned that the NYPD had five more days to catch the culprit before he made a motion that the state police be sent in.

Sounded good to me, I thought, licking my thumb and turning the page. I would be more than happy to let a trooper from Schenectady take a shot at cracking the case. In addition to the mayor, the papers, and the department top brass, I was almost starting to want me off this case, too.

I knew the odds were we'd eventually catch up to this monster. I'd caught up to every one of them so far. I knew I should believe the numbers on the back of my baseball card, and yet I was getting very worried.

Especially about Angela Cavuto.

There had been no word yet from her kidnapper, no demands. No news was definitely not good news. The one bright spot was the new sketch of the kidnapper the department artist had made with the help of Mr. Cavuto. They'd redballed it to the Public Info Division this morning to get it out on the newscasts, so maybe we had a shot. How much of one, I wasn't sure. But at least it was a start.

After another few minutes, I checked the time on my phone and got out of the car, leaving it right in the middle of the Seventh Avenue bus lane. If I got towed, maybe they'd let me get back to my vacation, I thought, as I took the escalator from the sidewalk down into Penn Station.

I really didn't think anything could cut through my darkening mood until I saw Emily Parker's smile and wave on the crowded underground train platform. She looked even better than I remembered, tall and porcelain-skinned, her eyes as bright and blue as ever. Her neatness and earnestness and energy were contagious. I think I actually smiled back as we came face-to-face.

We hugged, and she even gave me a peck on the cheek. Not exactly FBI protocol. It felt good.

"Finally some backup," I said, grabbing her bag. "Honestly, Emily, you are a sight for these sore eyes."

"It's nice to see you, too, Mike," she said giving my hand another squeeze. "It really is. I'm glad I came. You look great."

"Yeah, real *GQ,* I'm sure," I said, rolling my eyes "The bags under my eyes are bigger than your overnight."

"But such handsome luggage," she said, giving my cheek a playful tug.

I grinned back at her like a fool. Demonstrative attention from good-looking women was never a bad thing. Our reunion was off on the right foot. So far, so good.

"What do you want to do first?"

"Brainstorm," I said, leading her toward the stairs. "But we're going to need to use your brain. I fried mine about three days ago."

Chapter 50

Twenty minutes later, Emily and I were standing in the center of Major Case Squad's open bull pen on the eleventh floor of One Police Plaza. Phones kept ringing across the stuffy, beat-up empty office space, with nobody to answer them. Every single one of the task force's forty-plus detectives was out chasing down leads on the now *three*-pronged case. There was no rest for the weary in this summer of insanity. Nor any in sight, for that matter.

Beyond the cluster of cluttered desks, we parked ourselves in front of a decidedly low-tech rolling bulletin board. Pushpinned onto it was a huge map of the city, along with the printouts of each crime and crime scene. In the very center of the board, the new Xeroxed sketch of the kidnapper stared back at us like a spider from the center of its web.

With her arms crossed, Emily stared at the board silently, absorbed, an art critic before a new installation.

"Give me the vitals on the abduction, Mike."

I slowly went through what had happened to Angela Cavuto.

"According to the father," I said, "our guy is white, right-handed, walks with a limp and a cane and is thin and about five eleven." Cavuto also said he was cultured and polished. Not only was he wearing a tailored suit, but he spoke quite convincingly about hedge fund investing."

"I can't believe it, Mike," Emily told me as she took a rubber-banded folder out of her bag. "I spent yesterday pulling reams of stuff about famous New York crimes, hoping this wasn't true, but I think it must be."

"What have you got, Emily?"

"I think this guy's done it again. This

abduction is another copycat. A carbon copy, in fact."

"Of what? The Lindbergh case?" I said, confused.

"No. There was another heinous kidnapping way back in the twenties—in Brooklyn, no less. At the time, they called it the crime of the century. A sociopathic murderous pedophile named Albert Fish was dubbed the 'Brooklyn Vampire' when he abducted and killed a girl.

"And Mike, his MO wasn't just similar. From what you just told me, it was *exactly* the same. Posing as an employer, Fish answered the ad of an eighteen-year-old boy seeking work and ended up leaving with his ten-year-old sister under the pretense of taking her to a birthday party."

"F——— off! No!" I yelled as I collapsed into a chair.

Emily nodded.

"Tell me, did he give the father something?" she said.

"Strawberries and some goop," I said.

"Pot cheese. Right. Shit! It's the same

thing! The Mad Bomber, then the Son of Sam, now the Brooklyn Vampire. This guy's just pulled off a third famous crime. Mike, this isn't good. This Fish guy was evil personified. He made the Son of Sam seem like a volunteer at a soup kitchen. He was one of the worst pedophiles and child murderers of all time. He didn't just kill his victims. He would cannibalize them as well."

I punched the desk beside me, then my thigh. Then Emily and I sat there silently listening to the *whoosh* of the air duct. On the board, a picture of Angela from last year's Cavuto family Christmas card smiled at us from beneath a glittery halo.

Chapter 51

I was with Emily, putting on some coffee about an hour later, when I heard a strange, gut-wrenching call come over the break room's radio.

There was some kind of disturbance uptown. An unconscious, unresponsive child had been found in a store on Fifth Avenue. When I heard the name of the store repeated, my blood went cold.

"What, Mike? What is it?" Emily said, straining to listen.

"They found a little girl uptown at FAO Schwarz, the famous toy store across from the Plaza Hotel. Not good, Em. It's on the same block as the CBS *Early Show,* the locale of the bombing on Tuesday."

There was a more massive crowd than usual out in front of the landmark toy store when Emily and I arrived after a long, twenty-minute ride uptown. Two radio cars and two ambulances spun their lights in front of the freaked-out-looking tourists and moms and little kids.

A veteran Nineteenth Precinct sergeant whose eye I caught shook his dismal face before I was three steps out of my car.

I showed the cop the picture of Angela.

"Tell me this isn't her," I said.

"Marone a mi," the cop said, the smoke from his cupped cigarette rising like incense as he crossed himself. "It's her. They found her in the back. The clerk thought she was just sleeping."

Emily and I both turned as a car squealed up behind my cruiser. It was a black Lexus with tinted windows. I had my hand on my Glock when its door was flung wide open and a man got out. A man with red hair and even redder eyes.

It was Kenneth Cavuto, Angela's father.

"No!" I yelled as Cavuto bolted toward the store's entrance.

I managed to get there a second before him. No way could I let Angela's dad see his little girl. Not here. Not like this.

Apparently the distraught father had other plans. I'm not a small guy, but Cavuto shoved me off my feet like I was an empty cardboard box. I grunted as I fell forward and my chin hit the concrete.

I got back up and ran after Cavuto into the empty store. I bolted down some steps past museum-quality displays of giant stuffed animals: ostriches and horses and giraffes. I was scrambling past the Puppet Park when I heard a sound that stopped me.

It was a scream in a pitch I'd never heard before. I looked at Emily. She shook her head. We both knew what it was. It was the sound of Cavuto's heart breaking.

It took me, Emily, and three uniforms to get Cavuto off his daughter. I actually had to cuff him. He started crying soundlessly as he banged his head against the polka-dot-carpeted floor.

"Go out to your truck and get something to knock this poor son of a bitch out, would you?" I yelled at a gawking EMT.

I noticed only then that my chin was bleeding. I put my thumb on it to stop the drip as I turned and looked at the girl. She was sitting in a stroller with her eyes closed, her white-blond hair the same shade as the oversize polar bear on the shelf beside her.

I turned away and got down on my knees next to the father and placed my hand on his sobbing back.

I opened my mouth to say something. Then I closed it. What was there to say?

Chapter 52

The evening light was just starting to change as Berger steered the Mercedes convertible into the line for the car wash at East 109th Street. He stared up at the fading blue of the sky above the construction site across the street. What he wouldn't give to be in his tub right now, humming on Vitamin P as the sun descended toward the Dakota.

He turned as an unshaven bubble-butted old white guy knocked on his window. Berger thought it was a homeless person until he realized it was one of the car wash employees.

"What?" the guy asked in a Russian accent as the window buzzed down.

"The works," Berger said, handing him a crisp twenty.

"Interior vacuum, too?" Gorbachev wanted to know.

"Not today," Berger said with a grin before zipping the window back up.

Berger sighed as the machinery bumped under the car and began towing him through the spinning brushes and water spray. What a bust of a day.

The girl wasn't supposed to die. The plan had been to torture the parents over a two-day period with the ruse of a ransom and then kill her. But that was all blown to shit now, wasn't it?

It had been the Valium. The girl had had some kind of allergic reaction as he was taking her from the taxi to the Mercedes that he had parked in Brooklyn Heights. By the time they were back in Manhattan, she was gone. He'd screwed up, made his first mistake. He could kick himself.

Oh, well, he thought, as the lemony scent of soap filled the car. He had to stop beating himself up about it. No mission went perfectly. He smoothed out the fiber-optic camera cord sewn into the lining of his jacket. At the very least he'd gotten a little more footage.

Anyway, he didn't have time to dwell on his failures. So much to do, so little time to do it. He'd just have to go on to the next thing. He needed to keep heading in his two favorite directions, onward and upward, and hope it would all come out in the wash.

As the car wash spat him back out into the driveway, he rolled down the window and tossed something into the trash can by the fence.

The Elmo juice box spun as it arced lazily into the can's exact center. Boots the Monkey followed.

"Swish! Nothing but net, and the crowd goes wild," Berger said as he popped the clutch and squealed the Merc out into the street.

Chapter 53

After his preliminary, the ME took me aside by a stack of Buzz Lightyears and said it looked like an overdose of some kind. I turned away as a crying female ME assistant knelt by Angela, getting ready to move her. Her father, mercifully sedated, was out in an ambulance on East 58th. I wished I were as well.

"What do you think?" I said to Emily as we stepped along the rows of toys for the exit. "Does this dump fit in with the Fish case in some way?"

"No, actually," Emily said. "They found his victim's remains in an abandoned house upstate. My gut says our unsub screwed up, probably botched the dosage, trying to keep her quiet."

"Sounds about right," I said as we arrived back out in the street. I was hoping the outside air would make me feel better, but the crowds and heat only made me feel shittier.

"Guess our copycatting friend isn't Mr. Perfect, after all," I said.

We left the agonizingly sad and angering crime scene about an hour later. I took Fifth Avenue south from FAO Schwarz and hooked a right at 34th, by the Empire State Building.

"It's weird," Emily said, squeezing the empty water bottle in her hand as she stared at the sketch. "He's definitely culturally sophisticated and yet he also has military training, judging by his bomb-making skills. Interesting combination."

"Don't forget. He's also quite the New York City crime buff," I said.

"Speaking of which," Emily said, turning and taking out a folder from her bag.

"You guys probably thought of this, but before I hopped on the train, I printed out a custom map for all the crime scenes of the Mad Bomber and the Son of Sam that I could scratch together off the Web. There are dozens in Manhattan, the Bronx—everywhere except Staten Island. It's a long shot, but beefed-up patrols at some of these potential target neighborhoods might get us some luck."

I smiled at the neat Google pinpointed map and then at Agent Parker. Emily was exactly what this case needed: a new set of eyes, some new blood, some enthusiasm.

Back at the office, a stocky, young black detective dressed like Gordon Gekko all the way down to a pair of silk moiré suspenders, almost tackled us as we got off the elevator. His name was Terry Brown, and he was the squad's latest rookie out of Narcotics.

"Mike, finally," Terry said, waving for us to follow him. "I just got through the toy store security tape. I think I might have something. You have to see this."

We followed Terry down the hall and into one of the tiny interview rooms where he was banished until Maintenance found him a desk. Through a corridor of stacked file boxes, we huddled together at a folding table as he pressed the play button on his laptop.

He fast-forwarded through people browsing among the toy-filled shelves and then hit pause as a man with a stroller entered the frame.

"There he is. Now watch."

The man came closer, pushing the same pink Maclaren stroller Angela was found in. I let out a whooshing breath. He was wearing a Yankees cap and a pair of aviator shades, but it was him, the guy from the sketch! For the first time, I was actually face-to-face with the man who was responsible for killing eight people over the past few days and terrorizing another eight million.

He wheeled her into a corner. He took a cell phone out of his pocket and actually took a picture of her with it. What really burned my ass was how he actually stopped then and glanced up at the security camera and smiled as he left the store.

"That son of a bitch," I said. "He knew the camera was there. He's taunting us now."

We played it over and over again, trying to get the best shot. It turned out to be the one of him smiling.

"I did good?" Terry Brown asked hopefully.

"You keep this up, Terry," I said to the pup, pumped for the first time all day, "not only will I get you a desk, I might even throw in a chair."

Chapter 54

After firing our latest finding to the AV guys on the third floor, they blew up the image and did a terrific side-by-side with the sketch. Even better, the Public Info Office said they'd hustle and get it into today's evening news cycle.

We left headquarters around six, and I took Emily over to her hotel to check in. It turned out there was a rooftop bar and lounge at the Empire Hotel on West 63rd, where she was staying, so we decided on an early supper. While she freshened up, I went and had a drink at the spectacular outdoor bar.

As I waited, I leaned against the roof railing and texted the latest happenings and progress to my boss, Miriam. I was even feeling enough compassion to let Cathy Calvin in on the latest development, along with explicit instructions that she didn't hear it from me, of course.

I put away my phone and from twelve stories up watched the lights of Lincoln Center and upper Broadway come on as the paling sky went dark. I stared down on the corner, where a couple of hard hats were feeding fiber-optic cable into a manhole. I envied how perfectly content and oblivious of the world's problems they seemed. No psychos to worry about, no dead kids, no bosses or papers or mayor asking for their heads on a plate. Probably making time and a half, too, I'd bet. Was the phone company hiring? I wondered.

I spotted Emily as she came out onto the patio. She'd taken off her jacket and let her hair down.

We grabbed a table in a quiet corner and ordered off the bar menu.

Over some Kobe Sliders and ice-cold Brooklyn Lagers, we caught up with each other. Emily told me about her daughter's trials and tribulations over learning how to swim at her town pool. I was going to tell her about the ancestral Irish feud my family was engaged in out in Breezy Point this summer, but I decided it was better if she thought I was at least a little bit sane.

I pulled my chair over to Emily's side of the table as we showed each other cell-phone pictures of our kids.

After another round of Brooklyns, I told her about my meeting with the Son of Sam.

"Do you really believe he doesn't know what's going on?" Emily asked.

"If he's a bullshit artist, he's a good one."

"Better than you," Emily said, smiling over the rim of her beer bottle.

"Heck, probably even better than you," I said, smiling back.

Our conversation went back and forth smoothly, almost too easily. Were there some sparks between us? I'd say so, considering I felt like I could have sat on that patio drinking beer and staring out at the bright city lights with Emily for about the rest of my life. I wanted to arrest the waiter when he came over with the check.

Reluctantly back in the elevator, we stopped at the seventh floor for her room.

"See you tomorrow, Mike," she said after an awkward moment in which I probably should have said something like, "Hey, how about a nightcap in your room?"

"Tomorrow it is," I said.

She tugged my tie before bailing out into the corridor.

Idiot, I screamed at myself in my mind.

"Em," I said, painfully stopping the sliding elevator door with the back of my head.

"Yes?"

"Thanks."

"I haven't done anything."

"Oh, believe me," I said. "You have."

Chapter 55

I wasn't sure what time it was when I woke up, sweating in the pitch black of my beach house bedroom. It was early. Way too early, in fact.

After a few minutes, I knew there was no way I was getting back to sleep, so I decided to make use of my brain being on and sneak back into work while everyone was still asleep. Besides, it was Friday, and it would give me a chance to finish up early and beat the weekend traffic back. That was my story, anyway, and I was sticking to it.

The sun was just coming up behind me as I rolled into lower Manhattan. Beside a newsstand I saw that the cover of the *Post* showed the security video shot of our suspect under the headline "THE FACE OF EVIL." For once, the press had gotten it right. I couldn't have said it better myself.

It was so early, there was actually a complete lack of press corps outside HQ. The early bird outsmarts the worms, I thought, as the groggy security guard lifted the stick to the parking lot.

In the empty squad room, I found a stack of messages on my desk, left there by the night shift. I was hoping for a tip from posting the security footage and sketch on the news, but there were just fifteen crackpot confessions and two psychics offering their help.

I moved them to my circular spam file in the corner of my cubicle where they belonged, then made a few quick calls to the cops we'd posted at all the previous crime scenes.

There was no traction there, either. The killer hadn't come back. When I clicked open my e-mail, I learned that forensics had been unable to pull any latents off the stroller poor little Angela was found in. Despite our progress, it seemed we were still far out in the weeds on this one.

As I looked around the empty office, I decided to do something smart. I sat and tried to think of what Emily Parker would do. I decided that she'd take a deep breath and look at the whole thing patiently, clinically, and without frustration. Though it seemed like a pretty impossible task, I decided to give it a shot. I put on a fresh pot of coffee and came back and cleared my desk.

The first thing I did was slip on my reading glasses and go through the files that Emily had compiled for me on copycat killers. One of them stood out prominently, a copycat serial killer in New York City during the early nineties.

His name was Heriberto Seda, and he was a deranged young man from East New York, Brooklyn, who had killed three and wounded four others with homemade zip guns. Notes to the police found near the victims claimed that he was the famous San Francisco Zodiac killer from the sixties transplanted to New York. When he was finally caught, he told police that he identified with the Zodiac because he'd terrorized a city and never been caught.

"I needed attention," Seda said. "For once in my life, I felt important. I was lonely, in pain. I have no friends."

With that premise in mind, I got a fresh cup of coffee and laid out the case files for the six incidents. Four of them had been in the mode of George Metesky, the Mad Bomber. Two of them had been approximations of the Son of Sam, and the latest had copied the Brooklyn Vampire, Albert Fish.

Could our guy actually identify with all three? I wondered.

I sipped coffee and sat back in my office chair, staring up at the drop ceiling and thinking about it. It didn't seem likely. It seemed to me that although all three were violent weirdos, each was deranged in his own special way. The Mad Bomber had been a disgruntled employee of Con Edison, mostly seeming to seek revenge. The Son of Sam was more like Seda, a low-status publicity seeker who killed out of a twisted sense of empowerment, craving fame and attention. Albert Fish was more along the lines of a classic sadistic psychopath, like Ted Bundy, with no real interest in fame and who got off sexually on inflicting pain.

I lifted a pencil and twirled it between my fingers. How could one person not only seek revenge and twisted, freaky peekaboo thrills but also relish inflicting pain all at the same time?

He couldn't, I thought, as I tried to stick the pencil into the ceiling and missed. It didn't make any goddamn sense.

Chapter 56

That's when I pulled the second-smart-
est move of my morning. Instead of just
thinking like Emily Parker, I took out my
cell and called the real McCoy.

"Hey, Em. Sorry to call you so early,"
I said when she picked up. "I've been
looking at your notes on that copycat
Seda. He ID'd himself with the Zodiac,
right?"

"Uh-huh," Emily said, still groggy.

"Well, if our guy is doing the same
thing, how can he feel empathy with all
three New York nuts? I mean, one's an
organized technician, and one's a dis-
organized catch-me-if-you-can loon.
And the third one is a classic violent
sadist. How can that be?"

"That is weird," she agreed. After a yawn she said, "Maybe two of the modes are just a smokescreen for the real one."

"But which one is real and which are the smoke?" I said.

"The only communication he made with you was about the bombings, right?"

"You're forgetting the Son of Sam letter he sent me."

"True, but that was almost a photocopy of Berkowitz's letter."

"You're right," I said. "Also, since we haven't even seen any publicity-seeking taunts or manifestos sent to the media, I don't think his heart is in copying Berkowitz."

"I'd lean toward Metesky, too," Emily said. "Our guy is definitely detail-oriented, and not only was the library bomb the first crime, it was the only one that didn't have a copycat message."

"It's revenge, then?" I said. "This guy is trying to get back at the world for Lawrence? But what about the social skills that Cavuto attributed to him during their meetings? Berkowitz and Metesky were loner, loser types, while Fish was a married guy who was sly, manipulative, and charming. If someone is capable of channeling Cary Grant, how do they become a wound-up, light-'em-and-run sneak creep like Metesky?"

"But he has to be somewhat of a loner," Emily argued. "How does Mr. Life of the Party prepare his bombs and clean his collection of vintage weapons without friends or family getting suspicious?"

I slumped in my chair. Trying to figure this guy out was like trying to build a castle with quicksand. Yet we were almost onto something. I could feel it.

My office chair made a snapping sound as I suddenly sat straight up.

"Wait a second. He is detail-oriented, isn't he? This guy is all about the details. That's about the only thing we know about him."

"Yeah, and?"

I pulled out the sheets that showed the addresses of the historical crimes and compared them to the locations of the present spree.

"Emily, you know what I think? I think

our guy is meticulous enough to have copied these crimes even better than he has. If he wanted to just reenact the crimes, he could have done the exact same thing at the exact same locations, but he didn't."

"Why not?" Emily said.

"Maybe it's not about the copying at all," I offered. "Maybe the copycatting concept itself is the smokescreen. We need to take another look at the victims. Maybe the connection is with them."

Chapter 57

The rest of my day was nasty, brutish, and *long*.

Running with our new theory to find some connection between the victims, Emily and I split up and proceeded to try to interview as many of the victims' families as we could. Every session had been grueling. All the family members I sat down with were still confused and angry, raw with loss and grief. Laura Habersham, the mother of the girl who'd been killed in the Queens lovers' lane double murder, actually cursed me out before collapsing onto her knees in tears at her front door.

I didn't blame her in the slightest. I just helped her up and asked my questions and went on to the next poor soul on my list.

By the time I was finished, I'd spent twelve hours driving hither and yon through NYC's gridlocked outer boroughs and only managed to track down the families of four of the eight victims. Even so, it was a ton of data to crunch, a ton of potential connections. That was police work in a nutshell—too little or too much info.

Around ten p.m. that night, sweating, bone tired, and yet unbowed, I cornered 91st Street onto steamy West End Avenue. Stumbling over the opposite curb in the dark, I just managed to catch the sliding Chinese takeout and six Dos Equis I was balancing on top of the file box I was lugging. When my phone went off in my pocket, instead of stopping to answer it, I continued to soldier on toward the awning of my apartment house a block and a half away. Beat-ass tired cops in motion tend to stay in motion.

Since there was no way I could make it out to Breezy tonight alive, I'd have to make the best of it, crashing in my apartment alone.

My building's front door was locked when I arrived. Which was sort of aggravating considering how much my pricey prewar building charged for twenty-four-hour doorman service. Instead of putting down the heavy box, I turned and knocked on the thick glass with the back of my thick skull.

I almost fell down when the door was flung open suddenly two long minutes later.

"Mr. Bennett. I'm so sorry," Bert, the whiny evening-shift doorman, said hastily, tightening his loose tie. "Everyone else in the building is marked in, or I would have been standing right here at my post as usual. I thought you and the kids were away. We weren't expecting you back until next week."

I watched the short, old doorman yawn as he continued to make no attempt to help me.

"Yeah, well, you're looking at what they call a working vacation, Bert," I said as I walked around him.

Bert actually stopped me again halfway to the elevator to load me down

even more with piled-up mail and pack-
ages.

"Don't worry, Mr. B. Your secret is
safe with me," the old codger whispered, winking at my six-pack of suds.
"I've been reading about your case in
the *Post*. Who could blame you for hitting the sauce a little?"

I rolled my eyes as the door finally
slid shut and the elevator began to take
me upstairs.

Just what I didn't need in my life, another elderly wiseguy. And I was looking forward to a Seamus-free night,
too.

Chapter 58

I dropped the file box of victim data with a thud in the stuffy air of my apartment foyer and stood for a strange moment, just listening. After the usually thunderous chaos in our rambling three-bedroom apartment, silence was an almost unique experience.

Sorting through the mail, I smiled at the return address of a cardboard tube that had arrived. I went into the big boys' room and put up the action-shot Mariano Rivera Fathead that I'd gotten for my son Brian's birthday. Brian was going to go nuts when he saw it.

"Just me and you tonight, Mo," I said to the life-size wall cling as I left. "Welcome to old guy's night in."

I proceeded to turn on all the window air conditioners to high. Coming back through the living room, I lifted what looked like a plaid horseshoe off the floor. It was one of the girls' Catholic school headbands, I realized. I twirled it in my hand before placing it on a coffee table littered with Jenga pieces and *Diary of a Wimpy Kid* books.

Taking a load off on my beat-up couch, I reflected on all the craziness of the past fifteen years of family life. It was a blur of big wheels and videos and kitchen tables covered in Cheerios, a lot of tears, more laughter. We'd converted the three bedrooms into five by using the high-end apartment's formal dining room and half of the large, formal living room. Formal anything pretty much sailed out the window onto tony West End Avenue for Maeve and me once our incredible expanding family moved in.

The funny thing was, I wouldn't have had it any other way.

How I'd gotten my guys this far while putting away bad guys and keeping my job and a sliver of my sanity, I'd never know. Actually, I did know. Their names were Maeve, Mary Catherine, and, as much as I hated to admit it, Seamus.

Back inside my bedroom, I listened to the string of messages on the answering machine. The most recent one was by far the most intriguing.

"Yes, um, eh, he—, hello? Mary—Mary Catherine?" some fellow with a charming English stammer said. "It's Jeremy Griffith. I, um, spoke at your class? I, um, do hope you don't mind that I hunted down your number from the instructor. I don't normally do things like this, but I—well, I'm here at this atrocious party, and I couldn't stop thinking about those insightful links you made between German Baroque and Nordic Classicism. To be honest, I can't remember the last time I met someone who actually knew who Ivar Tengbom was, let alone would admit to being his number-one fan. Anyway, are you doing anything this week? I have another dinner with some MOMA people coming up on Friday and thought, eh, maybe you'd like to, uh, tag along. There, I've said it. If you can make it, wonderful. If you can't, well, my and Ivar's loss. Here's my number."

"Sorry, old chap," I said, immediately deleting with extreme prejudice Mary Catherine's Hugh Grant–like suitor. "Looks like you're going stag."

Was that wrong? I wondered, staring at myself in the mirror. I turned away. It most certainly was, and I most certainly didn't care.

Chapter 59

I showered, tossed on some shorts, and brought a beer and my phone back into the living room.

"Hey, Mike," Mary Catherine said when I called Breezy. "I was just about to call you. You're not going to believe this. No Flaherty incidents, no stitches, no one even got sunburned. Even Socky the cat seems ready to twist by the pool tonight. How are you holding up? Are you on your way? I'll save you some pizza."

"Don't bother, Mary," I said, toweling off my wet hair. "I'm actually at the apartment. This case is looking like an all-nighter. Hey, I forgot to ask you. How was your art course this week?"

"It was terrific," she said. "This really bright, young Oxford professor came to speak to us, a world-renowned expert on German architecture. He was really funny."

"German buildings are fine," I said, "but I'm more into Nordic Classicism myself."

"I didn't know you liked architecture, Mike. Were you peeking at my books?" Mary Catherine said.

"Bite your tongue, lass. Not all cops are meatheads."

"I'll have to remember that," she said after a beat. "I'm afraid it's too late to talk with the gang. They're all asleep."

"That's okay. Just apologize and kiss them good night for me, okay?" I said.

"No problem," Mary said. "Who are you going to kiss good night, I wonder?"

"What?" I said, startled. "What's that supposed to mean?"

"Nothing, Mr. Bennett. Have fun all by yourself in the city tonight," Mary Catherine said and hung up.

I stared at the phone. Then I cracked

the cap on my beer. Sauce-hitting time had officially arrived.

"Nothing, Mr. Bennett," I mimicked in a pretty good Irish accent as I tossed my phone at the opposite couch.

Chapter 60

I put on the TV with the sound off as I sorted through my notes and the case files.

It was a lot of paper. There was still so much to get through, so much to absorb. I wasn't even sure if we were wasting our time with our latest theory. The very real threat of yet another insane, pointless copycat killing wasn't exactly helping my concentration.

I was getting up to exchange my beer bottle for a coffee cup when my phone rang. I grabbed it from the couch.

Lo and behold, would you look at that? I thought, glaring at the screen. It was my boss, Miriam. Did the woman never sleep?

"Bad news, Mike," she said when I made the mistake of accepting the call. "I just got off the phone with the commissioner. It looks like he wants to go in a different direction with the task-force lead. Major Case is out. Manhattan North Homicide is in. We're both still on the task force, but he wants to, quote unquote, refresh the supervising investigative angle."

"Refresh what? With the Manhattan North scrubs? He's going to pull the plug on us now? Just when the ice is starting to break?"

"I know, Mike. This is just a bunch of backroom bullshit. The chief of detectives is just screwing with us because he can. We'll still run the task-force meeting tomorrow, but then that's it. I just thought you should know."

"I'm sorry. I feel like I let you down, Miriam," I said.

"How do you think I feel? I pulled you off your vacay only to get you jammed up. Don't take this to heart. You're still my go-to. Sometimes you just can't catch a break quickly enough."

I hung up, trying to absorb what I'd

just heard. I was letting out a breath as my text jingle rang. It was Emily.

Hey, u still awake?

I'd almost forgotten that Emily was still out pounding the pavement. The original plan was to meet back up for dinner to brainstorm and crunch every-thing we'd learned, but she'd been tied up in an interview when I'd called ear-lier.

Just barely, I started texting back, but then remembered I was over the age of twelve and actually called her instead.

"Hey, yourself," I said when she an-swered. I decided not to tell her the devastating news about my impending public demotion. She'd find out tomor-row along with the rest of New York.

"I thought we were supposed to meet and compare notes," I said.

"The best-laid plans of mice and Feds, Mike," Emily said. I could hear traffic in the background. "Turn left in two hundred yards," Emily's GPS sys-tem said in its annoyingly calm com-puter voice.

"I actually got lost after visiting one

of the Grand Central bombing victims' families. Newark is tricky with all those parkways and turnpikes."

"You're in Newark?" I said in shock. "What are you, nuts? I gave you all the Manhattan victims so you wouldn't have to go too far, country mouse."

I couldn't believe how far and fast Emily was going on this. This wasn't even her case, and she was putting in a superhuman effort. It was because it was my case, I realized. Not only had she volunteered, she was going above and beyond to make me look good.

"What's wrong with Newark?" she said.

"Nothing, if you happen to like drug gangs and gun violence. You should have called me."

"Please. I actually just got off the George Washington Bridge," Emily said over the GPS blathering something about the right lane. "That's somewhere near you, right? Are you too beat for a powwow?"

I perked up a little. The case was still mine until tomorrow. Maybe I might pull this off after all. Suddenly, Mary Catherine's comment about whom I'd be kissing good night crossed my mind.

"I'm wide awake, Emily," I said. "Ask that damn thing if it knows where West End Avenue is."

Chapter 61

In the glittering light of a cut-crystal chandelier, Berger lifted a warm mussel to his eyes like a jeweler with a rare gem. From the corner of the room, the piano played a cadenza from Mozart's piano concerto no. 20. In D minor, if Berger wasn't mistaken. And he wasn't mistaken, since, like Wittgenstein, he had the gift of perfect pitch.

Berger expertly parted the warm shell with his thumbs and scraped free the slick, pale yellow meat. The loud, guttural sucking sound he made as he popped it into his mouth momentarily drowned out the Mozart.

Berger slowly chewed, maximizing the mouth feel. He loved fresh mussels.

So tangy, so of the deep blue sea. The mussels tonight had been accented with a simple and perfect broth of lemon, white wine, and tarragon. The damask napkin tucked into the collar of his shirt was absolutely drenched in the heady broth. It actually heightened the experience.

Most nights, he liked a variety of food courses, but sometimes, like tonight, a fancy would take him, and he would fixate on one item sometimes for hours at a time.

It was like a contest of sorts, a culinary marathon.

He swallowed and burped and dropped the empty mussel shell into the brimming bowl beside him. So many mussels, so little time.

He was lifting up the next dark sea jewel when the music changed. Waiters came in from the kitchen pushing an immense white birthday cake on a rolling silver tray. The sparklers on top sizzled brightly in the dimness of the dining room.

"Nous te souhaitons un joyeux anniversaire," the staff sang. *"Nos voeux de*

bonheur profonds et sincères. Beau-coup d'amour et une santé de fer. Un joyeux anniversaire!"

It was *"Bon Anniversaire,"* the French version of the "Happy Birthday" song.

Berger waved his mussel along to the music like a conductor's baton. It was their way of saying good-bye, he realized. This was his last meal.

After the song was over, and the staff was about to depart, Berger rang his seafood fork loudly against his wine-glass.

"No, no. Please. Everyone wait," Berger said. "Sommelier, please. Glasses for everyone, including yourself. Fetch the champagne."

A moment later, carts piled with antique silver ice buckets were wheeled in from the kitchen. Inside the buckets were bottles of '97 Salon Le Mesnil Champagne, the best of the very best. Behind the champagne came the entire staff, all the servers, the table captain, sommelier, maître d', the chef and prep cooks, even the dishwasher.

Berger nodded. Corks were popped. Glasses filled.

"Over the years, you have treated me with such service, such grace," Berger said, raising his glass. "The happiest moments of my life were spent here in this room with you. You have provided me with a luxury, in fact, an entire life, I would never have had or even dreamed of without your impeccable assistance. For that, allow me to say, Skol, Salud, Sláinte, and L'Chaim to you all."

The servers smiled and nodded. The sommelier and maître d' and the chef clinked glasses and drank and set their glasses down. One by one, everyone filed past and gave Berger their happy regards before departing.

The maître d' and chef were the last ones to leave.

"My brother, the caterer, will come tomorrow for the tables and chairs, sir," said the maître d'. "It's been a pleasure coming here, into your home, all these years to serve you in this unique way. I hope you were happy with our approximation of a fine dining experience."

"You did a wonderful job. Truly excellent," Berger said, impatient to get back to his last plate of mussels.

"Mr. Berger, please just allow me one more moment," Michel Vasser, the tall, bearded chef said. He was a native of Lyon, had trained at le Cordon Bleu, and had actually won the Bocuse D'Or in the early eighties.

"It really has been a pleasure serving you over the past ten years," the talented chef said. "You've been more than generous, especially in your compensation package, and I just wanted to say that—"

As the man prattled on, Berger could take it no longer. He lifted the bread plate beside him. It made a whistling sound as it whizzed past the chef's ear and smashed against the wall.

"Au revoir, mon ami," Berger said, waving the asshole away.

He waited until he heard the front door open and close before he cracked open another shell.

Chapter 62

"Hey, did a toy come with this Happy Meal?" I asked as I stole a French fry from the Mickey Dee's bag on the dash of Emily's Fed car.

"I wouldn't know. That bag was there when I signed the car out," Emily teased as she flipped through my notes.

We were now parked down at the West 79th Street Boat Basin. On the dark mirror of the water we could see bobbing sailboats, the black mass of an anchored tanker, and the romantic chandelier-like lights of the George Washington Bridge off to the right. It was a nice secluded parking lot right smack on the Hudson. A notorious lovers' lane, and I knew we'd have it all to ourselves, since we had yet to catch the still-on-the-loose Son of Sam copycat.

As usual, Emily looked amazing, buttoned up in her business-hottie-with-a-nine-millimeter style. She looked fresh as a daisy, even though she'd been busting her tail all day. I could think of worse people to hang out with in a prime make-out spot.

I spat the cold fry into a napkin and looked over at my attractive FBI colleague with feigned hurt.

"Back to business now. Question one: You spoke to the Bronx stabbing victim, right?" Emily said.

"If I don't answer, will you waterboard me?" I said.

"I'd watch my step if I were you."

"Fine, Aida Morales. Yep, spoke to her. She had a complication with one of her stabbing wounds, so she was actually still at Jacobi Hospital."

"Did you show her the sketch and Photo Pak of the suspect?"

I nodded.

"She actually spent a lot of time with him, so even though he was wearing a curly Son of Sam wig when he attacked her, she was pretty sure it was the same guy."

Emily wrinkled her brow at the pages.

"What, if anything, about the victims' families jumps out at you as a possible link?"

"Not much," I said, looking out at the water. "Especially on the surface. I mean, we have eight victims, right? Aida Morales, the four people killed in the Grand Central bombing, the double murder of the professor and his lover in Queens, and poor little Angela Cavuto. Four females, four men, five of them blue-collar types, three a little more up-scale. You couldn't get a more disparate bunch."

"But like we agreed," Emily said, "only two of the people who died at the news-stand—the owner and the girl who worked there—can be considered targets. The officer who was killed wasn't on his regular post, and the homeless man wasn't known to frequent the area."

"Okay, fine," I said. "Six victims, then,

but there's still no obvious connection. Maybe we're digging a dry hole."

"Family dynamics are one thing we haven't fully looked into, Mike. We have to keep looking."

Emily stared at me and then started flipping through my notes again. To make myself useful, I started looking through hers. The interview parameters were extensive: socioeconomic status, brothers, sisters, parents, birth order, status of parents, employment history, education.

When the words started to blur, I slapped the folder closed.

"I'm not feeling it. I can't think here. Start the car. I know just the place."

Chapter 63

I directed Emily and told her to stop under the beacon of a green neon harp. It was the Dublin House bar on 79th Street, where I'd celebrated my twenty-first birthday.

"You can think better here?" she said.

"What do you mean?" I said, leading her inside. "The library's closed. Besides, haven't you heard? People leave bombs there."

The no-frills Irish pub hadn't changed a bit. I went to the jukebox and put on "The Black Velvet Band," which was the theme song of my childhood.

My NYPD detective father, Tom Bennett, used to bring me here on Saturdays sometimes when my mom went to visit her sisters back in Brooklyn. He'd ply me with Cokes and quarters for the pinball machine as he drank with his fellow Irish cop cronies. They used to call my dad Tony Bennett sometimes for his occasional habit of breaking into song when he was three sheets to the wind.

My mom and dad died in a car accident on the way down to their Florida condo the week after I graduated from college. They were buried together out in Calvary Cemetery in Queens, but it was here that I came when I wanted to visit.

Something, maybe the dustup with the Flahertys, was reviving a lot of my melancholy Irish childhood. My current professional woes certainly weren't cheering me up. I could handle having the press coming after me—that was their job. But getting the back of the commish's hand was the straw that broke the camel's back.

Or, hey, maybe I was having a midlife crisis. One night all alone in the big city, and I was sinking quickly into dad-olescence. I decided to roll with it. I continued to the bar and ordered us two shots of Jameson and two pints of Guinness.

"Let me guess. This is St. Patrick's Day in July," Emily said.

I winked at her and dropped the shot glass into the pint glass and tipped it back until the only thing left was the foam on my lips.

"Just trying to wake up," I said, wiping the back of my hand over my thirsty mouth. "What are you waiting for?"

She rolled her eyes before she dropped her depth charge as well and sucked it back with impressive speed.

"Hey, you got a little something on your lip," I said right before I kissed her.

I don't know which of us was more shocked at my forwardness. To top things off, she started kissing me back, but I suddenly broke it off.

"Okay, then," she said, looking at me funny. "You feeling all right, Mike?"

I shrugged. It was a good question. Unfortunately, I didn't have a good answer. Like the rest of the city, I was having one weird summer.

"Maybe we should call it a day," I said, dropping a couple of twenties on the bar and heading for the door.

Emily followed me back out, and we drove back to my building in silence. When I reached for the car door, it was Emily's turn to lean in and kiss me. There was a pregnant, hot, wavering moment when I thought some clothing was going to get torn, and then she ripped her tongue out of my mouth and shoved me toward the door.

Wiping lipstick off my face, I looked over at my building, where Bert, the doorman, stood avidly watching the proceedings. Of course *now* the son of a bitch was at the door.

"Hot and cold, cold and hot," she said. "I don't know, but I guess this just doesn't feel right for me right now, Mike. I don't know what it is, but I feel like we're not doing ourselves or each other justice. You should probably get out of here before I do something we'll both regret," she said.

I nodded. I knew what she meant. We

were friends, not to mention intuitive work partners. If we went much further, we'd be putting that in jeopardy. Or something. Right?

I wasn't sure how to reply, so I just said okay and opened the car door.

It was right then and there, standing in the street with Emily's brake lights flashing off, that it occurred to me. *Justice*. Some synapse in my brain finally fired, and the connection we were looking for materialized in my mind like a constellation from a group of random stars.

"Emily, wait!" I yelled as she pulled away.

She didn't stop. I actually had to run after her. If it hadn't been for a red light, she would have gotten away.

"Are you crazy?" she said when I opened her door.

"Listen. I got it. You were right. It *is* the family dynamic," I said as the light turned green.

"What?" she said as a cab honked behind us.

"What?" she said again after she'd pulled the FBI sedan to the curb.

"It's the mothers," I said, leaning across her and grabbing the interview sheets we'd been working on. I pulled out two of them, my finger racing down the rows.

"Look here. The mothers. Mrs. Morales and Angela Cavuto's mother, Alicia, both went to the same school. They both went to the John Jay College of Criminal Justice."

"Holy shit," Emily said. "Wait."

She shuffled some more sheets.

"Here it is. Right here! Stephanie Brill, the girl who died in the bombing at the Grand Central newsstand went to John Jay as well. Her stepmother said she had taken classes there before dropping out. Is it a city school or something?"

"Yes. And think about it. Criminal justice—that would totally jell with where you might find someone obsessed with crime! This is it, Emily. I'll call the squad and Miriam. We need to bring the mothers in tomorrow first thing."

Chapter 64

Emily and I were at my desk rereading homicide folders and sharing a Red Bull by eight-thirty a.m.

Every once in a while, I looked up from my case file and found myself glancing over at the back of Emily's still shower-wet coppery brown hair. Things were definitely looking up. Now that I'd finally made a much-needed break-through, we were back on track.

When I glanced over at her again, I found myself wondering what the line of her bra strap beneath her white blouse would feel like under my finger.

My shenanigans were acting up again apparently. Bad shenanigans.

"What? What is it?" she said, slowly

turning and completely busting me. Feds can be pretty crafty, too, apparently.

I shook the empty Red Bull can in my hand without blinking.

"Coffee?" I said.

I had just grabbed a couple of mugs when Miriam came in through the Major Case Unit's battered bullpen door.

"You need to make some calls and stall the morning meeting," I said before she made it to her cramped office. "Did you get my texts?"

"Don't worry. I got your texts," she said, dropping her bag onto her desk. "All eight of them. Tell me something, though. What if this John Jay thing is a spurious connection, Mike? What if nothing comes of it?"

"Then we get drop-kicked off the case as scheduled," I said. "What do we have to lose?"

"I don't know. My next promotion?" Miriam said dismally.

As I left, I knew she was only kidding. My boss was as stand-up as they come. She hadn't once brought up how slowly things were going, despite all the heat she was getting. Which was a lot, considering our squad room was a short elevator ride away from the commissioner's office upstairs.

Emily and I didn't waste a moment getting the rest of the task force up to speed on our newest theory during the morning skull session. Most of the cops coming off the night shift even stayed for the festivities.

"In reviewing the cases, Detective Bennett and I discovered a number of traditional offender personality types that just didn't fit together," Emily said in front of the cluttered case board. "So we decided to look more closely at a link between the victims, and last night, we think we found one."

"What link?" Detective Schaller from Brooklyn North said.

"We're not exactly sure yet," I said, "but it turns out that the Grand Central bombing victim Stephanie Brill went to the John Jay College of Criminal Justice at the same time as the mothers of both the murdered little girl, Angela Cavuto, and the Bronx stabbing victim, Aida Morales."

"The *mothers* of the victims went to John Jay?" said newbie Detective Terry Brown. "So our guy kills the kids for maybe like a revenge thing or something? That's cold."

Some confused grumbling from the packed room full of cops and Feds followed, but I noticed more than a few thoughtful nods. There weren't many wallflowers in our open-forum meetings. The fact that no one in the room full of dedicated professionals could come up with a glaring reason that my idea was stupid was a good sign. Maybe we were onto something after all.

Spoken too soon, I thought, as a scrub-faced young female ATF field agent, sent in to bolster our Bomb Squad, cleared her throat.

"New York City actually has a college for criminal justice?" she said.

"Gee, pa, those skyscrapers look just like corn silos, don't they?" some NYPD veteran detective from the back of the room chimed in.

"That's enough, people," I said over the chuckles. "I know you're all about as punch drunk-on this as I am. But things are finally coming into focus."

I pointed toward the caseboard at the picture of the cop killed in the Grand Central bombing.

"We all know why we're here. It's time to bring this thing home."

Chapter 65

Two teams of Major Case detectives were immediately dispatched to the bursar's office at John Jay to go over student records. Emily and I had to stay back for the 9:30 meeting we had set up with the two victims' mothers, Alicia Cavuto and Elaine Morales.

We'd just been notified by security downstairs that the women had arrived, when a tall, gawky woman with a striking resemblance to Caroline Kennedy came into the squad room and headed directly to my desk. Her name was Jessica Cook, and instead of American royalty, she was the cybergeek cop assigned to the task force from the Computer Crimes Unit.

"Mike, Emily, I think I got something on the John Jay lead already," she said. "A nibble, at least. Come and check this out."

We rushed with her across the hallway to Computer Crimes and into her closet-size cubicle. Tacked to the wall above her monitor beside a South Park calendar was a crayon drawing of a racing cop car with the words NYPD MOM on the door.

"I've been busy hitting deeper and deeper serial-killer fan sites ever since I started impersonating some of the names from the David Berkowitz correspondence," Jessica said as we stood in front of her screen. "The worst by far is this feed called DankDungeonNYC. I just got this instant message from a new friend who calls himself Manacle Max after I mentioned I was a John Jay grad."

I read off the screen.

John Jay? U must know the Collector then. What an admirable freak. Always wants the worst. Always pays top dollar.

"This is incredible," Emily said.

"Type in something like 'I haven't seen

the Collector in years. What's he up to these days?'" I said.

Jessica put it in and hit enter.

The message spat back a moment later

After he was fired u mean? Nothing was the last I heard, the lucky prick. I wish I was independently wealthy. Enough about him. Let's meet. U said u have atrocious homicide scene shots? So do I. I'll show u mine. U show me urs. LOL!.

"Fired? He worked there!" Emily cried. "He was an employee or a professor at John Jay. Has to be!"

"NYPD Mom to the rescue," I said, giving Jessica a high five.

Chapter 66

Beyond enthused for the first time since the case began, I sped with Emily back to the squad room. When we turned the corner, the elevator door at the end of the hallway opened.

A wiry male uniform from the HQ security detail downstairs exited with a tall, white woman and a squat Hispanic woman in tow. Both women looked tired and lost, completely grim-faced. I didn't have to read their visitor badges to know they were Mrs. Cavuto and Mrs. Morales.

Emily ushered them into one of the interview rooms as I ran and poked my head into my boss's office.

"Computer Crimes just pulled a lead

off a serial killer site that's making John Jay look even better," I called to her. "Some freak let it be known that some other rich freak who liked to collect sick, bloody crime-related shit was working there at some point but got fired. No name yet, but we're about to sit down with the mothers of the two victims to see if they can fill us in."

"What are you waiting for?" Miriam said, lifting her phone. "Get into that interview room and start pumping. I'll tell Brown to start scouring the staff rolls for people who got canned."

I turned off my phone as I entered the interview room, where Emily sat with the distraught mothers. Attractive, stylish, blond Mrs. Cavuto looked like she was taking the loss of her four-year-old daughter fairly well until you picked up on her extremely glassy eyes and sloppily applied makeup. Stocky, in a striped MTA uniform shirt, Mrs. Morales just looked like she wanted to hit someone.

As I sat, I could see from Emily's face that something very good was up.

"Mrs. Morales, please tell my partner what you just told me," Emily said.

"Alicia and I actually know each other," Mrs. Morales said, patting Mrs. Cavuto on the elbow. "Back in the nineties, we took a night class together at John Jay."

I shot Emily a look, squashing the urge to give her a high five. They'd been in the same class! This really was the connection we'd been gunning for! We'd struck absolute gold!

"Not only that, but our teacher was a sick, slimy weirdo. His name was Berger. Professor Berger."

"Berger," I said. "Are you sure?"

"Positive," Mrs. Morales said, nodding.

"It's true," Mrs. Cavuto said, quietly looking up at me with her empty blue eyes.

I thought of something then.

"His name wasn't Lawrence, was it? *Lawrence* Berger?" I asked.

"Yes," Mrs. Morales said, nodding vehemently. "That was it. Lawrence Berger."

"Excuse me one second," I said, popping out the door and poking my head back into Miriam's office.

"The lid just ripped off this thing. We got our Lawrence! Tell Brown to look for Berger. Lawrence Berger. He was a professor at John Jay."

I rushed back into the interview room. "I can't tell you how important the info you just gave to us is," I said. "Do you have any idea why Berger would do something like this? Hurt your families?"

"It's because we got the twisted son of a bitch fired. He got canned 'cause we objected that he was getting his rocks off," Mrs. Morales yelled, standing up.

"Come again?" Emily said.

"He set up a secret video camera in the ladies' room next to the class," Mrs. Cavuto said. She took a tissue out of the box on the table and began shredding it.

"Exactly," Mrs. Morales said. "There were strange noises from time to time in the ladies' room, and finally one day in the cafeteria between classes, Alicia and I and a woman named Stephanie put our heads together and realized we had all heard it. We took it to the administration. A week later, Berger was investigated, found out, and ultimately fired."

"Wait. What about Stephanie? Stephanie Brill, I think it was. Where is she?" Mrs. Cavuto said. "Did he go after Stephanie's family? She signed the complaint as well."

"Stephanie Brill died in the recent bombing at Grand Central," Emily said.

"He comes up to my neighborhood and stabs my *daughter?*" Mrs. Morales said, staring at us in disgust. "He didn't even have the cojones to come after me?"

"What was the name of this class?" I said.

"Abnormal Psychology," Mrs. Cavuto said, meticulously tearing her tissue.

There was a knock, and my boss threw open the door and gestured for me to come with her.

"This is it, Mike," Miriam said, handing me a printout. "We've got an address on Lawrence Berger. You're heading uptown, the Upper East Side. The son of a bitch lives on Fifth Avenue."

Chapter 67

"Ladies, thank you so much for coming," said a linebacker-size Emergency Service Unit sergeant as he folded open the rear of a shiny black Ford Econoline SWAT van in Central Park an hour later.

Two more vans just like it were parked in a wagon circle in our staging area behind the Metropolitan Museum of Art. More than two dozen Emergency Service cops and members of the FBI New York Hostage Rescue Team and NYPD Bomb Squad were now ready to close this case with extreme prejudice. With one cop already dead and a perp with sophisticated bomb-making skills, all stops had been pulled out to take Lawrence Berger down.

Emily and I climbed into heavy Kevlar vests as a short, grizzled, wiry black man with huge forearms and a Bic-shaved jarhead shook our hands painfully.

"Agent Hobart!" the Hostage Rescue Team leader introduced himself in a drill sergeant's near-scream. He tilted the Toughbook computer on his lap in our direction.

On it were photographs of Berger's elaborate prewar building a couple of hundred feet to the east. Close-up shots showed its even more impressive stone penthouse. It was amazing, like a monumental baroque palace in the sky, complete with columns and setbacks and gardens.

"Feast your eyes on Berger's quote unquote apartment," Hobart called out. "It's a three-level, seven thousand-square-foot penthouse."

I couldn't believe it. *Seven thousand square feet? In the Silk Stocking District?* How was that even possible? I thought.

"That's right," Hobart said, eyeing me. "I said seven thousand square feet."

"Shit, boss. I gotta get me a gig at John Jay," called back an Odd Job–looking, stocky Asian cop sitting in the van's passenger seat.

"Shut up, Wong," Hobart said savagely. "These shots were just taken from our scout snipers on the roof of the building across Seventy-seventh Street. As you can see, all the drapes are drawn, so no help for us there. The building super told us there's at least seven bedrooms, three hundred and sixty degrees of outside terraces, two separate staircases, and even an interior elevator. It's basically a maze. A nightmare for a breach and search."

"But great for cocktail parties, I bet," Wong said.

Hobart gave him a dirty look before continuing.

"The super also said Berger's a recluse, and he hasn't seen him in years. Said he hires his own contractors and staff who must have signed confidentiality agreements because they don't even talk to the doormen about what goes on up there. Berger basically does whatever he wants because he's, by far, the largest shareholder in the co-op. We've also been up on his phone for the last hour. No incoming or outgoing calls. Quiet as a mausoleum."

"Kind of looks like one, too, doesn't it?" I said.

Hobart nodded.

"If it were up to me, I'd go in at two a.m. with night vision. As it is, we're going to cut the electrical power to the apartment right before we breach, in case Mr. Mad-Bomber-Ass got something rigged."

Hobart turned and addressed the crowd of black-clad men around us.

"Remember, people, once the door is down," he called out, "three teams will split up. One per apartment floor. Berger Meister could be anywhere, hiding God knows what, so I want room-to-room sweeps that the fucking upstairs maid would be proud of. Also, check with your team's bomb tech before you even think about touching anything. Capiche? Good. Now it's hurry-up-and-wait time.

All we need is the green light from the pencil pushers."

For the next fifteen minutes, we listened to the SWAT guys lock and load and exchange terms like "tactical action parameters," "secure coms," and "mission capabilities." Sitting on a greasy steel bench along the wall of the stifling van, Emily and I tested our earpiece radios and quick-checked our own weapons.

I glanced out the van's one-way tinted window a hundred feet to the west, where the Ancient Egyptian stone obelisk known as Cleopatra's Needle stood against Central Park's bright blue sky. On the path beside it, a pudgy female jogger went by, followed by a dog walker pulling a ten-dog pack.

I don't know which was higher, the temperature, my adrenaline, or the tension. I was pumped that we were finally onto Berger, but also wary. I'd seen Berger's meticulous handiwork firsthand. Not only was he smart, efficient, and completely cold-blooded, but we had zero intel about the place where he was holed up.

We weren't pulling a crackhead out of a closet, I thought, staring at the photo of the creepy penthouse. It was more like we were reaching into a black hole in the ground to pull out a viper.

"Alpha One, we have a go," a voice in my earpiece crackled, a long, hot five minutes later. The van roared to life and swung hard to the right with a squeal of tires.

"Woo-hoo! This is it, y'all!" Officer Wong called out with an enormous grin as he adjusted his tactical helmet's chin strap. "We're moving on up to a deluxe apartment in the sky-high!"

Chapter 68

What seemed like a rapid heartbeat later, Emily slid into me as the van fishtailed with a shriek of brakes. My head almost hit the ceiling as the van crossed Fifth Avenue and hopped the curb in front of Berger's building.

The back doors popped open, and Emily and I quickly followed the tactical team across the sidewalk and under the hunter green awning. When my eyes adjusted to the dim lobby, I spotted the doorman pressed against the wall beside an immense oil painting, his hat on the floor between his feet, his white-gloved hands in the air. A sign beside him said ALL VISITORS MUST BE ANNOUNCED.

"Not today, friend," Hobart said, handing the guy back his hat.

Everyone froze in place as the wood-paneled elevator door at the far end of the lobby dinged open. Half a dozen laser sights trained on a tall, gorgeous young couple in business attire. Before they could open their mouths, they were taken facedown onto the Oriental carpet.

"They're clean, Chief," Wong said, tossing Hobart the young business guy's wallet.

A broad, black-haired man wearing blue work clothes and wire-rim glasses appeared from a door beside the elevator.

"The back elevator is here, officers. This way," he said in a thick Eastern European accent as he waved at us frantically.

A contingent of men was left to secure the lobby while we went through a dusty back hall and packed into a film noir–era freight elevator.

"This is so crazy, so crazy," the super kept repeating as he operated the manual elevator.

Damn straight, I thought. There was absolutely no joking now or even talking as we watched the floors slide by with a disturbing sound of rattling chains.

At the top floor, we came out into a dingy, narrow, windowless hallway lit by a single hanging bulb. This was definitely the service entrance. A hand signal from Hobart halted us at the corridor's bend beside some garbage cans. Two men rushed forward and knelt beside the lock on Berger's apartment's back entrance, placing the breaching explosive.

They ran back, and Hobart radioed down to some of his men now in the building's basement.

"In position," Hobart said.

"Roger. Pulling the switch. The juice is off. You're a go," a cop radioed back.

Hobart nodded. Then one of the commandos tapped a stapler-like detonator, and Berger's back door was blown to smithereens with an enormous crunching blast.

The next few moments were a chaos of running men and shouts.

"FBI!" Hobart screamed in a voice that sounded like it could have knocked the door down on its own. "Down! Down! FBI! Everyone on the floor!"

Behind the SWAT team, Emily and I entered over the remains of the still-smoking door into a high-ceilinged kitchen. Instead of the granite counter-tops and high-end cabinets I was expecting, there were well-used indus-trial-size stoves and stainless-steel countertops. But that head-scratcher was nothing compared with the dining room.

A dozen tables were covered in linen and set with formal place settings and unlit candles. For some reason, all the china and crystal and silver set out made the room look unbelievably creepy. There was even a grand piano on a stage in the corner. It looked like we'd walked into a restaurant.

"Talk about not knowing what we're going to find," Emily said, shaking her head.

We passed into an even larger wood-paneled living room. There was an incredible amount of art on the massive mahogany walls. A mix of museum-quality sketches, photography, what looked like a Renoir. Modern stuff.

"There's more paintings than wall space," I said.

We were stepping toward the stairs at the opposite end of the room when we heard shouting from above. There was an enormous chandelier-rattling thump followed by a blood-curdling scream.

"What is this? Why are you in my house? What the hell are you doing?" I heard as I arrived on the next floor at the commando-filled doorway.

Then I looked inside.

"No," I said, staring in wide-eyed wonder.

Emily bumped into me to look in as well.

"What the hell?" she said, shaking her head.

"You're hurting my back. I have a bad back," said the man on the floor—the tremendously fat, naked man lying face-down on the floor.

Chapter 69

I gagged as a waft of the stifling room's horrendous body odor slapped into me. I started coughing. I was surprised I didn't throw up.

Whoever the morbidly obese man was, he certainly wasn't the suspect from the witness statements or sketch or the surveillance video.

We'd screwed up, I thought as I lowered my gun.

"God, somebody get a sheet, huh?" Emily said, holstering her service weapon as she averted her eyes.

"And a case of Lysol," Wong said, covering his nose and mouth as he finished cuffing him.

Reluctantly, I went into the room and

tore a filthy sheet off the bed and covered the guy's backside with it. It barely fit. He was easily six hundred pounds. Maybe even seven. The ESU guy actually had to use two pairs of handcuffs to secure the fat bastard's wrists.

I knelt down beside him.

"Lawrence Berger?" I said.

"Yes," he said, lolling his large head in my direction. "Oh! Wow! Michael Bennett. I didn't know you were here. My God. This is so surreal."

Emily and I exchanged baffled looks.

"I know you?" I said.

"You gave a lecture on homicide investigation to the general assembly at John Jay back in 'ninety-three, was it?" Berger said, looking into my eyes. "Your wife was there with you. A tall, pretty Irish lady. Tell me, how is your wild Irish rose these days? Oh dear, what am I saying? The article about you in *New York Magazine* said she died. Well, she's in a better place. My deepest condolences."

Before I could punch the man in his mouth, Hobart hauled back hard on his handcuffs.

"Ahhh! My wrists!" Berger screamed, tears in his eyes. "Ow! Stop it! That hurts! What are you trying to do? Break my arm? Didn't I tell you I had a bad back?"

"I look like your chiropractor, fatty?" Hobart said in the man's ear. "Watch your mouth before I fill it with my combat boot."

Berger nodded as he turned slowly toward Emily.

"Don't tell me you're Agent Parker. You guys have teamed up again? I feel honored. Nice core. Pilates?"

"That's it," Hobart said, tugging back hard on the cuffs again.

But instead of screaming again, Berger did something as surprising as it was horrifying.

He broke into giggles.

"You call this pain?" Berger said, smiling back at Hobart after a beat. "I've paid more than you make in a week for far, far worse, Brown Sugar. What were you going to do with your combat boot again?"

This was taking a bad turn. Getting

weirder and weirder. Hobart let the cuff chain go as if it were on fire and wiped his hands on his pants.

"Where were we again?" Berger said, turning back around to face me. There was an oddly chipper tone in his voice now.

"Who the hell is this, Berger?" I said, showing him the sketch and FAO Schwarz surveillance photo.

Berger squinted at it.

"That would be a crappy rough semblance of Carl, I think," Berger said.

"Carl?" Emily said. "Who the fuck is Carl?"

"Carl Apt is my friend," Berger said. "My very close friend and companion. I know what you're thinking. Longtime companion, aka gay lover, but no. Not that I didn't make some overtures. Strictly business, Carl is. Pure as the driven snow and twice as cold."

"Carl what? Works for you?" I said, trying to piece things together.

"Kind of," Berger said. "It's complicated."

"I say we gag this turd," Hobart said.

"Where is he? Where's Carl right now?" I said.

"Where Carl usually is, silly," the fat man said, rolling his eyes. "He's upstairs taking a bath."

Chapter 70

Outside Berger's bedroom, Emily and I raced behind Hobart and a few SWAT and bomb guys to a circular staircase at the end of the hallway.

"If this sick-ass individual really is up there, he knows IEDs, so keep your eyes peeled for trip wires," Hobart called back to us as we quickly began to ascend in single file.

IEDs? Trip wires?! I thought, wiping sweat out of my eyes. I couldn't believe this insanity. We'd found Berger, taken him down, and yet this thing *still* wasn't over?

Of course not, I thought as we corkscrewed upward toward the penthouse's third floor. It wasn't over until the fat *lady* sang.

It was noticeably hotter in the upstairs hallway. Dim, with the curtains drawn, it reminded me of an attic. A bizarre, mazelike one with ornate crown moldings and paneled walls and more art. Strange art, too, I thought, scanning the walls filled with photographs of hellish landscapes and oil portraits of melting people. We passed a large room nearly filled with hideous primitive sculptures.

Sweat dripped from my nose and from the grip of my Glock as we slowly went down the hallway. Emily was pressed close behind me, her Glock 23 pointed toward the ceiling, her palm flat on the back of my Kevlar vest.

Everyone jumped in unison as we heard a loud, electric *clack* and a deep humming from behind the wall we were walking beside.

"Excuse my French, but what the fuck?" Emily said.

"Must be the building's elevator machinery," Hobart whispered over the com link.

"Can anyone loan me a fresh pair of

boxer shorts?" asked one of the commandos.

A moment later, Hobart and his men paused by an open doorway on our left. When I arrived beside them, I was surprised by a breeze.

That wasn't the only surprising thing. Inside was a bathroom. The most enormous white-marble bathroom I'd ever seen. It had a sunken tub, a fireplace, and French doors that opened onto a massive stone balcony. A soft breeze fluttered the bubbles in the tub along with the tiered flames of candles that blazed in the enormous fireplace.

"Where the hell is this creep, already?" Hobart said, sighting his submachine gun at the tub. "Did Calgon take him away?"

We followed Hobart out onto the balcony. A tar beach this was not. Talk about a million-dollar view. Over the ornate granite railing in front of us was nothing but Central Park's trees and the distant, iconic towers of the Dakota and San Remo apartment houses on Central Park West.

"What have we here?" Hobart said,

kneeling down at the terrace's south end. A rock-climbing rope was knotted expertly around one of the stone balustrades, its other end pooled onto the roof three stories below.

Hobart cupped his mike with his fist.

"I want a team on the roof at the base of the penthouse pronto. Be advised, it looks like our guy has bugged out, either into the building or onto one of the fire escapes."

I followed Hobart's gaze. He was right. Looking down below on the roof of the building, I spotted the openings for at least two fire escapes. If our man Carl had bolted the moment we'd knocked the door down, he could have gotten down to the ground floor by now or onto the roof of one of the block's adjoining buildings.

Shit. We would have to go floor by floor now or maybe even building by building. It was possible he could even have gotten away.

I immediately called Miriam.

"I got good news and bad news," I told my boss. "We found Berger, but apparently the guy from the security camera is his accomplice. Not only that, but he just went Spider-Man on us. We're going to need Aviation on the block here, eyeballing the rooftops."

"On it," my boss said.

"Wait up. What's this?" Hobart said, suddenly climbing over the railing on the north side of the balcony and hopping down.

Five feet below the terrace around the side of the penthouse was another balcony with a massive garden of potted palms and shrubs and exotic plants. Beside the garden, alongside the building itself, was a suburban-type garden shed. Hobart raised his foot to kick its door in, but then thought better of it.

Brian Dunning from the NYPD Bomb Squad popped a gum bubble as he climbed down and stepped forward. He took a digital video recorder out of a bag and worked its fiber-optic camera under the door's bottom crack.

"It's okay. Clear," he said after a minute.

Still, a tense, collective breath was held as he opened the shed's door.

Most of the dim room was taken up

by a massive worktable. The flashlight taped to Hobart's MP5 played over a soldering iron and bricks of what looked like modeling clay.

"That's plastic explosive," Dunning said, waving his arms frantically, warning everyone back. "Enough to crater this roof. We need an evac of the penthouse and the roof right now."

Chapter 71

An EMT guy with long black headbanger hair stood beside a stretcher in the hallway outside Berger's bedroom when we hurried back downstairs.

"What do you mean ASAP?" he was saying to a cop as he pointed down at Berger with an incredulous expression. "You don't need me, you need to call a piano mover with a boom crane."

Due to the evacuation condition, everyone pitched in. Everyone except Emily, who I noticed was suddenly conveniently absent. Very much like a beached whale, Berger was rolled onto a comforter and on the count of three was hoisted by ten groaning first respond-

ers out of the room and the apartment
into the freight elevator.

Downstairs, I hustled the doorman,
whose name was Alex Rissell, into the
coatroom off the lobby. We needed
info—and quickly. For all we knew,
Berger could have been totally bullshit-
ting us about Carl.

Alex seemed to have calmed down
from our initial storming of the building.
I walked over to Emily as she unfolded
the surveillance photo of Carl Apt and
showed it to him.

"Does this man live in Mr. Berger's
apartment, Alex? It's really important,"
she said.

"Holy crap! I saw that picture in the
Post," the doorman said, scratching at
a zit on his pasty double chin. "I didn't
think anything of it, but you're right. It's
him. It's Carl Berger."

"You mean Carl Apt," Emily said.

Alex gaped at us.

"His name is Apt? I thought he was
Mr. Berger's brother Carl. That's what
we were told. We all called him Mr.
Berger."

"Whatever," I said. "Was this Carl guy upstairs when we came in?"

The doorman nodded rapidly. "The board says he's been in since last night."

"How long have Berger and Carl been living here?" Emily said.

"Berger grew up here. Carl came much more recently. I'd say about five years ago," the doorman said, nervously flicking at his zit again.

"Where did Carl come from?" Emily said.

"I don't know," the doorman said with a shrug. "But I do know that when he moved in, Mr. Berger stopped going outside. Mr. B was always an odd duck, but after Carl came, he went full-tilt cuckoo. Started having all his meals catered. Mr. B was always rotund, but holy crap! I hear he's a real whale now, am I right? I mean, break-the-boxspring, TLC-show fat. Imagine what a scandal this is going to be for his family, especially his famous brother."

"What are you talking about?" I said.

"You don't know?" the doorman said, surprised. "Lawrence Berger's brother is David Berger, the Oscar-winning Hollywood composer. The whole Berger family are, like, rich and famous geniuses from way back.

"Lawrence's grandfather was Robert Moses's right-hand engineer or something, and his father was some kind of A-list computer-whiz business guy. The old super told us that, before the older Berger died, Bill Gates and Steve Jobs showed up here one night for a birthday dinner."

I blinked at Emily. Bill Gates? Could this case get any weirder?

"Does Berger have any vehicles, other residences?" Emily said.

"Let's see. They have an estate in Connecticut. The address is around here somewhere. Mr. B never went, but Carl went every other weekend in that slick Merc convertible of his. He keeps it at the garage around the corner on Seventy-seventh. Mr. Carl is the cold, silent type, but I'll tell you one thing, he always slips me a crisp, warm twenty just for packing the trunk. He really kill all those people? Planted bombs?"

"Who knows? Thanks, Alex," I said, going back to the lobby.

Outside I spotted Hobart.

"EMT says fatty-fatty-two-by-four is healthy enough for questioning," he told me. "They're taking him over to the One-Nine Precinct."

"Good," I said. "Any sign of Carl?"

"We're doing apartments and the house-by-house on the building side of the block, but so far not a whisper," Hobart said with a shrug. "Ain't that the way? Fat fell down and broke his crown, but so far, Skinny is still winning the race."

Chapter 72

Still dripping water from his wet hair, Carl Apt hung on in the shaft of the building's front elevator.

He had been hanging on for the past forty minutes on a vertical beam using a rock-climbing method known as laybacking. With the fingers of both hands and the soles of both bare feet gripping the cold metal, he hung sideways with the side of his butt and lower back pressed against the brick of the elevator's shaft.

Grabbing only the kit bag the moment after the authorities blew the door down, he was completely nude. Inside the duffel bag was everything he needed—a pistol, his ATM cards, five hundred Percocet, and a change of clothes. The bag dangled in the breeze along with the rest of him, eighteen stories above the hot, pitch-black pit of the elevator shaft.

Every once in a while, he had to shift his grip and foothold to avoid cramping, but he wasn't worried yet. One thing he knew was pain, and he wasn't even in the ballpark of his threshold yet.

What he needed now was a hole. A place to get inside of and stay until things cooled down enough for him to move again. Until dark at least. He knew just the place, too. He'd get to it in a few minutes. Despite the sudden turn of events, he was completely calm. He'd been planning everything in his mind, every contingency, for the past year.

A silver blue electric spark flashed down from above as the elevator motor clacked on, and the cables in front of him began to whir.

After a minute, the top of the elevator began to approach. It stopped ten feet below him, police radios squawking as the cops inside got off.

Now was his chance. He shimmied

down the girder and onto the top of the elevator as silently as a cat. His toes squished in the cable grease. The now-empty elevator started heading down toward the lobby.

Now for the tricky part, he thought as the floors fell away.

When the elevator car got to three, he stood and stepped off the top of the elevator car onto the lip of the second floor's elevator door. He waited for the door of the elevator to open onto the lobby before he popped the release lever at the top of the second floor's door and stepped out onto the landing. As he let the door slide back, he wrapped his bag's handle on the shaft-side door release.

He waited on the furniture-filled landing of the second floor, staring at the two doors of the A and B apartments. Now was the bugger, he knew.

He would have to wait until the elevator went back upstairs in order to open the door and actually get underneath the elevator. It was the only way of getting into the basement undetected. That's where his hole was. His life now depended on getting down into the building's basement.

He glanced at the apartment doors, his hand on the suppressed 9-millimeter Smith & Wesson semiauto in his bag. If someone came out, he would kill them. On that note, if the police came to the second floor, he would also be forced to have it out right here, right now. He'd go for face shots at this close range, grab one of the automatic rifles, go down to the lobby, and go balls to the walls. Shoot his way out or die trying.

He smiled. It wasn't such a bad plan, definitely not a bad way to go. If he was anything, he was a warrior, and like all warriors, what he ultimately wanted was a good death.

One way or the other. It was up to the fates now. It was completely out of his hands.

Chapter 73

Carl waited. Watching, listening. After a minute, he heard more police radios and then footsteps going into the elevator one floor below. He heard the elevator door whir to a close, and the car began to ascend with a mechanical hum.

He tightened his grip on the pistol as the car seemed to slow down. But then it was past the second floor and going up.

Excellent, he thought. So far, so good.

When he heard the elevator stop somewhere far above a long minute later, he yanked on the strap of his bag and opened the door onto the elevator shaft. He leapt onto the vertical girder he'd been hanging onto and began lay-backing down as silently and quickly as he could. Past the lobby door, he jumped the last ten feet into the well of the el-evator. There was a small door in its corner that led into the basement. He pushed it open and climbed out and then closed it quickly behind him.

He pulled out the gun and ran quickly down a corridor alongside dusty stor-age bins. He made a turn past the boiler room and came to a thick steel door at the end. He banged on the door with his fist once and then again.

Carl stuck his gun in the face of the ugly girl who opened the door. Her stained bathrobe was loose enough at the collar to reveal a tattoo of a butter-fly beneath her dirty collarbone.

"What is this? Who are you? You have no right to be here," she said in broken Slavic-accented English as she flinched from the gun.

"I'm an American citizen, bitch, unlike yourself. Now, shut your mouth and move," Carl said.

It had taken Carl six months of living

in the building to realize the super had turned one of the basement rooms into an apartment for Eastern European illegal aliens. It was the smell. He had caught a whiff of it when he came down to put away luggage in Lawrence's storage bin. He had smelled the same rank stench of bad sausages when he was in Delta Force and had body-guarded state officials in the Bosnian War.

He knew the building's super was a Serb the moment he first met him. Probably fleeing some war crime, from the way the beady-eyed guy operated. You wanted work done? Garbage taken away? He always got paid first.

In fact, Carl wouldn't be surprised if the girl in front of him was a whore, paying off her smuggling fee on her back. All this in the basement of a Fifth Avenue luxury high-rise, Carl thought with a grin. Economies within economies. Capitalism at its finest. USA, land of the free, where the streets were paved with gold.

All that aside, here was his hole. He had arrived. He would be safe for the next twelve hours at least. The police wouldn't search here. Since his job and his green card depended on it, the crafty mobster Serb super would never allow it.

Carl waved the girl inside with the gun, grabbed the back of her dirty housecoat, and shoved her forward toward the sound of a TV.

Inside the small room, he pushed the girl into a pale, bald old man with a regal-looking gray mustache who was cutting a swarthy teenager's hair with an electric buzzer.

"Drago mi je," Carl said with a smile. It meant, nice to meet you, or something like that, in one of those utterly confusing Yugo languages. It was the only scrap of nonsense he could remember from his boots on the ground in Eastern Europe.

The gray walrus's mouth dropped open. Why not? Shock was probably the appropriate reaction to seeing an elevator grease–covered naked man pointing a gun at you. Carl noticed that a rerun of *Full House* was on the corner TV. A pre-anorexic toddler Olsen twin was saying something cute and sassy.

Carl waited for the canned laughter to start before he shot the girl in the back of her head and threw her across the lap of the seated teen. It turned out the old man had some fight. He managed to throw the buzzing razor at Carl's face. It missed by only an inch, making a sound like frying grease as it sailed by. Carl smiled again as he shot the feisty old codger right in his proud gray mustache.

Carl watched the man go down in a heap. When he turned, he saw that the teenager was still seated, making a two-handed begging gesture as the dead girl spasmed and bled out in his lap. There was something artistic and powerful about the whole thing, a sense of the tragic here in this single-hanging-bulb-lit shithole basement room, a low-rent *La Pietà* under way.

"Drago mi je," Carl said again and put a bullet in each of the kid's closed eyes.

Chapter 74

It was almost an hour later when Emily and I arrived at the Nineteenth Precinct house to interview Berger.

Berger's building and block were still a chaos of running SWAT guys and bomb techs when we left. Worst of all, there was still absolutely no sign of Carl Apt. It was like he had disappeared into thin air.

Emily and I had a quick pre-game powwow in the tight cinder-block hallway outside one of the precinct's first-floor interview rooms. Through the one-way mirror, we stared at Lawrence Berger where he reclined, looking quite relaxed on a massive wheeled stretcher. He still had his shirt off, but someone had managed to fit a pair of Tyvek pants on him.

As I watched him, I was barely keeping my anger under control. Berger seemed to actually enjoy wallowing in the crimes committed and the repulsiveness he radiated. Though he was obviously mentally disturbed, I was having trouble giving a shit. I was sick of craziness, sick of this case, especially sick that it was still open.

We finally decided that I would go in first to warm him up.

"Remember, Mike," Emily said as I left. "This guy's a predator. He's all about manipulation, domination, control, and displaced rage. Don't let him get under your skin."

"Well, if he does," I said as I left, "just give me a minute or two before you try to pull me off him."

"Hi, Lawrence," I said, smiling, despite my fury as I stepped inside. "Can I call you Lawrence?"

"Absolutely, Detective," Berger said, looking around the old precinct's dingy space. "I used to be an auxiliary cop here, can you believe it? After my shift,

I would go to cop bars to watch Yankees games and check out the badge bunnies with the guys. They called me super-buff behind my back, but I didn't mind. I was like a mascot, one who was always good for a round."

"That's really interesting, Lawrence," I said. "But actually I wanted to ask you some more about Carl. We looked for him upstairs in your apartment, like you said, but he wasn't around. Where would Carl go, do you think? To your weekend property in Connecticut?"

"Maybe," Berger said, squinting. "But I doubt it. To tell you the truth, I think you'll have a hard time finding him. He grew up in terrible poverty in Appalachia, and when I met Carl, he was living on the street near Union Square Park. He called it "urban camping." Carl's ex-military, he likes things hard. He claimed he was in Delta Force before getting kicked out. I think he actually enjoys pain. He's a pretty singular individual."

"In what way?" I said.

"Well, for one thing, he wasn't formally educated, but he has a truly keen intelligence. After I got him off the street,

I introduced him to things. Art. Litera-
ture. I even sent him to City College. He
absorbed everything instantly. He was
like a sponge."

"Wow," I said.

"'Wow' is right," Berger said. "We
used to stay up late, sometimes all night,
just talking about everything under the
sun. What we loved. What we hated.
When I opened up about some of my
darker tastes, like my obsessions with
the bloodiest crimes of the century, Carl
was always cool with it, always non-
judgmental."

"You guys were good buddies," I said,
wishing I had some aspirin.

"Yes. We were friends," Berger said.
"Is it that hard to believe that even
someone as disgusting as me could
have a friend? Carl proved it when I
found out I was going to die. Did I tell
you? I have a congenital heart condition. Coupled with a little excessive
snacking. You can laugh, Mike. That's a
joke."

I smiled, thinking, *You're a joke*.

"Anyway, a few days after I heard the
bad news about my heart, Carl said he

had a surprise for me. The best gift anyone ever gave anyone. He laid out his
plan to take out my enemies and to en-
tertain me at the same time. I was in-
trigued. I didn't know if he was just kidding. You get to be my size, stuck in
bed all day, you get bored. But then I
saw an article in the paper about the
bomb in the library, and I knew he was
actually doing it! Carl did everything he
said he'd do and then some."

I glanced at the mirror, where Emily
was watching. What Berger said made
some sense. It certainly explained why
we had had trouble putting things together. It had never been just one mo-
tive from one perpetrator, but an odd
mix of several odd motives.

"You didn't think to come forward?"

Berger shrugged. He looked away
and began examining his fingernails.

"Must have slipped my mind," he
mumbled.

"And you readily admit everything?" I
said, staring down at Berger. "You freely
admit your involvement?"

"Proudly so," Berger said. "Write it

up, Mike, and get me a pen. I'll be more than happy to sign on the dotted line."

It was odd as I turned on my heel to leave, but I suddenly wasn't angry anymore. I refused to let Berger's evil and his twisted ridiculous pathetic feelings affect me. I was suddenly able to see him for what he was, a pile of human wreckage. I was just a garbage man trying to get through the rest of my shift.

"Be back in five, Lawrence," I said, my smile not forced now.

I actually felt happy. Happy that I would soon be out of here and back with my family. This mistake of a man forgotten by the time I finished my shower.

"Thanks for being so forthcoming. I'll be right back with that statement and that pen."

Chapter 75

In the dusty back room of the precinct house, Lawrence Berger lay sideways on a steel-reinforced hospital cot that had been loaned to the NYPD by the Brookhaven Obesity Clinic in Queens.

The chamber's fluorescent glare glistened off the layer of sweat on his pale face. He gazed with unfocused eyes at the wall beside him in a kind of rapture.

At first, when he'd been rolled into the pen, the strangeness of his new surroundings, the unclean taste of the stuffy air, and the stench of burnt coffee and old sweat and urine had been so overwhelming that he'd thrown up all over himself. The officers who were in charge of the holding pen let him lie in his vomit for over an hour before getting him some napkins and a new sheet.

Berger endured the humiliation by remembering the fate of the great throughout history who suffered at the hands of their inferiors. From his near-photographic memory, he conjured up Jacques-Louis David's *The Death of Socrates.*

He thought about Detective Michael Bennett. He'd actually been following Bennett's career ever since the St. Patrick's Cathedral hostage situation. For some time, he'd felt a kind of psychic link with the man, an almost metaphysical twinning. Confessing to him of all people had been like a dream come true, the icing on a long- and painstakingly planned birthday cake.

But now the party was coming to a close, wasn't it? he thought with a sigh.

And yet, through all his suffering and ponderings, he kept coming back to one thing. The only thing. What it always came down to in the end.

His family. His granddad and dad and brother. His beloved flesh and blood.

His grandfather, Jason Berger, had been a great man. World War I hero, brilliant civil engineer, businessman, and politician, he'd been essential not only in the development of the United States interstate highway system but also in the designing of many of New York City's bridges and parkways.

His father, Samuel J. Berger, had continued the familial tradition of greatness by being one of the first visionary businessmen of the computer age. The company he started, Berger Applications, had been one of the first venture capital firms in Silicon Valley and had, as billionaires so modestly put it, "done quite well."

Then came David. David was Berger's older brother, and if anything, he was the most talented Berger of them all. By the age of nine, his talent for musical composition had gained him an unheard-of admission to Julliard. By the time he was forty-five, his legendary career as a Hollywood composer paled perhaps only to the iconic John Williams's.

David easily would have earned more than the one Oscar he had but for his vocal disdain for the movie industry. All he wanted to do, and all he did, was make beautiful music. Sometimes in his La Jolla mountainside home. Sometimes in his villa in Burgundy. Lawrence had never been invited to either one, but he had seen pictures in an *Architectural Digest* article, and they were very nice.

David truly was a simple and gracious man. As simple and gracious as their father and his father before him. They were all examples of human potential fulfilled. They were Bergers, after all. All except for him, of course. Lawrence. Poor, sad, slow, embarrassing Lawrence.

Berger smiled up at the ceiling of his jail cell.

It had taken a century for all of the Berger family's amazing societal and global accomplishments.

If all went as planned, and it seemed

like it would, he would successfully undo every last Berger triumph in a week.

Sorry, Grandpap. Sorry, Dad. Sorry, Bro, Berger thought with a shrug of his shoulders. *Look on the bright side. The Berger name will be remembered. Just not the way you wanted.*

Lawrence's last gift would eventually be delivered to his saintly, talented brother. It was the film footage of all of Lawrence's meticulously plotted crimes. It wasn't complete yet; there were a few choice scenes that needed to be added, but he was confident in its success. He couldn't have left his final wishes in more competent hands.

The film was for David to ponder over, to wonder about, and, hopefully, to eventually score.

Lawrence knew he was no Spielberg, no Scorsese or Coppola, but perhaps when all was said and done, his brother might one day come to understand that he, Lawrence, had a little talent, too.

Was that too much to ask?

Chapter 76

Berger snapped out of his reverie when his longtime lawyer, Allen Duques, opened the door to the holding cage.

Duques, a partner in a global 100 Lexington Avenue corporate firm, handled all of his dealings. The stocky, aristocratic-looking, middle-aged lawyer looked positively lost when he spotted Berger behind the mesh. The attorney screeched a folding chair over in front of the cage's wire and hesitated before sitting, as if reluctant to muss his immaculate blue serge suit.

"Tell me it isn't true what the authorities are saying, Lawrence," the preppy gray-haired attorney said, thumbing off his BlackBerry. "These killings and the

Grand Central bombing—you've admitted your involvement? I don't understand."

Berger's basset-hound jowls jiggled as he shook his head.

"I'll try to explain in a moment, Allen, but first, did you bring it? The caviar?" Berger asked hopefully.

He'd been devouring tin after tin of Iranian Special Reserve in bed right before he'd been arrested. The thought of lighting into one last can of black gold had been girding his spirits.

"Of course, Lawrence, but unfortunately they searched my attaché when I came in. It was confiscated, I'm sorry to say. I'd say it had to do with that policeman who lost his life in the Grand Central bombing. You'll find no friends here, I'm afraid."

Berger immediately began to cry. In his mind, he pictured Dali's *Christ of St. John of the Cross,* Jesus on the cross as seen from above in a darkened sky, hovering over a body of water.

"Lawrence, are you okay?" Duques said. "I think we should seriously consider an insanity defense. I'm quite… worried about you."

"Can we talk about it tomorrow at the arraignment, Allen?" Berger said when he finally managed to pull himself together. "I'd really like to be alone now, please."

Berger rolled back toward the wall after his lawyer promptly left. As he grimly perused the primitively sketched genitalia and plethora of four-letter words scratched into the plaster, he heard a sudden clapping. From somewhere beyond the closed metal door, a television was playing a sporting event. He could hear a crowd cheering, an announcer's excited voice, more clapping and euphoria.

A sudden cold pierced the center of his chest like a bayonet. He thought about his life. What he had done to himself. What he had done to others.

He put his right thumb and index finger into his mouth like he was going to whistle. Instead, he thumbed off the cap of one of his molars, the third in on the top left, and carefully slipped out something from the hollow of it.

Up to the light, he held what looked like a small red jelly bean. It was a special gel sac with liquid inside it. It was actually a poison pill, an extremely lethal cocktail of cyanide and codeine.

It was time for his contingency plan. The one that even Carl didn't know about.

It was over for him, Berger thought, looking at the pill. In the sanctity of his citadel, he'd imagined that he could stare society coldly in the eye and laugh. Faced with actually doing it, he knew there was no way.

He thought about how disappointed Carl would be in him. Because the plan they'd agreed on wasn't actually over. All that had happened so far was supposed to be only phase one.

Once Berger was dead, his will would immediately be contested by his sister in Minnesota. All of his assets, including the murder slush fund he'd given Carl access to, would immediately be frozen. Carl, perhaps the only real friend he'd ever had, would be hung out to dry.

It couldn't be helped, Berger thought, quickly putting the pill into his mouth.

Berger surprised himself. Instead of his usual waffling, he bit down and swallowed readily. He thought he might throw up again at the sudden bitterness, but he breathed slowly and carefully until he felt better and the room began to dim.

Chapter 77

Everyone was asleep when I came home after midnight, and they were still snoozing when I came out of my bedroom dressed for work at the ungodly hour of five a.m.

Well, almost everyone, I thought, spotting a light coming from the living room. I went in and saw the lamp on by the empty reading chair in the corner. I was about to click it off when I heard some giggling from behind the chair.

I leaned over. It was Bridget. In her *Phineas and Ferb* pajamas she was sitting Indian-style on her pillow with the latest *39 Clues* book open in her lap.

"Hey," I whispered.

"Hey, Dad," she said without looking up.

"Um, what are you doing out of bed so early?"

"Reading," my daughter said, a tacit "duh" hanging in the air.

"Don't you want to sit in the chair?"

"I can't," Bridget said, turning the page. "I have to read in secret because of Fiona. MC is sponsoring a contest to see who can read the most books by the end of the summer, and I think I'm one ahead of Fi-Fi. If she sees me reading, she'll try to catch up. I want to lull her into a sense of complacency."

I blinked and nodded. Of course. Even reading was competitive in a family of ten. Well, at least in a family of ten as crazy as mine.

"What do you get if you win?" I asked.

"Dinner and a movie with Mary Catherine. Just the two of us."

Sounded good, I thought. I made a mental note to swing by the library on the way home.

"Well, carry on with your lulling," I said as I smooched the top of her head and headed for the front door. "Good luck. I think."

It was still dark when I climbed into the car and drove away from the house. Somewhere around the Brooklyn-Queens border, I pulled off the express-way and got some takeout from a diner. Back outside, surrounded by rumbling semis in the darkened parking lot, I checked in to the squad from my car.

There was no news, which in my high-profile case was actually bad news, since it meant Berger's buddy, Carl Apt, was still missing. There still wasn't sign one of Apt or of the Mercedes convert-ible Berger kept in a garage around the corner from his apartment.

Worst of all, there were no records of a Carl Apt in any of the city and state databases, no last-known address, no Social Security number, no driver's li-cense. Nada. Maybe I should start read-ing the *39 Clues,* I thought as I restarted the Chevy's engine, because no matter what we did, this ugly, baffling case just didn't want to die.

I was up on the elevated expressway with the sun finally coming up over the decrepit Queens skyline on my right when I got a call. It was from Steve Makem, the desk sergeant at the Nineteenth Precinct.

"What's up, Sarge?"

"You're the primary on Berger, right? Well, heads-up. They just went in to take him to his arraignment and found him in the holding tank, unresponsive."

I was having trouble absorbing what I was being told. Remembering my recent near-death driving-while-phoning experience, I lowered my cell as I pulled over onto the right-hand shoulder.

"Hit me again there, Steve," I said.

"EMTs are inbound, but I saw him, Mike. Humpty had a great fall out of his stretcher. His face is a bright strawberry red like I've never seen before. I don't know what, but something happened. Something bad."

Chapter 78

Something bad had happened, indeed, I thought, twenty siren-blaring minutes later as I burst into Berger's holding cell in the back of the precinct.

Berger had fallen out of the bed. Also, his butt had fallen out of his sheet again, I couldn't help but notice, to my horror.

The EMTs were long gone, replaced by the thin, birdlike female Medical Examiner I'd worked with before named Alejandra Robles.

As Alejandra went through her routine, I stared down at the massive dead man. He'd had everything—education, wealth, the coolest apartment in Manhattan—and decided on this? Setting off plastic explosives? Killing children?

Committing suicide? He was the most inadequate person I'd ever come across, and that was saying a lot.

The worst part of it was that it all felt almost scripted. The people who'd been killed seemed like they'd been bought for Berger's fifteen minutes of slimy fame.

I tried not to think about what it meant, about what kind of future the human race was heading toward. But I couldn't help it.

Alejandra knelt in front of Berger, pointing a flashlight into his mouth.

"I take it he's having trouble saying ah," I said.

"You take it correctly," she said, beckoning me over. "I think it was poison. Cyanide, I'd guess by the bright red rash, but we won't know until the toxicology."

She held the light over his upper back teeth.

"Check this out," she said, directing me to peer into Berger's pie hole. "See that molar? That's not a cavity, Mike. It's a fake tooth. That must be where he hid the poison. Can you believe it?"

After Berger was rolled out, I called Emily Parker at her hotel from the hallway outside the precinct detective squad room upstairs.

"If you thought the pantie bomber was crazy, have a seat," I said when she answered.

"You found Carl?" she guessed.

"Nope," I said. "It's Berger. He's gone. Killed himself. He had poison in a hollowed-out tooth, a cyanide pill most likely, like a Nazi spy. How's this for an epitaph? 'Lawrence Berger, weird in life, weird in death, weird in the hearts of his countrymen.'"

"Wait. Did you say *cyanide?* Hold on. Let me get my notes. Crapola! He's done it again. It's happened before. Maggie O'Malley, a nurse dubbed the 'Dark Angel of Bellevue,' swallowed a cyanide pill after she was accused of some baby murders in the early nineteen twenties."

"I need to watch more of the History Channel," I said squeezing my temples.

Book Three

THAT'S WHAT FRIENDS ARE FOR

Chapter 79

A noontime three-car pileup halted the traffic on the Sunrise Highway two miles west of Hampton Bays, Long Island.

Behind the wheel of the Mercedes convertible, Carl Apt watched a Suffolk County Highway Patrol cruiser drive past on the grass center berm to his left, followed by an ambulance. Frowning, he slipped on his designer aviator shades. He cranked the A/C as he pressed the button for the automatic hardtop.

Why had he pushed it? he thought, watching the cop's bubble lights spin. He knew he should have ditched the car already.

He held his head in his hands. Christ,

he was exhausted. The sun was like an ice pick in his eyes. He'd had a splitting headache since four a.m., when he'd climbed from the basement through a sidewalk grate on the 70th Street side of Berger's building.

What he wouldn't do for one last soak in his penthouse bath.

As he waited in the dead-stopped traffic, he glanced at the motorists around him. There were a lot of Range Rovers and Cadillac sedans. What was it Lawrence had called loud-mouthed, showy people from Long Island? LIDS. Short for Long Island Dimwits.

After a few minutes, from three cars behind him, a group of lug-nut teens with gelled hair, no shirts, and bottle tans started making some noise. A painful thump of rap music bass began to emanate from their tricked-out convertible Mustang.

"Anywhere, anywhere, woo-whooo, woo-whooo," they sang along to The Show's instant summer classic. A fat girl wearing a bikini top and short shorts stood in the passenger seat, threw her hands above her head, and started grinding her hips.

"Real slow, real slow, woo-whooo, woo-whooo," her mutt friends intoned.

A bead of sweat rolled down Carl's temple as he eyed them in his rearview. He felt like taking the Steyr AUG sub-machine gun from under the blanket in the foot well beside him and emptying all thirty 5.56 NATO rounds into the car. Roll out, put it to his shoulder and bear down full auto with the bullpup machine gun. Gel the ginzo driver's hair with his own blood before blowing out the bitch's tattooed spine, ending her pole-dancing career and having her piss in a bag for the rest of her miserable life.

Why stop there? he thought. After he raked the Mustang, he could easily kill thirty or forty more people sitting in their cars before the Gomer Long Island cops down the road figured out a response. Turn the LIE into the DOA. Sounded like a plan.

Instead, he let out a breath and popped a Percocet as the traffic started to move. After another minute, he saw a cutout in the berm and spun a U-turn.

He pulled off the southbound high-way at the next exit. Strip malls began to appear, followed by box stores. He pulled into the Roanoke Plaza in River-head and cruised up and down the aisles of the massive parking lot.

When he found a '90-something Buick in a Target parking lot, he squealed out of the lot. Half a mile east, he pulled back off the road into a small, dumpy-looking strip mall that had a pizza place, an optometrist, and something called Edible Arrangements. He drove around the rear of the low, decrepit building and parked the Merc beside a Dump-ster.

He got out and locked up and began walking back toward the Target parking lot. Halfway there, he stopped into an Ace Hardware store and bought a set of jumper cables, a can of lighter fluid, and the largest flat-blade screwdriver he could find.

"That'll be nineteen-ninety-nine plus shipping and handling," the red-vested fool behind the counter said.

Carl stared at the LID without speaking.

"Just kidding," the clerk said sheepishly as he handed him back his change.

When he got back to the Buick parked outside Target, Carl jammed the screwdriver into the slot of the window and broke it as quietly as he could. He unlatched the door and popped the hood. With the jumper cables he'd just bought, he ran a line from the positive battery node to the red coil at the back of the engine.

With the engine now powering the dash, he knelt in the open driver's-side door and cracked the plastic steering column with the flat blade of the screwdriver. Then using the metal blade, he crossed the now-exposed terminals for the solenoid and the battery. The engine chugged for a moment and then grumbled to life.

Carl flicked glass off the seat before slipping behind the wheel and pulling out.

He drove back to the Merc, unlocked the door, and soaked the interior with the lighter fluid after he transferred his bag and the assault rifle to the Buick. He lit a book of matches. He winced as he tossed them into the beautiful, six-figure car's front seat.

He looked around at the piece-of-crap Buick for the first time as he pulled out back toward the highway. McDonald's soda cups everywhere. A Jets Snuggie blanket covering the rear pleather seat.

He popped another vitamin P, then thought about it and popped another. His cheeks bulged as he inhaled and let out a long, aggravated breath.

Chapter 80

Carl pulled off the LIE into East Meadow, Long Island, an hour later.

He cruised the Hempstead Turnpike. Narrow streets of capes and split-levels, fast food, a driving range. His LeSabre fit right in.

It took him twenty minutes to find the address and parked across the street. There it was. Twenty-four Orchard Street. It looked like just another Long Island dump, but he knew it was actually more. He knew that many women had been killed behind its walls, that their bodies had been cut up in its garage.

He'd been thinking about doing another Brooklyn Vampire murder, or maybe the Mad Bomber, but then he'd remembered Lawrence's library and decided on a new string of killings. Lawrence was going to be so happy when he got the news.

Carl smiled as he thought about his friend. He'd killed for his country in the Special Forces. Called in air strikes in Bosnia, shot stinking goat herders in Afghanistan from as far away as eight hundred yards. But actually killing for something he cared about was another thing entirely.

Lawrence was his soulmate, his liberator, his master entire.

They'd taken into account that he would probably be captured. But instead of abandoning their efforts, Carl was going to redouble them. Their joint homage to the great murders and murderers of New York would keep occurring in bloodier and more horrifying ways during Lawrence's incarceration and trial. It would be the topper of the longest, most audacious crime spree of all time.

All the killing so far had been just for Lawrence. It had been Carl's pleasure.

The least he could do, after all. Twelve years earlier, Lawrence had found him panhandling on Park Avenue. He'd cleaned him up and put him through City College, where he'd studied English lit, especially the classics.

He knew all about law enforcement profiling, how he was supposed to be inadequate, looking for power, for meaning in his pathetic life. What a joke! He wasn't doing this for himself. He was a warrior, a real catalyst for history. Besides, people like Lee Harvey Oswald really had changed the world with one pull of a trigger.

But he shouldn't get ahead of himself. First things first, he thought as he pulled out.

It was time to put a smile on his good buddy's face.

Chapter 81

After I picked up Emily at her hotel, we spent the morning interviewing members of Berger's catering staff. A fruitless morning, as it turned out. All they knew about Berger were his odd eating habits. About Carl Apt, the waiters and cooks knew nothing at all.

We did manage to contact the Connecticut state troopers and have hidden surveillance put on Berger's Connecticut estate. I didn't think Apt was dumb enough to show up there, but you never knew.

We'd just sat down at DiNapoli's on Madison Avenue for a breather when I saw the headline crawl beneath the Fox

News Channel anchor on the bar's muted flat-screen.

"Wealthy Murder Suspect in Police Custody Found Dead."

I immediately lost my appetite. I didn't need to hear or read the rest of the story to realize Lawrence Berger's demise had hit the speed-of-light news cycle running. Emily and I had actually been in the middle of debating how to play the media with Berger's suicide. We'd been planning to sit on things for as long as it took to lure Apt into a trap, but as I stared at the TV, it was looking more like we were the ones who'd just gotten played.

I got a call as we were about to order. I didn't recognize the number. I picked it up, anyway.

"Detective Bennett, I need to speak with you," said a French-accented voice.

I realized it was Berger's chef, Jonathan Desaulniers, whom I'd spoken to this morning.

"What's up, Jonathan?"

"There's a girl, Paulina Dulcine," he said in a panicked voice. "She is a friend of mine. She would sleep with Mr. Berger on occasion. I apologize for not recalling this during our interview. It happened on and off for about three years. You mentioned Mr. Berger perhaps killing people who had crossed him, and after I spoke with you, I thought of her."

"She crossed him?" I said. "How? What happened?"

"Well, for a long time they had a tender relationship. He would purchase fine jewelry for her. But one day he asked her to do something to him that she thought was odd, and she started laughing. He ordered her to leave him, and they never were together again. I think Mr. Berger felt humiliated.

"The reason I'm getting in touch now is that I called Paulina today. While we were speaking, I heard a scream and then nothing. She hasn't picked up since."

"What's her number and address?" I said, waving for Emily to follow as I jumped up.

Twenty minutes later, we screeched up in front of a thirty-story high-rise

building in Battery Park City with another team of Major Case detectives
and two more uniforms.

"Paulina Dulcine. Is she home?" I
yelled at the concierge as we ran inside.

The slight, effeminate black man's
jaw dropped to the collar of his black
Nehru jacket.

"Paulina, um, no. I thought I saw her
leaving her apartment when I was deliv-
ering dry cleaning."

"She didn't leave through the lobby,"
said the female concierge beside him.

"She must have gotten her car in the
basement garage," the thin black guy
said, opening a door.

We ran down a flight of stairs into the
dim cave of the concrete garage. The
concierge pointed to the crowded corner on the left.

"It doesn't make sense," he said,
pointing across the lot. "That blue car.
The Smart car. That's hers."

We went over to the tiny car. Half a
snapped key stuck in the lock. Emily
knelt down and pulled a purse from un-

derneath the driver's door. She opened it and found a Gucci wallet.

"It's hers, Mike," Emily said, opening the wallet. "Paulina Dulcine's. He got her. We're too late."

Chapter 82

"You know, there was a case of tag-team killers we learned about at Quantico," Emily said when we got back to the squad. "It was a textbook case of these guys, Oden and Lawson. One was a psycho rapist, the other a schizophrenic. Oden raped a girl and then handed her off to Lawson, who killed and mutilated her. Each had his own thing."

"And your point is?" I said, still stinging from our near-miss of Carl.

"In this case, Apt is just killing off Berger's enemies in the way that Berger wanted. He was like the caterers we spoke to, following specific orders. I see all Berger here. No Apt."

"You're right," I said. "Even though the murders seem sadistic, they're really not. The're really set pieces, like elaborate assassinations."

"That's it, Mike. Apt seems like an assassin, cold, calculating, competent. I still can't figure out what's in it for him. Money? Maybe he's just crazy. Who knows?"

"No," I said. "You're onto something. There's something in it for Apt. There has to be."

"You sound so sure. How do you know?"

"The fourfold root of the principle of sufficient reason," I said. "Anything perceived has a cause. All conclusions have premises. All effects have causes. All actions have motives."

"My goodness, aren't we going all Aristotle suddenly?" Emily said, smiling for the first time that afternoon. "Or are the four folds from Thomas Aquinas, you Irish church boy?"

"Arthur Schopenhauer, actually," I said, faking a wide yawn.

"You read Schopenhauer?" Emily said, raising an eyebrow.

"Just at the beach," I said.

I was ducking a tossed empty Gatorade bottle when my boss came out of her office.

"They found her," Miriam said. "Paulina Dulcine. Get up to the Fifty-ninth Street Bridge."

She was actually under the 59th Street Bridge beside a York Avenue Mobil station. We bore right onto a little service road and down a ramp toward the East River. At the end of a parking lot beside an abandoned heliport, crime scene tape was wrapped around a chain-link fence.

Beyond the fence, half a dozen cops were spread out on the rock-piled shore. On the jogging path that ran under the bridge, a crowd had formed. I spotted a twelve-speed cyclist in a full-body Speedo beside a gaggle of Jamaican nannies leaning on their Maclaren strollers. They looked bored, like they were waiting for the good part to start.

"How did the call come in?" I said to a tall, elfish-looking young uniform working the crime scene log.

"By pay phone," the kid said.

"Amazing," I said.

"That someone called it in?" the young cop said.

"That someone actually found a working pay phone in Manhattan."

The jokes were long gone by the time Emily and I stumbled over to a yellow crime scene marker down by the water's edge. It was next to a paint can. Beside the can, a burly uniform cop was squatting on the rocks, smoking a cigarette. His dazed, despondent expression couldn't have been more disturbing.

This wasn't going to be pretty, I thought as I finally walked up to the can.

I didn't want to look down. I didn't want to add another nightmare to my list. I'd seen too many already.

But it was my job.

I looked down.

I was rocked to my center. All rationality abandoned me for the moment. The mind doesn't register such things easily.

Inside the can was Paulina's head. Her face was turned skyward, her eyes open. She looked up at me almost pleadingly. She looked like she was buried underground or like she'd been trying to climb through a ship's porthole and had gotten stuck.

Some very sick son of a bitch had somehow rammed the girl's decapitated head into the can.

Emily came over and put her hand on my shoulder.

"We need to get this guy, Emily," I said after a silent minute.

Emily suddenly whipped out her iPhone.

"What are you doing?" I asked.

She furiously pressed and rubbed at the screen, oblivious of me.

"I knew it. This is it! Joel David Rifkin. Parts of his first victim were found in the East River! It says it right here. The woman's head had been cut off very neatly and stuffed into an empty paint can."

"Who was Rifkin again?" I said.

"A serial killer in the nineties from Long Island," Emily said. "He was convicted of murdering nine prostitutes. He beat them with something heavy and then strangled them and mutilated their bodies. Some say it was closer to twenty victims. Apt is onto another New York killer."

A shadow passed over us. I looked up. It was the Roosevelt Island tram. We both watched the red cable car as it sailed precariously though the air out over the darkening water.

"Maybe there was some odd bond between Berger and Apt," I said, thinking out loud. "Like a cult sort of thing. Apt seems programmed. Berger had him completely brainwashed."

"Maybe that's a good thing," Emily said as we started for the car. "Maybe when Apt finds out Berger's dead, he'll snap out of it. Come to his senses."

"We can only hope," I said, failing to shake Paulina's face from my memory.

Chapter 83

Late Sunday afternoon found me on the back deck of my not-so-palatial Breezy Point vacation house. Boogie boards and blown-up flotation devices of every description were scattered around me while from the sun-bleached railing flew about as many beach towels as there were flags at the UN.

I was back in my element, my green zone.

Home Chaotic Beach Home.

In my atrociously ugly neon green surfing shorts, I sent my bare feet upward toward the bright blue sky as I lay back in my zero-gravity beach chair. I even had a half-full can of Tecate securely holstered in the drink holder. The only downside, I guess, were the bright red crime scene photos that stared up at me from the open murder folder in my lap.

I stared back, forcing myself to examine again the remains of Paulina Dulcine. The Medical Examiner's Office had said that the poor woman's teeth had been pulled out with a pair of pliers. From Emily's notes I knew Joel David Rifkin had committed the same savagery on his first victim in the early nineties. I tossed the file onto the picnic table beside me and let out a breath. Carl Apt was nothing if not a stickler for details.

As if I weren't depressed enough, one of my Major Case Task Force buddies had just texted me the latest rumor that Chief McGinnis wanted a personal who-what-when-where-how-and-why session with me and Emily about the murder of Paulina Dulcine. Another carpet call. Sounded fun, not to mention productive. I couldn't wait.

I'd just finished my beer and was having a staring contest with a shady-looking seagull perched on my rusty rain gutter when my phone rang.

I smiled as I looked at the number. It was from me, apparently. Someone inside the house behind me was playing a joke at my expense.

"Detective Bennett, NYPD. Who is this? Who's wasting my time?" I barked in my best tough cop voice.

"Yes, uh, hello, Detective," said Eddie in a low, badly disguised voice. "I'd like to report a crime."

I'd specifically told them I had to work and to leave Daddy alone, but the natives were getting restless. And who could blame them? I hadn't been around much for the past week.

I was about to hang up, when I spotted something on the picnic table beside me, and I suddenly had a better idea.

"Well, you've called the right place, sir," I said as I quietly stood, lifting the Super Soaker water gun from the table before I trotted down the deck steps. "Name the felony, please."

"Well, it's a kidnapping," Eddie said

as I quickly came around the side of the house.

I stopped at the hose bib and loaded the gun with water before I hopped over the railing onto the front porch.

"Kidnapping? Well," I said as I peeked through the screen door at the backs of Eddie and a cracking-up Trent at the phone in the kitchen. "That's a serious crime. What's the victim's name?"

"Pants," Eddie said, not missing a beat. "John Pants."

Trent guffawed as he punched Eddie's leg. I had to stifle my own laugh as well. Eddie was a funny kid. Maeve and I always said we should have made Eddie's middle name Murphy. They definitely seemed to be in much higher spirits since that Flaherty kid had been put back on his leash.

"Mr. Pants. I see," I said as I silently opened the front screen door. "Now, what relation is he to you?"

"Well, he's my father, actually," Eddie said. "We haven't seen him in a few days. It's really not like him. Well, actually it kind of is. We seriously think he might be a workaholic."

"You're in luck, sir. I think I know the location of Mr. Pants," I whispered as I took aim from the kitchen doorway.

"Where's that?" Eddie said.

At the last second, Trent, who had been bent over, laughing, stood up straight, his head tilted slightly like a deer at a cracked twig.

"RIGHT BEHIND YOU!" I yelled as loudly as I could.

Eddie dropped the phone as Trent screamed. Before they could breathe again, I let them have it.

"Oh, I'm sorry. Am I getting you jokers wet?" I said, dousing them with the Super Soaker's twin barrels.

Trent got the worst of it, by far. He looked like I'd poured a bucket of water over his head by the time he squirmed away, screaming.

"What in the name of Jesus, Mary, and Joseph?" Mary Catherine said as she came running from upstairs.

"They started it this time, I swear," I said as I hid the water gun behind my back.

Chapter 84

After I swamped out the kitchen, I decided to put death on hold and give Mary a break, so I took the kids down to the beach.

There must have been a storm coming or one out at sea, because the water was particularly choppy. Some of the blue-gray Atlantic waves were as high as five feet. Tall enough for some pale surfers to be out there among the shore fishermen's lines.

There were at least a dozen cops and firemen and phone guys hanging ten Queens-style. New York City was the last place most people would think of as a place to surf, but you could pull it off, once you figured out how to fit the board on the A train.

I sat on the shore, watching the little guys goof in the shallows, shoveling for sand crabs with their heels the way I'd shown them. I remembered being a kid doing the same thing with all my cousins.

One time, I remembered, a couch — a bright '70s-orange couch — washed up with a breaker, like a floor model from an underwater Ethan Allen. I also remembered pausing to watch the Concorde head out of Kennedy for Europe. You didn't watch it so much as stand in awe of it, trying not to wet yourself once you caught the high, terrifying, bone-rumbling scream of its supersonic engine.

When I turned to watch the swimming "bad teens," as Chrissy and I called the older kids, I saw that Seamus was out with them. At one point, the septuagenarian actually stood on a boogie board. For about a millisecond. He somersaulted once and almost again in the air as a wave swatted his skinny butt into Davy Jones's locker. The lifeguard went batty, blowing his whistle. A moment later, Seamus broke the surface with his hands in the air like a victorious prizefighter.

I couldn't stop laughing. You can't hurt a fool.

I signaled Seamus ashore to do the babysitting in order to show him how it was done. Which was odd, since I had absolutely no idea. I goofed on the boogie board for a while until the ocean stole it.

Instead of fretting, I decided to surf the way God intended with my just awesome bod NYC freestyle. That is, until an evil wave tried to make off with my Hawaiian jams. I managed to retrieve them with a last-ditch hook of my right foot.

"Mr. Pants, indeed," I mumbled, tightly retying the string.

"Trouble?" someone said.

When I looked up, my jaw dropped almost as hard as my pants just had.

Mary Catherine had decided to join us, after all. In a bikini. A new red bikini, I noticed. I knew all of Mary's swimwear, and the article she was almost not wearing was definitely new. As a detective, I was trained to pay attention to details.

I tried to be nonchalant, as if my nanny showing up dressed like a Maxim pinup girl was about as exciting as waiting for the crosstown bus.

"Trouble?" she repeated as she brushed past me, all blond and tan and thin scallops of red.

She disappeared into a wave a moment later. Heading back for Ireland, with my luck. She very well might have been a mermaid returning to sea.

"Just breathing," I finally said.

Chapter 85

A couple of hours of saltwater frolic later, I was back at the grindstone in my outdoor office. I was still barefoot, of course, and my hair was still wet, but I was wearing jeans and a T-shirt now and had replaced my beer with a massive mug of French vanilla coffee.

Even with the caffeine kick, it took me a while to ramp up. I had to work to get some indelible images out of my head first. Every time I closed my eyes, I saw water sluicing off Mary's back, her beautiful face laughing as she lay on the towel beside me, her eyes closed, her tan cheek powdered with sand.

Magical visions every one, the hardest of all to shake.

To linger on such things was fraught with danger, I knew. A massive land mine of buried feelings had built up since my wife had died, and thinking about Mary Catherine in this manner was like taking a jog right through the middle of it. I did it, anyway. Of course I did. Every cop is at least a little bit suicidal.

Hard as it was, eventually I had to get down to brass tacks. I rubbed my eyes for a few minutes, putting back on the armor, and guzzled some coffee. Then I flipped the murder folder open and re-entered the land of the dead.

I read over everything meticulously. What I was most interested in was the connection between Berger and Apt. What had drawn them to each other? Was it a cult thing, like Emily had suggested? Could just two people qualify as a cult?

Mary Catherine came out after a while and refilled my mug. She'd gotten changed as well, unfortunately.

"You didn't have to do that," I said, smiling. "I appreciate you keeping the savages at bay. Speaking of which, why is it so quiet?"

"The older guys went to a fireworks show, and Seamus took the peewees to miniature golf. They'll bring back pizza."

"We're alone? Heck, what are we waiting for?" I said, starting to stand. "I'll get the beers, and you take a seat."

She put her hand on my chest.

"Not so fast, slacker. I got the kids out of here so you could have some peace and quiet. You need to work. You need to catch whoever it is you're chasing, and take off the rest of this dwindling vacation for real. At this point, I want to catch him just so you can have a break. It feels like I'm at work just looking at you."

"Why are you so nice to me?" I said.

Mary Catherine's smile lit up the back porch.

"You know, that's funny. I keep asking myself the same question," she said.

I reluctantly went back to my wretched reading. As I pored over the case files,

I was again struck with regret over not being able to keep Berger's death out of the press. If Apt really was brainwashed, we could have used it to somehow lure him in.

But had we lost it after all? I suddenly wondered. What if we set up some sort of memorial service? Maybe something in Central Park, across the street from his building. A chance for all his friends and family, if he had any, to pay their respects.

I heard the phone in the kitchen a few minutes later. I didn't want to know who it was. The commissioner, probably. Someone in a position of authority, without a doubt, ready to dole out more responsibility or more punishment. I wanted neither.

It turned out I was wrong. It was actually worse.

"It's that woman from the FBI," Mary Catherine called out coldly from the back door.

I sat up as if I'd just been busted doing something.

"Uh," I said. I forgot I had given her

the number of the beach house just in case my cell battery died.

"Take the call, Mike," Mary Catherine said. "She's practically drooling on the other end. 'Is Michael there? Can I speak to him, please? Is this Mary Catherine?'"

"Hello?" I said, back in the kitchen.

"I hope I'm not bothering you, Mike."

"Pity the thought," I said. "What's up, Emily?"

"You know how we're having trouble placing Apt in the databases? Well, I think I found out why. I just got a call from an agent friend on the Joint Terrorism Task Force. A cousin of his might have some information on Apt. She wants to set up a meeting for Monday."

"Why can't this cousin tell us over the phone?"

"She works in Intelligence, Mike. As if this case needs some more intrigue. Apparently, the CIA has something to do with this now."

Chapter 86

Gershwin played from a piano as Apt shook another peanut into his mouth. A $19 cocktail called a Whiskey Smash sat untouched on the black-granite bar in front of him.

The place was the Bemelman Bar in the luxury Carlyle Hotel on Madison Avenue, only a few blocks from Lawrence's apartment. Carl knew it was risky to come here, but he didn't care. The white-jacketed waiters, the art deco furniture, the dreamy lighting. Like the Tea Garden at the Plaza Hotel, and the 21 Club, it was one of his favorite places in the city.

He looked at himself in the bar mirror. Form-fitting Dior Homme black polo,

Raf Simmons skinny black jeans, chunky gold Rolex Presidente. Confident, stylish, a sense of moneyed swagger. He fit right in, didn't he? Which was quite odd when you considered where he'd come from.

He would have said he pulled himself up by his bootstraps, but he hadn't been able to afford boots. He'd had to pull himself up by the dirt on his bare feet. He'd grown up in Appalachia in a place called Manette Holler, Pennsylvania, near the West Virginia line. His family had been backwoods poor, living in a trailer butted up against a junkyard. His half-toothless, alcohol- and drug-addicted mother worked sporadically at the truck stop Burger King when she wasn't turning tricks with the semi drivers in the parking lot out back.

His Uncle Shelly was the owner of the junkyard. The sadistic son of a bitch used to beat him just for the hell of it. After a while, he'd almost gotten used to it. Once he got to school, the bigger kids would try to beat him, too, but they had nothing on his malicious uncle.

The military was the only way out of

Manette Holler for him, and he took it at seventeen. The 82nd Airborne Rangers had been like a dream come true—three squares and a place to sleep. They'd taught him to kill and how to survive in the wilderness. He was a quick study.

He'd still be serving his country in the Special Forces if they hadn't royally fucked him over. But once out, he went underground. Eastern seaboard, Key West to Maine. Wandering, living on the streets or the Appalachian Trail, riding the freights.

He would have done that for the rest of his life had he not met Lawrence. Not only had Lawrence discovered that he had dyslexia but he'd actually taught him how to beat it. At the age of thirty, Carl had been introduced to reading. Lawrence had been his benefactor and his tutor, like Aristotle was to Alexander the Great.

He thought about all the books and meals and discussions he had enjoyed. How wonderful to read quietly by his window as the wind howled through the trees of Central Park. The drives up to

Connecticut in the fall on Route 7, the Mercedes's engine purring. He could have done that for the rest of his life. Happy, alone, living the good life, the clean, dry life of the mind.

But then Lawrence was diagnosed, and they learned his enormous heart was failing. He'd thought that all the good things had come to an end. That's when Lawrence came to him with a not-so-modest proposal. If Carl eliminated all of Lawrence's enemies, his education and aesthetic discoveries would continue for the rest of his life, courtesy of Lawrence. Once the last of the people on Lawrence's list was eliminated, Carl would receive the number to an account in Geneva.

After all, he'd killed for his country for no more than his mother had been paid at the Burger King. Killing for his friend with a $20 million inheritance was a no-brainer.

Apt ate a couple more peanuts, his eyes moving left to right then right to left, the scan of a hawk perched on a utility pole. He stirred his drink and continued to people-watch at the tables. A nipped-and-tucked divorcée on the prowl. A well-groomed, swarthy little Prada-wearing fuck with three gorgeous Asian women. A black male model in a white sport coat who kept trying to catch his attention.

Then he spotted her, a busty pale blonde in her late twenties sitting at the other end of the bar. There was a sexy, slutty, Old World Hollywood glamour about her, Marilyn Monroe.

Carl knew her name wasn't Norma Jean Baker but rather Wendy Shackleton. She'd made Berger's list for showing up from an escort service for Lawrence one night and taking one look at him and turning on her heels. The whore had totally rejected his good buddy before he'd even had a chance to open his mouth. She'd hurt Lawrence's feelings very badly. Bad move.

Carl made eye contact as he carried his drink over.

"Good-bye, Norma Jean. Though I never knew you at all," he sang, taking her hand as he sat down beside her.

She laughed demurely.

"I'm sorry," he said, letting her go after a second. "How forward of me. My computer company just went public, and you're just about the most glamorous-looking woman I've ever seen. You could be Marilyn herself."

"You're very kind," she said, checking him out with approval. "Are you staying at the hotel?"

"Yes, I am," Apt said. "I actually rang the opening bell down at the stock exchange this morning. It's been one of the most exciting days of my life, and I need someone to share it with. Please, please, please, let me buy you a drink."

"Sure, sure, sure," she said, giggling. "What a gentleman."

"Are you looking for some company tonight?" she said in his ear when her $20 dirty martini arrived.

"Oh," he said, feigning surprise. "Oh, wow. You're um..."

"Working. Yes," she said, nodding, smiling. "Does that bother you?"

"Bother me? I'm bothered, all right. Hot and bothered in the best way possible. How does it work?"

"You're not a cop, are you?"

Carl laughed and took a sip of his Whiskey Smash.

"Hardly," he said.

"I didn't think so. How does it work? Let's see. You give me a thousand dollars, and I give you a lovely night you won't forget."

"Heck, let's get to it, then," Carl said, taking her hand again.

She banged his bad knee as she was pulling out her bar stool.

"I'm so sorry," she said.

"No problem," he said, his eyes tearing with the pain. She was going to pay for that, Carl thought.

His limp became more pronounced as they left the bar and headed for the opulent lobby's elevator.

"Are you sure you're okay?"

"Old war injury," Carl said. "Don't worry. Everything else works fine."

"Glad to hear it. What should I call you?"

"My employees call me Mr. Rifkin," Apt said. "But you can call me Joel."

Chapter 87

Monday morning, I sat at my desk at One Police Plaza still as a Zen master, breathing slowly, eyes closed, mentally prepping myself for my upcoming reaming at the task force meeting.

After reading the morning papers, I needed the meditation. Berger's lawyer, some fool named Allen Duques, was crying false arrest and police negligence and was insisting on a thorough investigation into his client's death. Only the *Post* piece happened to remind everyone that his client was a child- and cop-killing wacko.

I was thinking about getting into the lotus position to counteract all the bad karma when there was a knock on my cubicle wall. I reluctantly opened my eyes. Then I smiled. It was Emily Parker.

"Mike, are you...okay?" she said.

"Fine," I said.

"Good, because my friend's cousin is downstairs waiting for us."

"Oh, right. The spook," I said, standing.

"Shh," Emily said. "The walls have ears."

Outside on the street half a block east, a massive silver Lincoln Navigator sat idling. A bony, attractive brown-haired woman sat behind the wheel. Even more unexpected was the six-month-old in the car seat behind her.

"Mike, Karen. Karen, Mike," Emily said as we climbed in.

Emily grabbed shotgun while I was relegated to the backseat next to the baby on board. I flicked some cheerios off the leather before I sat.

"Please tell Mike what you were telling me, Karen. You worked with Carl Apt in Intelligence, right?"

"I did," the thin woman said, checking her mirror.

"How about the baby?" I said, smiling at the cute little girl.

"She's a civilian," Karen assured me with a smile. "I worked for the Company until a year ago. Now I'm a Larchmont soccer-mom-in-training. Who knows what tomorrow will bring? Love makes you do some damn strange things."

"I know what that's like," I said.

Emily shot me a look from the front seat.

"I thought it was Carl when I saw the security shot in the *Post*," Karen began, "but I didn't come forward because of national secrecy, yada, yada, yada. But after the recent death of that woman, I couldn't stay silent anymore. What I'm about to tell you is classified information. You didn't hear this from me. Agreed? In 2002 I worked in Yemen with the CIA SAD."

"Is that the stay-at-home-dad department?" I said.

"Special Activities Division," she said as we hooked a quick left down an alley-wide Chinatown street. "We were responsible for covert military raids on Al Qaeda targets. Carl was on one of our strike teams. He was the bomb tech. All the other Delta guys deferred to him for all things explosive. He actually won the Intelligence Star commendation in our operation when he used a predator drone to knock out a pickup truck loaded with bad guys who were coming in on our position."

"You're kidding me," I said.

"I made some phone calls," Karen said. "Carl, while great at war, wasn't too hot on the domestic front. He was working at Fort Bragg as a Delta Force trainer up until 2003, when he got into a beef with his new supervisor. He was about to be transferred out of the group, when the CO found some C-four wired to his car battery. When they came to ask Apt about it, he was gone. He'd bugged out."

"He went AWOL," Emily said.

"Not just that," Karen said. "A month to the day after he left, the supervisor didn't show up for work. They found him sitting at his kitchen table in his bathrobe with the top of his head blown into his bowl of Blueberry Morning. Coroner retrieved two .forty-five ACPs from his brain pan. He'd been double tapped, execution-style. No forced entry. Apt must have picked the lock. Delta Force SOP. Apt came back and finished the job."

That explained a lot, I thought. Apt's dedication, his bomb-making flair. It also explained the connection he had with Berger. Both warped bastards had been "wronged by the world."

"That's what I call Army strong," I said as the baby grabbed my thumb. "Do you know anything about Berger?"

"The rich fat guy?" Karen said. "Not a thing. I just thought I'd let you know who you're up against. Apt knows tactics, counterinsurgency. He's one dangerous son of a bitch. I said more than once that I was glad he was on our side. Only now he's not."

"Any family?" Emily said.

"Only family on his army record is a mother. Deceased."

I looked out at the street then turned and looked at the baby.

"You wouldn't know where Carl is right now, would you?" I asked the little girl.

Chapter 88

As Spy Mom dropped me and Emily off in front of One Police Plaza, I felt a tingle run up my side. Instead of my Spidey sense cluing me in to Apt's current location like I was hoping, it was just my cell phone that I'd left on vibrate.

"The good news is that you don't have to attend this morning's piss-and-moan session," my boss said. "One guess what's behind door number two."

I took the phone off my ear and just stared at it as I leaned back on one of the massive concrete bomb-blast planters out in front of the building.

"Another one?" Emily groaned.

"How? Where?" I finally said into the phone.

"The Carlyle Hotel," Mirlam said. "Madison and Seventy-something. Looks like a hooker, Mike. You need to get up there before the news vans. This guy just won't quit."

Emily and I got my car and went crosstown to Sixth Avenue and made a right. It was another sidewalk-scorcher of a day. The overtaxed A/C started spitting water by the time we made it to Midtown. As we approached 42nd, the traffic actually halted, and we did the stop-and-go thing in the white-hot glare. I thought there was an accident or maybe the president was in town, but it turned out to be just a traffic agent blocking off two right-hand lanes for no discernible reason.

"Are you freaking kidding me? Get the hell out of the way!" Emily screamed, practically climbing out of the passenger window to get a piece of the stringy white traffic lady as we roared past.

"And an abusive morning to you, too, Agent Parker," I teased as I gunned it, hoping the city worker didn't catch our plates. "You want to stop for an iced coffee? Or I could pull over and throw open a fire hydrant for you to cool down if you want."

"I don't know how you do it, Mike," Emily said, taking her pulse. "This city. This heat. No wonder everyone here is nuts."

"Present company most definitely included," I said, pointing at her.

We rolled east over to Madison and picked up the pace. Fancy boutiques with even fancier foreign names started sailing past. Emanuel Ungaro, Sonia Rykiel, Bang & Olufsen, Christian Louboutin. Were they luggage shops? Jewelry stores? Law firms? If you had to ask, you couldn't afford it, and I most definitely had to ask.

The Carlyle was between East 75th and 76th on the west side of Madison Avenue. It was also right around the corner from Berger's Fifth Avenue co-op building. Was Apt getting sloppier now? I wondered. Was he homesick? Or was he taunting us? If he was, it was working. I most definitely felt taunted.

We had to circle around the block in

order to double park on 76th near Fifth behind a patrol car. As we approached the Carlyle, I saw that a section of the hotel was actually under renovation. There was a sidewalk shed and an exterior construction elevator connected to the pale limestone of its north face. Outside the construction entrance, about twenty hardhats, half of them shirtless, were enjoying coffee and cigarettes and the passing women. They immediately shifted their attention to my partner as we passed.

The Carlyle had one of those lobbies that immediately makes you check the shine on your shoes and look to see if there are any spots on your tie. A piano played from somewhere as chandeliers the size of minivans glittered between palace walls of pristine white marble. The black stone floor was so highly buffed, I looked for a "Slippery When Wet" sign.

An almost-as-buffed short black man in a tailored blue suit immediately button-holed us by the check-in desk. The man looked incapable of perspiring, like he'd long ago had the offensive glands removed.

"I'm Adrian Tottinger," the manager said. "The um...unfortunate person is actually downstairs, where they're working."

It was hot again once we entered the hotel's drab concrete back stairwell. At the bottom of it, a uniform snapped his cell phone shut and led us along a stifling corridor past the hotel's kitchen and a rumbling laundry room.

Beyond some hanging plastic and another door, the section of the hotel under construction smelled faintly of an open sewer. The sound of nail guns and shouts rang from above as we walked over gravel to a corner where three more uniforms were standing.

The "unfortunate person" was lying in a large tublike pan used for mixing concrete. The woman had actually been cemented into the tub with just her head and arms and lower legs exposed. As if perhaps she'd mistaken the pan of ready-mix for a Jacuzzi and had fallen asleep.

She was pale and had white-blond

hair and a Marilyn Monroe or Madonna look. Even with most of her face beaten black and blue and her neck swollen and purple, she'd obviously been quite attractive. Now she was naked and dead and tossed like so much trash among the construction site's drywall screws and spackle-flecked-compound buckets.

"Let me guess. This fits with the Joel Rifkin profile somehow," I said.

Emily was already on one knee, reaching into her bag, flipping through her stacks of photocopied research.

She tore out a sheet.

"Rifkin's second victim was beaten and strangled."

"Check," I said.

"The dismembered body parts hidden in buckets of concrete."

"This isn't technically a bucket, but a pretty reasonable facsimile."

"Reasonable?" Emily said as the sound of hammers rained down from above.

Chapter 89

The hotel's security cameras turned out to be a gold mine.

Standing in a cramped, broiling basement security room, Emily and I watched a computer screen, where Apt, in living color, casually walked with the dead girl through the Carlyle's lobby.

"You grinning son of a bitch!" I said, clinking the screen with my finger.

Apt was wearing an expensive-looking polo shirt and jeans, dressed elegant casual, summer suave. He had on a chunky gold wristwatch. We'd already spoken to the clerk, who said Apt had paid for his $2,000-a-night suite in cash. Watching him head for the check-in desk, I thought Apt's overall demeanor seemed calm, self-confident, not out of place in the slightest in the insanely expensive hotel. The fucker.

The best video footage of all came from the camera in the corridor outside his room. At three a.m., a difficult-to-make-out man carrying something large wrapped in a sheet walked toward the rear service elevator.

"So he did her in the room, then," Emily said, nodding.

I nodded back.

"It still boggles my mind that he would take the time to prepare a batch of concrete in the basement and lay her in it. Imagine, you're down in that pit in the middle of the night. He even took the time to trowel it smooth and seamless with a craftsman's pride. I can see why this guy was a commando. He must have antifreeze for blood."

After we obtained copies of the tapes, we went up to the eleventh-floor room Apt had rented out. There was lavish furniture everywhere, an antique rolltop desk, a cream-colored sectional, gilt-frame mirrors. The window of the sitting room had an incredible view to the south, the Met Life Building on Park and the Chrysler Building.

We found the hooker's bag behind the chic sectional. Among a plethora of interesting trade equipment was a wallet with a New Jersey State driver's license. Wendy Shackleton.

"Do you think Jersey Girl Wendy here crossed Berger somehow, too?" I said. "Or is Apt maybe starting his own Dead People Club now? Branching out?"

"My money's on Berger," Emily said.

The CSU team was already in the bedroom. They'd found a bloody chair leg and blood spatter on the sheets and headboard of the bed. One of the techs told us they'd also found textbook-quality fingerprints on the chair leg.

"He's getting sloppy?" I said.

"No," Emily said, staring at the blood on the graphic canvas over the California King sleigh bed. "I'd say it's more that he just doesn't care if he leaves evidence. His main concern and number-one priority was staging the body, turning it into a copy of Rifkin's second victim. The girl was just his project material, modeling clay, oak tag."

We stared out the window as the techs clicked their cases shut, getting ready to leave. As we watched, the sun came out from behind a passing cloud and turned the Chrysler Building's iconic spire to molten silver.

"Not bad digs for a boy from coal mine country," Emily said.

"Berger transformed the lad," I said. "It's your classic rags-to-riches-to-mass-murderer story."

"What now?" Emily said as we kept standing there.

"How about we both resign, and I call room service for a bottle of champagne?"

"Don't tempt me," Emily said as she headed for the door.

Chapter 90

After a hot, frustrating ride back downtown, we headed directly up to my boss's office on the eleventh floor of HQ to show her the hotel's security tapes.

"The stones on this guy," I said as we watched. "This place makes the Plaza look like a Days Inn, Miriam. And look at him. He's walking around like he owns it. He even paid for his room with a sheaf of hundred-dollar bills."

"What's the progress on getting Berger's assets frozen?" Emily said.

"The wheels of justice move slowly. Actually, in the summer in this city, they come to a grinding halt," Miriam said, frowning. "Last I heard we'll have the warrants by the end of the day, but that's what they said yesterday. Berger's lawyer, Duques, is the executor of the estate. Why don't you swing by and appeal to his civic responsibility. It's a long shot, but maybe it'll get him to shut his damn mouth to the press for five minutes."

We took another leisurely roll in the baking midday gridlock back up to midtown. Allen Duques's office was in a glass pagoda-shaped building on Lexington Avenue across from Grand Central Terminal. I parked my unmarked in the middle of a bus stop across the insanely congested street and threw down the NYPD placard on the visor so it would still be there when we returned.

Duques's firm was on thirty-three. The outfit had the entire floor. Right out of the elevator, the name of his firm, Hunt, Block & Bally, stood in yard-high stainless-steel letters on the Brazilian Cherry wall.

"Mr. Duques?" said the brunette waif of a receptionist behind the glass door after we asked to see him. Her fine-boned model's face looked amazed, as if we'd just asked her to tell us the meaning of life.

"I'm sorry, but Mr. Duques is booked all day," she informed us.

"Yeah, well, this is important," I said showing her my shield.

"Really, really important," Emily said, flipping her Feds creds for good measure.

Even with all our magic badge power, we had to wait another ten minutes before another attractive flunky, who looked like she ate maybe every other day, showed up.

I trailed a finger along one of the exotic-wood-paneled hallways she led us down.

"So this is what the corridors of power look like," I said, nodding thoughtfully.

Around a corner, Duques stood in his office doorway, smiling pleasantly. The preppy bespectacled gent shook our hands before getting us seated in his plush office. He reminded me of the fancy hotel manager, polished and perfect, not a damn wrinkle in his white shirt even when he sat down. I, on the other hand, was sweating like a pig in a hot tub, despite the A/C. How did these rich guys do it?

"Now, what can I do for the NYPD and the FBI?" he said after we declined his coffee offer. The trim, middle-aged lawyer seemed affable and down-to-earth, which most likely wasn't easy for him, considering his socks had probably cost more than my shoes.

"We were wondering if you could help us," I said.

"I can try," he said, eyeing us carefully. "What's the problem?"

"We have reason to believe that Carl Apt still has access to Lawrence Berger's money," Emily said. "To be frank, we're working on a warrant to have Berger's assets frozen, but it won't happen until tomorrow at the earliest. We know you're the executor of Mr. Berger's estate, and we're here to ask you to freeze action on all accounts before anyone else is killed."

"Hmm. That's a tall order," the lawyer said, leaning slowly back in his chair. "You're assuming a lot. I'm not even sure I should admit that my client had a relationship with Mr. Apt."

"Crazy assumption, I know," I said, "considering your client admitted to it and to his guilt in his signed confession before he killed himself."

Duques took off his glasses and chewed on an endpiece.

"A signed confession that I'm going to fight to have expunged," he said.

"We're not here to bicker, Mr. Duques," Emily said.

She placed a sheet of paper on the lawyer's desk. It was a printout of Apt and the hooker at the Carlyle from the security tape.

"This morning, we found this woman dead at the Carlyle Hotel," Emily said, tapping the paper. "Apt paid two thousand dollars in cash for the room that he killed her in. We know Apt isn't independently wealthy. Berger took him in off the street."

"Allegedly," Duques said, raising an eyebrow.

"Right," I said, going into our folder and showing him a crime scene close-up of Wendy Shackleton's beat-in face. "And see, this is where Apt allegedly bashed in this young lady's alleged face with an alleged chair leg."

That's when I stood.

"I told you we're wasting our time," I said to Emily. "I told you we should have gotten the warrant first."

Duques stood himself as we were leaving.

"Wait, I'm sorry," he said, rubbing his eyes. "Of course, I'll help. We actually have a team working on the audit right now. I'll tell them to put blocks on all transactions. Also, if I find any discrepancies, I will let you know first thing. Though in all honesty, it might take a little while. Mr. Berger's estate is in excess of eight hundred million dollars."

"What's your cut?" I said, still in pissed-off bad-cop mode.

"Thank you, Mr. Duques," Emily said, getting me out of there. "I knew you'd do the right thing."

Chapter 91

Despite the charming Mr. Duques's assertions to do everything humanly possible, for the rest of the day, we put full-court pressure on the city DA's Office to speed things up on a warrant. Emily even placed a call to the FBI's New York Office White Collar Squad for any guidance they could give in cutting off Apt's money supply.

By 7:30, we hadn't heard back from anyone, but at least it seemed we were barking up the right money tree now. Also, no one else had been ritualistically killed—at least that we knew of. I love progress.

I was going to give Emily a ride back to her hotel, but she begged off, saying she needed to get some shopping done for her daughter.

"Get some sleep, partner," she said as we departed in the parking lot. "You're going to need it."

I turned down the police radio as I began my drive home and slid in a Gov't Mule CD that I kept in the glove box. A machine-gun roll of skull-whomping drums started up, followed by a soul-piercing electric guitar. The hard-wailing Southern rock turned out to be just what I needed to reduce my about-to-pop blood pressure. I turned it up as high as it would go as I punched my Impala toward the FDR.

My stress felt purged as I pulled into my beach bungalow's driveway an hour later.

"Finally. There you are. I was getting worried," Mary Catherine said as I crossed the porch and opened the front door.

"What's up?" I said.

"Did your phone battery die or some-thing? The phone's been ringing off the hook. Your FBI agent friend said something urgent just came up and to call her right away."

I quickly checked my phone. Emily had left three messages. I must have missed it over my head-banging.

I called her back.

"Emily?"

"You need to come back to the city right away, Mike. Karen from the CIA just called me again with new info that she said might lead us straight to Apt. She's coming to my hotel room. You need to get here as soon as you can."

"On my way," I said before hanging up.

"I take it you're not staying for dinner," Mary said.

I nodded and then glanced beyond the kitchen doorway at all the kids seated at the dining room table. Beside a cauldron-size metal pot, Juliana was passing out plates of pasta. That's when I inhaled the scent of garlic and olive oil.

Sweet glory of angels!

Mary had made a massive batch

of her world-famous meatballs and sauce.

I glanced at my phone.

Too bad I was going to have mine for tomorrow's breakfast.

Chapter 92

Starving and biting mad, I listened to some more Gov't Mule as I hammered back toward Manhattan's big-city bright lights. It was nine thirty on the button when I rapped on Emily's hotel room door.

She surprised me when she answered it. She was in a bathrobe.

"Hey, Mike," Agent Parker said, hurrying toward the suite's bedroom after she let me in. "Karen isn't here yet. Why don't you have a seat and a drink while I get changed?"

"Twist my arm," I said, spotting a six of Brooklyn Lager on a table by the terrace door.

I rolled open the sliders to her room's

small terrace and drank by the rail. The first beer was good. The second even better. Down on the street in front of the hotel, taxis were lined up back to Central Park West. One after the other, they pulled into the hotel's driveway, and well-dressed, smiling folks got into them on their way to a night on the town. With my drink, the sultry night air, and the romantic city lights, I felt like I was having one, too. Almost, at least.

I decided to raise my drink to them and the city at large. I was proud of them. They weren't going to let Apt ruin their night. That's what the Carl Apts of the world didn't understand, I thought as I took an icy sip. New York was just like the human race. Sure you could scare it, slow it down, maybe even halt it for a little while. But it kept right the hell on going. No matter what. That was the best thing about New York City.

"Mike, where are you?" Emily called behind me.

"Out here," I said, turning.

I froze in midspin by the terrace sliders. Inside the doorway, Emily wasn't wearing her usual Fed business getup.

She was wearing a midnight blue dress. A short dress that hugged her hips and showed a lot of cleavage. As I failed to close my gaping mouth, she fingered the string of pearls around her neck.

I was still stumped for a verbal reaction when there was a knock on the door.

"Is that Karen?" I finally said.

"I don't know. Go see," Emily said.

It wasn't Karen. It was two white-jacketed room service guys with two white-linen-covered rolling tables. On one table were two silver trays, on the other two silver buckets. They wheeled them both out onto the terrace and brought out two chairs. The older of the waiters smiled at me as he popped the champagne bottle's cork.

"Shall I open the other, sir?" he said to me as he filled two flutes.

"That won't be necessary," Emily said, tipping the man as she shooed him off the terrace and out of the room.

Chapter 93

"Um?" I said when she came back.

"I forgot to tell you. Karen's not coming," Emily said as she put a glass of champagne in my hand.

She sat down in a chair above the sparkling city lights and took a sip of her bubbly.

"In fact, she never was coming," she said. "I made it up."

"Why?" I said.

"Several reasons," Emily said, staring at me as she crossed her long legs.

She was wearing high heels, I noticed. Very high, very black, peep-toed ones.

"I'll tell you all of them as we eat,

Mike," she said as she lifted the lid of her tray.

"You should see your face," Emily said as I sat.

"I'd rather see yours," I said, shaking my head.

I devoured the dinner. I couldn't decide which was better, the perfectly cooked baby lamb chops smothered in lemon, parsley, and rosemary, or the white truffle–garlic mashed potatoes. The champagne we washed everything down with was cold crisp Veuve Clicquot. After the third glass out in the night air, I could feel bubbles dancing in my bloodstream.

Emily popped the other bottle and filled our glasses again.

"I'm still waiting for those reasons, Agent Parker," I said, smiling at her. "Why am I here? What the heck are you doing? What the heck are we doing?"

She set down the wet bottle carefully on the linen.

"Okay. First," she said. "Happy birthday."

"But it's not my birthday," I said.

"I know," she said, taking a little bow. "It's mine. My thirty-fifth, to be exact."

"No!" I said, reaching over and giving her a hug. "Happy birthday! Why didn't you tell me?"

A huge, beaming smile crossed her face as she gazed out at the city. In the dim glow of the building lights, her face took on an amber cast, as if she were made of gold.

"Ever since I got divorced, Mike," she said, still looking away, "I've dated some pretty great guys. But every time I feel myself getting close, I start thinking about this guy I know. This New York cop who, no matter how wise he is with his mouth, just can't quite disguise the sadness in his pale blue eyes, the light in them that's so bright yet somehow so sad."

In the warm breeze, the candle flame flickered between us and she looked at me full on. Her beauty was always striking, but never more than at that moment. Seeing her face and smile were like looking at a gift I'd given up on getting.

"For my present, I wanted you all

alone, Mike, for a couple of hours," she said, standing and lifting the bottle off the table. "No kids. No cases."

Her free hand found mine, and she tugged me up out of the chair and guided me into the room. She set the bottle down, closed the door, and pulled the curtain, and then she was in my arms.

"Just you," she said, kissing me.

We kissed for a while, standing. I could feel the goose bumps on her arms as I touched her. She shivered when I laid my palm on her bare back.

"I want you, Mike," she whispered a few wonderful minutes later. She took my hand again, this time tugging me toward her bedroom.

"I always have," she said.

We kissed on her bed for a while, and then she broke off suddenly and headed for the bathroom.

"Get the champagne from the other room," she said. "I'll be right back."

I went out and took the champagne off the coffee table. I was turning back to the bedroom when I stopped. Suddenly I couldn't do it. I didn't even know why. Pascal said that the heart has reasons that reason itself knows nothing about.

I placed the bottle back down on the coffee table. Instead of opening the bedroom door, I crossed the room to the hotel room door and left.

I looked back up at Emily's terrace one time as I walked out onto the street. Then I just shook my head and headed uptown, searching for my car.

Chapter 94

Savoring the last bite of his Magnolia Bakery cupcake, Carl Apt crumpled the wrapper and, without breaking stride, hook-shot it at the corner garbage can he was passing. It bounced off the light post a foot in front of the can before landing in the exact center.

Bank shot! Yes! Swa-heeet! he thought as he pumped his fist.

Wiping frosting off his nose, he continued to walk south down Christopher Street in Greenwich Village. He now wore a pair of black suit pants, a crisp white shirt, red silk Hermès suspenders, and an undone red silk Hermès tie. The point of buying the outfit at Barney's after killing Wendy was for him to blend in on the street, and it was working like a charm.

Except for his gun in the laptop bag strapped to his side, he could have been just another Wall Street hump trudging home from a busy day of destroying the world's economy.

Despite the APBs and whatever video the NYPD had of him, he knew he was okay. He knew how hard it was to catch someone with means on the move if he didn't want to get caught. With his ATM card and Lawrence's dough, he could walk around forever if he wanted. If he didn't do something stupid to get himself arrested, he would never get caught.

And the last thing he was was stupid.

He was on his way to one of his safe houses, the one in Turtle Bay, where he was going to gear up for tonight's grand finale. He could hardly believe he was almost done. There was only one more name to go. One more target. One more hit. It was a doozie, too. He was actually looking forward to it because it was the biggest, ballsiest challenge of all.

Spotting an HSBC Bank on the opposite corner, he remembered he was running low on cash. How much would he need? he thought as he crossed the street. Two hundred? Screw it, three. After all, it was only money.

"Hey, bruva. How about a dollah, bruva?" said someone at his elbow as he was carding himself into the alcove of the bank.

He looked up and shook his head, smiling.

He'd seen white street guys with rasta dreads before, but never a pudgy Asian. The short Chinese-looking guy even had a six-string guitar with a Jamaican flag on the strap.

New York was a trip. You never knew what was going to happen next. He was going to miss it.

"Maybe, bruva. We'll see," Apt said.

WELCOME TO HSBC, the screen of the ATM inside said. PLEASE INSERT YOUR CARD.

"The pleasure's all mine," he mumbled as he followed the instructions.

His account kicked out a thousand a day for expenses. Since he didn't have to use the whole grand every day, there was more than nine grand in it.

Tonight when he was done, it would have a lot more.

Eight million more, to be exact.

It was his big payday. His retirement money. The real reason he was going to such incredible lengths to take out everyone who had ever crossed his dearly departed and extremely wealthy friend, Lawrence.

He wiped the smile off his face. He had to stop thinking about it. After all, he wasn't done yet. Couldn't start counting those chickens. Couldn't get cocky now.

He typed in his card's PIN: 32604. It was the date he'd killed his Delta Force boss. The day he'd shown bad-ass Colonel Henry Greer who really had the bigger set of balls. Greer had tried to get him transferred, but he'd ended up getting himself transferred, hadn't he? Into the great beyond.

Apt was busy reliving his own Ode to Joy of putting two ACPs in the back of the big, ball-busting bastard's head, when a little screen popped up that he'd never seen before:

CODE 171. INVALID ACCOUNT.

He cocked his head at the screen like a poked rooster.

Huh? he thought. That was funny. Not funny fucking ha-ha, either. Not even a little.

He hit the cancel button, trying to get back the card to try again. But nothing happened. He tried it again, hitting the cancel button harder this time. Same result. Nothing. Shit. Why wouldn't it return his card?

He punched in his PIN again. Nothing.

He pounded the screen, clanging panic bells going off in his head. What the hell was this? What the bloody fuck was going on?

After a moment, the screen changed, and the PLEASE INSERT YOUR CARD crap came back up.

No! he thought, cupping his head with his hands. How could this happen? Without the card and the money, he was wide open, on his own, completely and utterly screwed. Something was wrong. Very goddamn wrong.

"How about that dollah, bruva?" said the Asian street musician, stepping in front of him as Apt exited the bank.

There was a *snick* sound as Apt whirled instantly. He embraced the man from behind, knife already in his hand, blade in, the way they'd taught him.

The derelict's guitar gonged against the sidewalk as the kid dropped to the sidewalk, holding his slit throat. Apt, already at the corner, calmly went down into the subway pit, Metro-carded through a turnstile, and hustled down the crowded platform.

A train came a second later, and he got on it without caring where it was going, his mind a blank screen of burning, pulsing, white-hot rage.

Chapter 95

Lawrence Berger's lawyer, Allen Duques, lived in New Canaan, Connecticut. His house was a nine-thousand-square-foot Tudor mansion on a fifteen-acre estate set back off an unpaved road filled with similar ridiculously ostentatious castles.

Apt knew this because he had been there twice, running errands for Lawrence. Apt knew Duques was the executor of Lawrence's estate, which was why he was paying him a visit.

Apt used an electrical meter to check the rear chain-link fence for voltage, then bolt-cut a hole in it, all the time listening for dogs.

Through the window of the massive

five-car garage was, of all things, a blue Mercedes convertible. It was an S65, even nicer than Lawrence's, with something like 600 horsepower.

Apt smiled at his luck as he checked the load in the suppressed Colt M1911 pistol. Instead of the rental car, which he'd left on the service road, he'd drive the German luxury rocket out of here when he was done.

He walked quickly around the perimeter of the imposing house until he spotted where the underground power and phone lines went in behind some azaleas. Sparks shot from the bolt cutter's blade as he snipped them both at the same time.

He started to pick the rinky-dink lock on the rear kitchen door, then decided instead to tap in its window with the handle of the bolt cutter. He was inside, approaching the dining room, when he saw it. A paper printout banner stretched chest high across the threshold:

MR. APT, I KNOW HOW UPSET YOU ARE. I AM NOT HOME. THERE IS A

CELL PHONE ON THE DINING ROOM TABLE. PLEASE HIT THE REDIAL SO WE MAY SPEAK. ALLEN.

A trick? Apt thought, listening very carefully. Duques was smart, almost as smart as Lawrence.

After a minute, Apt broke through the banner and picked up the Motorola in the center of the huge antique Spanish farmhouse table.

"Carl, I'm so glad you called," Duques said with audible relief.

"Where's my money, Allen?" Apt said.

"I froze the account. I didn't know any other way to contact you. There have been some developments."

"You have my complete, undivided attention, Allen."

"I'm sorry to tell you this, but Mr. Berger is dead."

Carl closed his eyes as he took a long deep breath. Knowing this was coming didn't make it hurt any less.

He opened his eyes and stared at the painting over the sideboard. It looked French Impressionist, but he could tell right away that it was actually a cheap

French Impressionist knockoff bought in Vietnam.

Carl swallowed, his eyes watering.

Lawrence had taught him that.

Lawrence had given him everything.

Chapter 96

"Was it his heart?" Apt finally said.

"No. It looks like he committed suicide. He had some sort of pill hidden in his mouth when he was arrested. At least that's what the police are saying."

Carl thought about that. Lawrence dying alone. His friend. It broke his heart. If only he could have been there.

"Carl, are you still there?"

"Yes," Apt said, hiding the sadness howling through him. "What now?" he said.

"First off, in case this is being recorded, I would like to state that I, Allen Duques, am in no way complicit with any illegal activities, but am merely in the process of dispensing the will of the Lawrence M. Berger estate, of which I am sole executor."

"Whatever," Apt said. "Where's the money?"

"Yes, of course. In front of you, down the hallway, is my den. Do you see it?"

Apt crossed the room and pushed through some French doors.

"I'm there."

"Excellent. On the leather couch are two valises."

Apt clicked on the desk light.

"The black suitcases?" Apt said, spotting them.

"Yes."

Apt opened them without checking for wires. The thought of Duques blowing up his anal-retentive-designed interior of his mansion was laughable. Inside the bags were hundred-dollar bills. Lots and lots and lots of them. Stacks upon stacks.

"I apologize for the cumbersome number of bills. I would have liked to wire it to the account of your choice, but I had a visit today from the authori-

ties that makes that extremely impracti-
cal. Lawrence actually anticipated as
much and had me make these arrangements as a precaution. I believe there's
a note for you in the bag on the left."

Apt opened it and slid out an expensive stationery card. Carl smiled at Lawrence's beautiful handwriting in his signature green ink.

Carl, my most excellent friend,
    *Thank you. Only you could make
my last days my best.*
    Never stop learning,
Lawrence

"Mr. Berger wanted you to be happy,
Carl," Duques said in his ear. "He always spoke of you so fondly."

Apt lowered the phone to wipe a tear
away with his thumb before tucking the
note back in the money bag. He was
beyond touched. The big guy had done
the right thing after all. His good buddy
had more than taken care of him. How
could he have doubted it for even a
second?

"Carl, before I forget. Mr. Berger left

a message for you. He said, and I quote, you needn't bother with the last name on the list. End quote. Whatever that means. He said you'd understand."

Apt thought about that. That didn't sound right. If anything, Lawrence had been *most* excited by the last name on his list. Did the Big L have a change of heart?

"You sure about that?" Apt said.

"He was quite emphatic about it. Consider your services rendered in full. Enjoy your reward. You've earned it. As this will be our final communication, it's been a pleasure knowing you."

"You, too, Allen. I have just one question."

"What's that?"

"Where do you keep the keys to the S Sixty-five?"

"My new car?" the lawyer sputtered. "Why? That has nothing to do with these arrangements."

"I thought we'd make a new arrangement."

"I don't understand."

"How's this?" Apt said. "I get the S Sixty-five and you don't come home to a smoking crater where this palace used to be."

There was a short silence.

"They're hanging on the back door to the butler's pantry," Duques said and hung up.

"Pleasure doing business with you," Apt said to the darkness as he back-tracked toward the kitchen.

Chapter 97

There was a large crowd waiting out in front of the Sugar Bowl when I rolled past around eleven. A live band was playing tonight. It was the last concert of the summer, I remembered from a flyer. An up-and-coming band out of Ireland called the Gilroy Stompers was being touted as the next U2.

I thought Mary Catherine might like to go for a goof.

I parked and went inside the Bennett compound. The tiny house was still and quiet. I found Seamus asleep in front of the TV. Instead of waking him, I tossed one of the girls' pink Snuggies over him, then took out my phone and snapped a picture of him. I couldn't resist.

I peeked inside the door of the girls' room and smiled. There was more bed in the room than floor space. I stood for a moment, watching them sleep. The sight of them lying so peacefully warmed me in the way only being a parent can. While my day might have sucked, they'd managed to tack on another hopefully happy memory or two, grown another day older.

Who knows? Maybe they'd even grown a little stronger, a little more capable of dealing with this chaotic world they would one day inherit. I hoped so. I had a feeling they were going to need all the help they could get, the way things were going.

Kids could be challenging, oftentimes a downright pain in the ass, but in rare moments they made you see that maybe you were trying after all. Maybe you really were doing the best you could.

Stoked from my warm-and-fuzzy moment, I went into the kitchen, searching for a beer. I was popping open a can of Miller High Life when Mary Catherine came in from the back porch, a book and a blanket in her hands.

A smile started and spread wider and wider over my face as I stood staring at her. Beer foam spilled over onto my hand, and I kept smiling. I don't think I can properly describe how happy seeing her made me.

She was tan and glowing and looked fabulous.

"You look...fabulous," I said.

"Yes, I do, Mike," she said. "Is that so surprising?"

"No. Fortuitous, is how I'd put it."

"For who?"

I was speechless for the second time that night. I was really losing my touch.

"Hey, you want to hear some rock music at the Sugar Bowl?"

Mary smiled.

I smiled back.

"You wake up Seamus," she said, rolling her Irish eyes. "I'll get my flip-flops."

Chapter 98

The safe house Apt had rented on 29th Street between Lexington and Third was a small brick town house that actually had a one-car garage. After he coded open the box on the sidewalk, he drove the S65 in and closed the gate behind him. He left the convertible running as he grabbed the money-filled suitcases piled on the front seat. This wouldn't take long.

In the back of the loft-style space's bedroom closet, he took out a North Face knapsack. Inside were several driver's licenses and passports with his picture on them.

He'd paid a hundred thousand dollars for them to a Canadian counterfeiter who'd just gotten out of jail. They were excellent forgeries, virtually indistinguishable from the real thing. He'd picked up a few things from the Intel people he used to run with in his other life. Names of folks who could get you things. Guns. Documents. Whatever. It was all about the networking.

As he shouldered the bag of documents, he glanced at the bulging garment bag above it. In it were the clothing and equipment and research he'd done to prepare for his final hit. He stared at it for a second, regretfully. All that recon for nothing. A shame, he thought, heading outside. Oh, well. Next life.

Back inside the garage, he sat for a moment in the front seat of the S65, thinking. He'd been planning on heading down to New Orleans, where a pretty girl he'd gone to City College with was living, but now he wasn't so sure. He'd stirred up one hell of a hornet's nest here with all these killings. What if the news had gotten to her?

He finally decided to ditch that idea

and head down the coast to Key West for some extended R & R. Dip his toe into the Gulf of Mexico until he figured out his next move. With the bulging suitcases beside him now, he could certainly take his time.

He hit the garage door and cranked the Benz. He sat in the car, listening to the purring thunder of its engine, as he stared out at the open road. It was a warm and lovely night. A haze hovered along the edges of the street lamps down the slope of 29th Street. It was one of those magical moments in New York when it feels like it's all yours: the buildings, the streets, all of it built for you, waiting on you, pivoting on you.

He kept sitting there. What the heck was he doing? What was he waiting for? He was done now. Time to hit the road and see exactly how free $8 million could make him. How good he could make himself feel.

But he didn't go. Instead, he shut off the car and hit the garage door down and went back inside. When he came out again he was holding the garment bag. He laid it down on the front seat on top of the money and stared at it.

He was probably being foolish, but he just couldn't leave things like this. Fuck what the lawyer, Duques, had said about Lawrence's having changed his mind. He knew what Lawrence would have wanted him to do. He understood the big man better than anyone. Maybe better than the guy understood himself.

Lawrence had done so much for him. It wasn't about the money. He realized it never had been. This was about friendship. About faith, respect. Lawrence had been the father he never had. You couldn't put a price tag on that.

Besides, he thought as he opened the garage door again and revved the engine.

He always completed the mission.

He unzipped the bag and took out the MapQuest sheet for the final target and turned on the Mercedes's nav system.

Point of start? the screen asked.

Manhattan, he typed.

Point of destination?

Apt's fingers hovered above the keyboard for a moment and then he typed it:

Breezy Point, Queens.

Chapter 99

It was a little after midnight when Carl Apt drove out from underneath the second-to-last stop of the A subway line in Rockaway, Queens.

A sign said the name of the stop was Beach 105th Street, but there was no beach in sight. There was just a razor-wire fence outside some sort of industrial plant. Some ant colony high-rises, an ill-kept ball field.

It got nicer the farther he drove south. Swept sidewalks. Neat lawns. Fireflies glowing beneath leafy shade trees. After a while, it flattened out the way it does near the water, sky suddenly everywhere.

The narrow side streets he started to

pass had little guard booth arms blocking car traffic and then that was it. The road just stopped. In front of him beyond a spray-painted guardrail lay the dunes, the silvery bulge and fall of waves, the open sea.

He made a U-turn, checking the GPS. When he was close, he spotted a closed IGA supermarket and pulled into its empty lot. Around the back of it near its loading dock, he tucked the Merc beside the beat-to-shit rusted trailer of an 18-wheeler.

He put the top up on the convertible before he opened the bag and got changed. Once dressed, he took an electric razor from the bottom of the bag and plugged it into the cigarette lighter with an adapter he'd bought at a Radio Shack.

Done, he clicked the razor off and checked himself in the rearview. He had a Mohawk now. He quickly slid on his aviator sunglasses and his vintage army jacket.

He was dressed as Travis Bickle, the anti-hero from Martin Scorsese's seventies classic movie *Taxi Driver*. Played by Robert DeNiro, Bickle, like Apt, was a soldier turned idealistic assassin.

It was elaborate fantasyland stuff, but that was just the kind of whimsy Lawrence really enjoyed.

For Detective Michael Bennett's death, Lawrence had chosen his most beloved New York killer of all.

The fiber-optic camera was now in the lining of his jacket. As usual, he was filming everything. The entire digital tape, including this last scene, the grand finale, would be going into a FedEx box as soon as he was done. David Berger, Lawrence's famous, saintly, genius musician brother out in California, would receive it the day after tomorrow.

Apt got out of the car. Sticking to the shadows, he hurried down Rockaway Point Boulevard until he got to Spring Street, Bennett's block. He started counting addresses after he made the left. The tiny, quirky, not-very-stable-looking houses were almost on top of one another, but he could actually hear the nearby surf.

He found himself liking the vibe of the place. As with all good beachside spots, there was something old about it, time-less. It seemed like a way station, an outpost at the end of things.

When he came to Bennett's place, he crossed the street and crouched in the shadow between two houses opposite and sat staring.

All the lights were off. Was Bennett asleep, dreaming sweet dreams after a long day of failing to catch him? It was looking like it.

He waited for almost half an hour. When he crossed the dark street, he saw that from its neatly painted porch rail an American flag was flying. Apt shook his head. Mike, Mike, he thought. Don't you know you're supposed to bring Old Glory in at night?

The cluttered back deck was baffling, like a Toys "R" Us fire sale. Blow-up air mattresses, water guns, a rusty bicycle. Careful not to knock anything over, he crept up the steps and peeked in the back-door window. A Reagan-era fridge, a massive table with breakfast bowls, spoons, and folded napkins all set out for the morning. He counted at least a dozen settings. What was up?

He was bent, scrub-picking the door lock, when he heard something behind him. The air mattress by the stairs had moved. Had the wind knocked it over? But there was no wind.

Then something cold and hard slammed down on top of his head, and he felt his legs give out and the deck rushing toward his face.

Chapter 100

His skull on fire and his vision blurring, Apt pulled himself up onto his knees.

He wiped his eyes. There was a kid in front of him on the top step of the deck. He had an aluminum baseball bat on his shoulder. He was Hispanic, maybe ten or eleven, wearing Yankees pajamas.

"Who are you?" the kid said, brandishing the bat. "I saw you come past my window. You're a Flaherty, aren't you? Why the hell can't you people leave us alone?"

Apt put up his hands as the kid feinted with the bat. He couldn't believe it. He'd come this far and some ten- or eleven-year-old punk had taken him out? With a bat? What kind of crazy father was Bennett, anyway?

"Wait. I'm not Flaherty," Apt said.

"Bull. You look crazy. What's that? A Mohawk or something?"

Apt stood up, holding his aching head, smiling. "I think there's been a mix-up. Are you Mike's kid? I work with your dad. I'm a cop, too."

The kid paused. Confusion eclipsed the kid's face.

Apt snapped his finger.

"Sorry. I keep forgetting how crazy I look. I'm actually undercover."

Apt watched as the kid's face softened, now filling with regret.

"Oh, I'm so sorry, mister. I didn't mean to hurt you. I thought you were somebody else. Why didn't you use the front door?"

"That was some swing," Apt said, stepping toward him. "Don't tell me you bat cleanup?"

"Uh-huh. Your head is bleeding. I'm really sorry. I'll get my dad."

"Actually, could you just hold up a second first?" Apt said and then suddenly clocked him. The boy flew back and ricocheted off the deck railing before he fell flat on his face, out cold.

Apt glanced at the kid, then at the house, thinking.

He lifted the kid over his shoulder and went down the deck steps toward the alley and the street.

Chapter 101

Whe my cell phone woke me in the dark, I rolled off the bed and stumbled around before finally fishing it out of the pocket of my pants.

It was a 212 number, which meant Manhattan. I didn't recognize it.

I was still so dead to the world that when I tried to answer it, I actually hung it up instead.

I wiped my eyes as I yawned. No wonder I was out of it. Mary Catherine and I had gotten back pretty late from the concert. If that wasn't bad enough, MC, Seamus, and I had stayed up watching a hilarious eighties Brat Pack–era comedy called *Heaven Help Us* about a Catholic boys high school in

1960s Brooklyn. I shared many of the same sorts of friendships and screwups and absurdities at Regis, a Catholic boys school in Manhattan. I couldn't remember the last time I'd laughed that hard.

The phone rang again as I was getting back into the bed. I managed to actually answer it this time.

"Bennett."

"It's three o'clock. Do you know where your children are?" a voice said.

That sat me straight the hell up.

"What?" I said.

"Dad?" Ricky said a moment later. "Dad, I'm sorry."

At the sound of Ricky's scared voice, I shot out of bed as if I'd been Tasered. A bunch of books and a radio flew off a shelf as I crashed my shoulder into it, blundering around in the dark.

Was this a dream? I thought, staring at the moonlit window in shock. No. It was a nightmare. I could hear the phone being taken from Ricky.

"Who the fuck is this?"

"You know who this is," the voice said. "And you know what you have to

do. Lawrence taught me. Now I'm going to teach you."

Apt!

"Carl," I said. "Please, Carl. I'll do
anything you want. Don't hurt my son."

"Come down to the beach due east
of your house, Bennett. No cops, no
gun. You have three minutes before I
cut his throat. Three minutes before
you'll be down on your knees, trying to
get his blood out of the sand."

"I'm coming, I'm coming!"

I dropped the phone, trying to think.
What could I do? The son of a bitch
sounded absolutely fucking insane, and
he had Ricky. I pulled on my shorts,
looked for a shirt, then stopped looking. There was no time.

"Mike? What is it? What's going on?"
Mary Catherine called after me as I
banged open the front door.

I decided I couldn't tell her. Apt had
said just me. He sounded way too crazy
to mess with.

"Nothing, Mary. Go back to bed," I
hissed.

"What do you mean nothing?" she
said, coming out after me. "It's three in

the God-loving morning! Where are you going?"

I didn't need this shit. Not now. She started following me. I didn't have time to explain. How could I stop her?

"Do I have to say it? I'm going to meet Emily, okay? Are you happy now?"

Mary stopped dead-still on the porch steps. It killed me to hurt her like this, but I didn't have a choice.

"How could you?" she said very quietly as I started to run.

"Just get back in the house!" I yelled.

Chapter 102

Please, God, I said as I sprinted. Please, please, please, let my boy be okay.

Calm, calm. I can handle this, I thought, trying to relax myself as I huffed. I could talk to Apt. Get him to release Ricky. God had given me that gift, the power to talk to folks, to calm them down, especially people who were hurt in some way. People with sick minds.

I'd negotiate for Ricky whatever it was Apt wanted. It was what I did. I had no choice.

Tears in my eyes, my lungs on fire, I crossed over the concrete path of the boardwalk onto the dark sand. I spotted a quarter moon out over the water.

On the horizon were red lights, tiny ship lights, so far away.

I was panicking, thinking I'd come to the wrong place. Then I spotted some movement by the lifeguard chair where Mary and I had made out.

Oh, my God! It was them. There was a man standing next to Ricky. He had a Mohawk and was wearing an army jacket and aviator sunglasses. Not only that, but he was holding a knife to Ricky's throat!

I couldn't really tell if it was Apt. He was just a crazy man. A crazy, evil man with my eleven-year-old son's life in his hands. Ricky was actually taped to the chair, I realized. Black electrical tape crisscrossed over his arms and legs, over his neck.

"I'm here," I said, falling to my knees about twenty feet away. My whole body was covered in sweat. "You win, Carl. Let's talk, okay?"

Apt cocked his head at me, his mouth tight and angry.

"Get up, Bennett! Get up, tough guy. Mr. Badass. Stand up like a man!" he said.

I slowly stood. "We can work this out, Carl," I said.

"Oh, we're gonna work this out, all right," he said. "What are you waiting for, Bennett? Come and get me!"

I stood there frozen.

That's when I noticed he had a baseball bat in his other hand. Ricky screamed as Apt turned and hit him in the back with it.

"You want me? Then come and get me!" he screamed.

I ran at him. It wasn't a conscious decision. Some force sent me hurtling forward through the darkness, my feet flying, my toes digging, kicking back sand. Both of my feet were off the ground when I dove at him. I don't think he expected me to reach him from so far away. I know I didn't. I saw shock in his face before I plowed into him as hard as I could, sending the bat flying.

Chapter 103

We both scrambled back up. I got up first and swung as hard as I could at his face. It was a good right. It felt the way it does when you've swung a golf club perfectly, two hundred yards pin straight down a fairway.

It would have probably ended things right then and there, but my swing was too high, and I heard my pinkie snap as I punched him in his thick-skulled forehead. I screamed as I hit him with my broken right hand again. I made contact with his glasses and nose this time. He screamed as I felt something squish.

I really thought I had him again, but then he was on me like some kind of wild animal, shrieking as he thumbed at my eyes and grabbed my face. His hands were like steel. He got his fingers deep into the muscles of my cheeks. It felt like he was tearing my jawbone off as he pushed me back.

A second later, as I was about to try another swing, Apt slammed into me, and I felt something punch quickly into my right side.

I looked down. There was a knife in me. I stared down at the steel blade, embedded through the waistband of my shorts just above my right hip, as blood began to pour out.

Chapter 104

I fell to my knees in the sand again. My whole body began to tingle painfully. I felt a stinging like pins-and-needles, only sharper, like a low-level electric current was running through me.

I had trouble thinking, trouble seeing. The surf was crashing behind me. I knelt there, afraid to touch the knife, beginning to shake as I bled.

Before I could form even the semblance of a thought, Apt kicked me in the side of the head. He was wearing steel-toed combat boots, and I immediately went down, my skull ringing.

"That's all!" he screamed as he reared back and kicked me full in my unprotected balls.

I threw up then. I was leaking from every orifice. Pain was arriving from all points at once.

I don't know how I got to my feet, but I did. I started running down the beach. I was the one he wanted, and I wanted him to follow me. I needed to get this fucking maniac as far away from my son as possible.

I didn't make it twenty feet before I was tackled from behind. I screamed. The knife had opened me up even deeper as I landed. It was in deep, the blade now scraping on bone.

"This all you got?" Apt said, turning me over and pinning my shoulders with his knees.

"You know what I'm going to do now?" he said. He went into his pocket and brought out something orange-tinged and gleaming.

No. Please, no, I thought. It was a pair of brass knuckles.

I went out when he hit me in the side of my face. When I came out of it, the bone near my eye didn't feel right. The eye itself felt like it was hanging wrong.

"This is what Lawrence wanted. Not for me to shoot you. Not for me to knife you, but for me to beat you to death. He wanted you to feel it, he said. What he wanted was for a hero, a truly good person, to feel what it felt like to be him, to be on the bottom, to be nothing. So don't blame me, Bennett. Remember, I'm just the errand boy."

When he swung again, he broke my jaw. My face, my entire self, felt cracked, like a jigsaw puzzle being taken apart.

Bleeding badly, almost unconscious, and barely able to breathe, I was going down heavily, like a foundering ship, when I heard it.

"Freeze!"

I didn't know whose voice it was. At first I thought it might have been God's. Then I recognized its familiar tone, its pitch, its power.

It was the voice of authority that they'd taught us at the Police Academy. It was a cop's voice, I realized. A sole cop's voice crying in my wilderness, and it was the sweetest sound I'd ever heard.

"Relax, relax. We're just messing,"

Apt said, raising his hands as he got off me.

Then I heard it again.

"Freeze!"

But the voice was different now. Same tone of authority, but from someone else. Incredible. It was another cop! The cavalry.

"Freeze, fucker!" called a woman a moment later.

"You heard her. Put your hands up!" called another voice.

"Down, down!"

Now I heard a litany of voices, a choir. I realized they were my neighbors. Breezy Point's Finest, a regiment of vacationing cops to the rescue.

"On your knees, shit-ass!"

What happened next was a blur. Apt screamed, and then there was a cracking sound. Actually several of them. Cracking and popping like firecrackers going off all around me, and I turned my face down into the sand like a fed-up ostrich and passed out.

"Okay, okay. C'mon, c'mon. Let's pick it up."

I woke up with a start, still lying facedown but staring at the blurring ground. I felt about twenty hands on me, running me across the sand. The face next to mine was Billy Ginty's, my neighbor, an anticrime cop from Brooklyn. I saw another guy from my block, Edgar Perez, a horse cop sergeant with a disabled kid. There was a big burly son of a bitch in a Mets jersey, and I realized it was Flaherty. He was holding me as gently as a baby, his face red as he ran.

My friends and neighbors, all of them heroes, were trying to save my life.

We suddenly stopped somewhere. I wanted to thank Flaherty, to apologize, but he shushed me.

"Don't you dare go out now," he said. "They're getting you a chopper. You're going for a ride on the whirly bird, you lucky dog."

"Mike, Mike," Mary Catherine said from far away.

From somewhere close by, I could hear Ricky crying. Oh, thank you, God. He was all right.

"Tell him it's okay. I'm okay," I said or attempted to. I gagged as I swallowed blood, salty and thick like metallic glue.

"Stop, Mike. Don't try to talk," Mary Catherine said, next to me now.

My cell phone started to ring.

"I got it. I got it. It's for me," I gurgled as I reached for it.

Then Mary Catherine took it out of my pocket and tossed it. My eyes fastened on it in the sand where it glowed on and off, ghostly and blue as it rang and rang and rang.

Then I looked up at Mary Catherine. I remembered how magical she had looked that night diving into the water. I wished we could both do that now. Walk down to the beach, hand in hand, go under the waves where it was quiet and dark, quiet and peaceful down in the tumbling warmth.

Epilogue

Epilogue

Chapter 105

I'm at the window in the bedroom of my apartment.

A strange nickel-colored light fills the streets. The streets are empty. No cars, no people. The lustrous light winks off endless rows of empty windows. Off to my right beyond the buildings is the Hudson River, but I can't see any current. Everything is as still as a painting. The curtains blow in on my face for a moment and then fall back, still, and I know time has stopped.

I'm sitting back against the headboard of my bed, which is funny because my bed isn't anywhere near the window, only now it is. Then I realize it's not my current apartment on West End

Avenue. It's actually my old place, the tiny studio Maeve and I rented on a sketchy run of Riverside Drive after we got married.

Just as I realize this, arms suddenly embrace me from behind. I want to turn, but I can't. I'm paralyzed. Hair stands up on the back of my neck as a chin rests on my shoulder.

Michael, a soft Irish-accented voice whispers in my ear.

It's my dead wife, Maeve. She's alive. I can feel the warmth of her hands, her breath in my ear, on my cheek. I check myself, feel my side where Apt stabbed me, feel my face for the dent in my fractured face, but everything is impossibly smooth. An incredible sadness rises in me like an overflowing spring.

No, she admonishes me when I start to cry.

But it's over, I cry.

No, she says again as a finger wipes away a tear and presses against my lips.

It's not the end. There is no end. That's the good part. How are all my babies?

I have trouble breathing, I'm crying so hard.

Baby, you should see Juliana. She's so brave and capable, just like you. And Brian, he's this huge, wonderful, polite young man.

Just like you, Maeve says.

And the rest of them. Eddie's so funny, and Trent. The younger girls have left me in the dust, honey. Pink is cool one second, then it's so babyish. I can't keep up. Oh, God, you'd be so proud of them.

I am, Michael. I see them sometimes. When they need me, I'm with them. That's another good part.

I reach out and suddenly hold her thin wrist. I move over to her hand, run my finger over her wedding ring.

I made it back to you. I knew I would. I never doubted it.

When she squeezes my hand back, my sadness evaporates, and I'm overcome with a pulsing warmth. I'm being filled inside and out with peace. Suddenly there's a pop, and a rushing sound fills my ears, like water roaring violently through a pipe. The bed starts to shake.

Will you show me everything? I say, holding on to her hand for dear life.

Of course, Michael, she says as she lets go of my hand. *But not now. It's not the right time.*

But I don't want to go back, I yell. *Not yet. I have so many questions. What about us? What about Mary Catherine?*

I know you'll be good to her, Michael, Maeve yells over the increasing roar. *I know you. You would never play with a person's heart.*

That's when I turn.

But Maeve isn't there.

Nothing is. Everything is gone. My room, the block, the city, the planet. There is nothing but the roar, and my breath and sight fail as it swallows me whole.

Chapter 106

First, there was just blackness and pain and a relentless chirping beep. It was like a bird had gotten inside of me somehow and was trying to peck its way out. Two large predator birds. One in my side, one in my face.

I opened my stinging eyes. Outside the window beside me, sun sparkled off an unfamiliar parking lot. On a highway in the distance, cars passed normally under a blue, cloudless sky.

A red-haired nurse with her back to me was moving some kind of wheeled cart in the corner. When I opened my mouth to call to her, I tasted blood again. I felt dizzy and weak, and nausea crowded up on me, and I slipped under again.

Next time I woke up, my eyes adjusted to the gray shapes. At first I thought there were people hovering above me, but then I realized they were balloons. Red and blue and shimmering Mylar ones. About as many as floated out of Carl's chimney in the movie *Up*.

I looked away from them, wincing in pain. My face and my side were hot and tight with an itchy, horrendous stinging. The head-to-toe tightness was the worst. I felt like a sheet being pulled apart.

"Thank the Lord. Oh, thank you, God," someone said. It definitely wasn't me.

A second later, Seamus's face appeared.

"Please don't tell me it's last rites."

"No, no, you've got at least another fifty years to suffer in this vale of tears, you crazy SOB. You scared the H-E-double-hockey-sticks out of us all."

"How long have I been out?"

"This would be day three."

"How's...?"

"Apt? Deader than dog excrement," said another voice.

Emily Parker appeared next to my grandfather.

"Mary Catherine followed you down to the beach. She said when she saw you fighting, she ran back and started ringing doorbells. I guess it pays to have half the police and fire department for neighbors when you're on vacation."

I nodded.

"How's...?"

"Your condition?" Seamus said.

I shook my head.

"Mary Catherine."

"She cried for two days," Seamus said. "But now I believe she's fine, Mike. She's one remarkable girl, or I should say, woman."

"It's true," Emily agreed. "She saved your life. And Ricky's. All of your lives. Feel better, Mike. Call me when you can. I have to go now. There's about a thousand people waiting to see you."

I squeezed Emily's hand.

"I'm sorry," I said.

"For what?" she said.

"For leaving the hotel."

She smiled.

"You're where you're supposed to be, Mike. I know that now."

The redheaded nurse came back then, looking pissed.

"Visiting time is over," she said as she shoved Seamus toward the door.

"Get better," ordered Seamus.

"I will."

"Promise," he called back.

I smiled.

"I swear to God, Father," I said.

I slept for another stretch. When I opened my eyes, it was dark and all my kids were there.

At first, I flinched. I didn't want them to see me this way. Their mother had died in a hospital bed. They'd seen enough horror in their young lives, hadn't they? But after a minute, I found myself smiling as I looked from concerned face to concerned face.

They were all trying to be brave and to make me smile, I saw. Mary Catherine most of all. A wall of concern and love and support was bearing down on me whether I liked it or not.

After a little bit, I smiled back through

my tears. I couldn't have helped it if I'd wanted to. Resistance was futile.

"Go give your Da a kiss," Seamus instructed my kids.

And incredibly, somehow, all at the same time, that's exactly what they did.

Books by James Patterson

FEATURING ALEX CROSS

Cross Fire
I, Alex Cross
Alex Cross's Trial
  (with Richard DiLallo)
Cross Country
Double Cross
Cross
Mary, Mary
London Bridges

The Big Bad Wolf
Four Blind Mice
Violets Are Blue
Roses Are Red
Pop Goes the Weasel
Cat & Mouse
Jack & Jill
Kiss the Girls
Along Came a Spider

THE WOMEN'S MURDER CLUB

The 9th Judgment (with Maxine Paetro)
The 8th Confession (with Maxine Paetro)
7th Heaven (with Maxine Paetro)
The 6th Target (with Maxine Paetro)
The 5th Horseman (with Maxine Paetro)
4th of July (with Maxine Paetro)
3rd Degree (with Andrew Gross)
2nd Chance (with Andrew Gross)
1st to Die

FEATURING MICHAEL BENNETT

Tick Tock (with Michael Ledwidge)
Worst Case (with Michael Ledwidge)
Run for Your Life (with Michael Ledwidge)
Step on a Crack (with Michael Ledwidge)

FOR READERS OF ALL AGES

Witch & Wizard: The Gift (with Ned Rust)
Maximum Ride: The Manga, Vol. 3 (with NaRae Lee)
Daniel X: The Manga, Vol. 1 (with SeungHui Kye)
Daniel X: Demons and Druids (with Adam Sadler)
FANG: A Maximum Ride Novel
Witch & Wizard (with Gabrielle Charbonnet)
Maximum Ride: The Manga, Vol. 2 (with NaRae Lee)
Daniel X: Watch the Skies (with Ned Rust)
MAX: A Maximum Ride Novel
Maximum Ride: The Manga, Vol. 1 (with NaRae Lee)
Daniel X: Alien Hunter (graphic novel; with Leopoldo Gout)
The Dangerous Days of Daniel X (with Michael Ledwidge)
Maximum Ride: The Final Warning
Maximum Ride: Saving the World and Other Extreme Sports
Maximum Ride: School's Out—Forever
Maximum Ride: The Angel Experiment
santaKid

OTHER BOOKS

Don't Blink (with Howard Roughan)
The Postcard Killers (with Liza Marklund)
Private (with Maxine Paetro)
The Murder of King Tut (with Martin Dugard)

For previews of upcoming books by James
Patterson and more information about the
author, visit www.JamesPatterson.com.

About the Authors

James Patterson has had more *New York Times* bestsellers than any other writer, ever, according to *Guinness World Records*. Since his first novel won the Edgar Award in 1977, James Patterson's books have sold more than 205 million copies. He is the author of the Alex Cross novels, the most popular detective series of the past twenty-five years, including *Kiss the Girls* and *Along Came a Spider*. Mr. Patterson also writes the bestselling Women's Murder Club novels, set in San Francisco, and the top-selling New York detective series of all time, featuring Detective Michael Bennett.

James Patterson also writes books for young readers, including the award-winning Maximum Ride, Daniel X, and

Witch & Wizard series. In total, these books have spent more than 200 weeks on national bestseller lists, and all three series are in Hollywood development.

His lifelong passion for books and reading led James Patterson to launch the website ReadKiddoRead.com to give adults an easy way to locate the very best books for kids. He writes full-time and lives in Florida with his family.

Michael Ledwidge is the author of *The Narrowback* and *Bad Connection,* and most recently the coauthor, with James Patterson, of *Worst Case.* He lives in New York City.